Friday, May 28, 2019: The Dance

Although there were a lot of things on his mind as Brendan slowly opened the gym doors on May 28, 2019, the one that was loudest and most prevalent was: I have a reason to be here. For in the last two years Brendan had lost Grandpa George to cancer and his father to some skank named Rhonda, and these losses made him feel less and less enthusiastic about his lot in life and more and more likely to avoid social situations that he couldn't control, of which this dance would surely qualify.

Grandpa had fought like hell against his colon cancer and remained Brendan's greatest role model. He had continued his chemo regimen while exercising more than he had in years, above and beyond the will of both his family and doctors. He'd walk three miles when he was advised to walk a quarter of one and come in still full of energy. He continued to drink and whiskey and watch Lightning games with Brendan, who lost Grandpa George one night after a crushing loss to the Canadiens in the playoffs. His last words to Brendan were, "We'll get 'em next game."

But those were far from the only words Grandpa George had left Brendan. All through his life he had been bombarded by both his mother and his grandfather with three-word sayings that Brendan's mother had at some point dubbed "Grandpa George-isms." When Brendan had asked him, "Grandpa. Why just three words?" his grandfather had responded with "Anything worth saying can be said in three words. Less bullshit then." As he got older these frank yet encouraging sayings felt to him like a favorite blanket or stuffed animal felt to other kids.

And the one he thought of now was **worst case scenario.** In this case, think of the worst thing that could happen, run through what that meant in your head, then prepare for it to happen. See it happen. Then realize that even IF it happened it wouldn't be that

bad. So that fit this situation perfectly, and Brendan was running the permutations through his head now.

Following this, Brendan was pulled to the place he dreaded to go but had to at some point every day. The "loss" of his dad. One night at the dinner table he sensed a tremor in the mood and looking up, saw both his parents staring at their plates. When Brendan asked what was going on, his parents exchanged a furtive glance at one another, which in retrospect Brendan felt was scripted for TV, and his father calmly stated that he was leaving Brendan and his mother. His mother's deer-in-the-headlights stare tore a hole through Brendan, and, coming only three months after Grandpa George's death, left him free-falling through floor after floor of an insane funhouse then finally crashing to the ground.

Despite these thoughts, when Brendan beheld the glory of the sixty-fifth annual Wildwood Middle School Sixth Grade Fire and Ice Dance, he felt connected in a way that he hadn't in nearly a year. Not because of the dance. He'd never been to a dance, couldn't dance, and didn't know what you did at a dance. He was there for one reason and one reason only. Caitlyn.

As he scanned the growing throng of excited, bubbly sixth graders, he saw dozens of boys wearing red and girls wearing blue, but no Caitlyn yet. He was a bit early, so he decided to check out the food stands to see what they were offering. The first he came up to was Devil's Delights, and there was a vat of bubbling chili, Taki's in a glowing red bowl, some kind of cinnamon candy, and little paper cups of hot sauce next to their labeled bottles with a sign questioning, "Are you ready to burn???" A woman in some kind of devil outfit tried to shove one in Brendan's hand but he skirted her with a quick "No thanks" and instead opted for the tiny cup of cinnamon red-hots.

Stepping away from the stand, he decided to check out the decorations. The basketball hoops raised to the roof trailed red and blue streamers, supposedly signifying fiery flames and icy tendrils. There was a makeshift dais at mid-court with a platform that was split into half red and half blue sides and corkscrew stairs for entry at either side, with the drama class's lights supplying the red and blue beams illuminating the sparkly material and sending small beams of color splashing across the ceiling. Brendan marveled at the steps, probably made in someone's garage for the occasion, but very WELL made. His dad could build anything, but right after the pair made a garage shelf that Brendan was extremely proud of his dad split. Two days later the crow-barred remains of it filled the top of the trashcan, which brought Brendan a small bit of closure.

Brendan could make out crowns that were perched atop a stand on either side of the dais, a male and a female crown, which would probably be adorning some popular kids' heads tonight.

He checked his phone. 6:45. The party didn't kick off until 7:00, but Brendan followed the lead of Grandpa George, who always said **ten minutes early.** This advice had rarely failed him. He sat down facing the stage and decided to check to see the starting lineups for the Rays series opener at New York. The stunning sweep of his beloved Lightning, who were 62-20 in the regular season, by the Columbus Blue Jackets last month was only assuaged by Caitlyn. But then, Caitlyn made up for a lot in his life.

As he pressed the home button on his phone and started to punch in his passcode, hands from behind him covered his eyes.

"Brendan Ellison. This is the police. You are under arrest." An object thudded onto the table.

Caitlyn released her hands and pushed his back gently. "Hey you," he said.

"Watcha doin' here so early, boy?" she said, sitting in the chair in front of him at the round table.

"You haven't figured out by now that I'm ALWAYS early. Like, to everything?"

He noticed then that the object was her camera. Caitlyn was one of only three photographers for the yearbook, with one of the others being her best friend and his longtime pal Kristen, and she had apologized to him that some of her time was going to be spent snapping photos for the yearbook. When Brendan tried to argue that they had already had their yearbook so what's the point of taking pictures of the dance, Caitlyn rebuffed him with, "Oh. You don't know Miss Thorssen. There is NEVER an event she doesn't cover. Even if it goes in NEXT year's book!" She turned her head to the left and when she turned back her face was lit.

"Hold on. I'll be right back. I spotted some dyed blue rock candy on a stick at the 'Feelin' It in Your Bones' stand that I've just gotta have before they're all gone."

She rose and Brendan was able to appraise her outfit, which took some time to completely figure out. She had on white stockings and white shoes, but the headliner was the dress, which was ice blue with sequins or sparkles or something for the main part, accompanied by a matching blue wrap that swirled around her when she moved. Her blonde hair was braided down her back. He finally got it: Elsa from Frozen. And he just noticed that her hair was dyed that same color of light blue. She grabbed a stick of the rock candy, stood in front of the stand, licked it, then closed her eyes, ran her hand slowly across her forehead, and swooned. Brendan laughed.

"Come on. It can't be that good."

Elsa flew back to the table and once again stood behind him and this time covered his eyes with her left arm. "Close your eyes. Open your taste buds. Prepare to be amazed." Brendan did as instructed and she gently with her right hand placed the tip of the concoction on his tongue. Brendan kept his mouth open. "Lick fool!" He licked. "So? Is it not the BEST thing you've ever had? Like, seriously?"

She fell into her seat and awaited his reaction. He scrunched his face into a thinking, worrying look, and said, "No. Not really."

"Oh. My. God. You're kidding. It's like the nectar of the gods, Brendan. What is WRONG with you?"

"It tastes like pure sugar, with I'm sure some blue dye #5 mixed in. And nectar is a liquid."

"Okay, so DRIED NECTAR if you want to get technical, and I cry 'Sacrilege!' You are clearly not WORTHY of this delectable treat, so I will keep it to myself." She nodded defiantly at him and Brendan smiled. "And it matches my dress."

"I'm so glad you're here, Caitlyn."

This shot through her and she stopped devouring the candy for a second. "You are so sweet. I'm glad to be here. With you." For not the first time, Brendan wondered what this gorgeous, fun, creative blonde would be doing with him, and quietly thanked the powers that be of his good fortune and tried to tamp down his ever-present insecurity.

And then she reached out and took his hand. This had only happened a few times, and this froze Brendan now. Caitlyn, seeing this, smiled and took his hand in both of hers.

"Don't be so scared, Bren. It's okay. I'm not gonna bite."

"It's . . . okay. It's more than okay. It's just . . . unexpected, each time." He tried a thin smile at her and she mimicked his.

"Hey, you two lovebirds," said Kristen Rothstein, slinging her camera onto the table. Brendan went to withdraw his hand from Caitlyn's but she wouldn't let him. He relaxed.

"What's up girl?" Caitlyn said, hugging Kristen, who apparently was dressed as Cinderella, to the best of Brendan's knowledge. This made him look down at his outfit, which consisted of a pair of jeans and a plain red t-shirt bought for the occasion.

"Hey Brendan," Kristen said, smiling. Although she knew Brendan better than Caitlyn did, he was still an odd choice. Caitlyn was always interested in the different, the unusual, so this hockey-playing, action movie-loving kid seemed unusual if not just wrong for her. Kristen and Brendan had been friends for years, and their parents knew each other, so she had spent parties and get togethers with him. But Brendan was always the kid that either shied away from conversation or left early or was on his phone--by himself. One on one, though, he would open up. But around most people, he always had some great internal struggle going on and was always guarded, afraid to say or do the wrong thing. Caitlyn was improving this, though. And he was pretty cute. That overcame a lot. "I see your cast is gone. Yay-uh."

"Just three days ago," he said.

"That'll teach you to let guys, what do you hockey players call it, pound you on the boards or whatever?" Caitlyn snarked. Brendan shrugged. "Come on, Bren. We're just messing with you. Lighten up," Caitlyn said.

"Yeah. You're used to this, right? Didn't you break that same arm in first grade? How'd that happen? I forget," Kristen said.

"Fell out of a tree," Brendan said, nodding.

"That's right. And didn't you have that at MY birthday party? And what, you couldn't swim or something, right?"

"I pretty much just sat and watched you guys playing three hours of Marco Polo. From my seat. Beside the pool."

"Sometimes I forget how long you guys have known one another," Caitlyn said.

"Besides, we're not all military kids who get to travel the world, now are we, Cait?" shot back Kristen.

"Hardly," she said. "I've lived in Ohio, Arkansas, and here in Jacksonville. Not exactly the WORLD now is it?" Kristen rolled her eyes then looked toward the stage.

"Hey Cait. Miss Thorssen's waving at us. Let's go see what she wants," Kristen said.

"Okay," Caitlyn replied. "Be back soon, Bren," she said, giving his hand a squeeze.

The two girls left, and Brendan noticed the gathering swarm starting to circulate, usually in groups of four or five, walking around to check out the different food and entertainment stations around the gym's perimeter. Brendan saw nearby some screens showing home screens of various games like Madden, Guitar Hero, Minecraft, and Animal Crossing, Caitlyn's personal favorite. He resisted the temptation of the beckoning PlayStation controller and the chance to direct the Bucs against the Saints and the hated Drew Brees and remained where he was.

He looked toward Caitlyn and Kristen and found them boisterously talking with the equally animated Miss Thorssen, planning and plotting their strategy of pictorial conquest of the dance. Brendan hoped she wouldn't be completely immersed in her job to his detriment. He had tried to imagine how this night would go, but his only comparison was other events and other nights with his friends, with no pressure, with no real intentions beyond just hanging out. This was unstructured, unscripted, and possibly even unruly. In other words: not fun for him. However, being with Caitlyn was the opposite of this. It wasn't entirely unpleasant, but it was entirely unsettling. Watching TV shows and movies of how guys and girls interacted really didn't prepare him for the real thing. Especially with his constantly surprising . . . "girlfriend." He liked the sound of that.

Out of the blue one day two weeks ago in Florida history class, during a test no less, Brendan had felt a piece of paper land in his lap. Looking down, he realized it was a folded note written on notebook paper. Momentarily flustered, Brendan looked first to the teacher, who was working on his computer and oblivious, then to his left, where Kristen was smiling at him, beckoning with her cupped palm repeatedly in expectation of his response. His focus now completely shot and being completely clueless why his friend would pass him this note, Brendan slowly opened it. The writing, unfamiliar to him, said, "Wanna hang out?" with boxes for a response of either YES or NO. When Brendan looked confusedly back at Kristen, she knew he misunderstood. She mouthed "Not me," and pointed to Caitlyn, who was immediately to her left. Brendan then folded up the note, pretended that he was focused on his test, and didn't look at Kristen, or Caitlyn for that matter, the rest of the period. Did this mean what he thought it meant? In the hallway after class, as he tried to slink away to PE as quickly as possible, Caitlyn stepped in front of him and said, "Well?" Her face was lit up like a child anticipating a Christmas present. How could he say no? He quickly nodded, mouth agape, and she scurried off, bounding back to Kristen excitedly. Did he just say yes to someone who, although he had thought she was cute ever since the first day she stepped into their class at Rollins Elementary in fifth grade wearing a pink dress and pigtails, would do that, pointedly, right in his face, in the hallway, at school?

This was just two weeks ago, but the effect on his life had made it seem far longer. He looked toward the teacher and her students, and as his girlfriend gave him that same smile now across the packed gym, a warmth spread through him.

"Mom, do I really have to go to this dance?" Chris said as the olive-green door of his mother's Range Rover closed behind him, certainly sealing his fate.

"Yes, you have to go. I really don't see what the big deal is here, Christopher. There will be video games and all your friends are there."

"Exactly. What is the big deal about me going? Why do you care?"

His mother turned the key and the car sprang to life. She exhaled deeply and looked over at him.

"It's not exactly a BIG DEAL, but you are keeping up appearances."

"Appearances? To what?"

"Chris, you know that your father and I are very involved in this community and have a reputation. It would be unseemly if our child didn't attend his sixth-grade graduation."

"Mom, seriously, it's just a dance. No one GRADUATES from sixth grade. And I am not a part of yours or Dad's 'community reputation.'"

"Regardless," she said, dismissing his protestations with a wave, "You're going." Chris rolled his eyes in her direction. "And besides, you might meet a girl at the dance."

"A girl? Mom, get real. And you keep calling it a dance, like anyone will actually be dancing there."

"It is called a dance because it is. The sixty-fifth annual Fire and Ice Dance. It's a tradition."

"A tradition that should have ended somewhere around the hippies I think."

"Your father and I first got together at a dance in seventh grade, I'll have you know. Just because it's middle school doesn't mean its meaningless."

At this point Chris knew it was pointless to continue, so he turned on the radio to a rock station and turned up the music and Led Zeppelin's "Over the Hills and Far Away" filled the car. This drew a frown from his mother, but she allowed him that small victory.

When they arrived at the school, Chris opened his door as his mother said, "I'll pick you up at—" as Chris shut the door ceremoniously with a two-handed shove.

Nine. The dance ended at nine. They had discussed this a few times already. Chris waved this understanding at his mom through the glass as the door closed and she slowly pulled away. As he was walking to the gym, he saw his friend Will, who didn't look any more thrilled than Chris to be here.

"Yo, Will."

"Hey man. What's up?"

"Where did you get those RED pants, dude?" Chris shrugged. "Hey, just don't blame me if middle-aged women tonight ask you where housewares is Mr. Target employee. That's awesome."

Chris had somehow momentarily forgotten the glowing red pants his mother bought for him. On the Internet. A month ago. Good old Mom. Always prepared.

"Yeah, thanks. Just what I wanted to wear tonight."

"But you are TOTALLY on the theme, my friend. And that studly pink shirt too? I don't know if I can be in your presence."

Chris saw that Will had on a red polo shirt, one that he'd probably had for a year rather than purchased just for this occasion, and beige pants. Probably like pretty much every other boy tonight. It SHOULD feel like a Target store meeting.

"Yeah, thanks buddy." Chris punched Will in the arm. Will retaliated, they called it even, and Chris opened the right double door to the gym.

It was close to 7:00 so the gym was pretty full. The boys quickly spied the video game setups and chose the one that had MLB The Show in the far-left corner of the gym to walk toward. When they arrived, they saw Dave and Mateo already in a game of Home Run Derby.

"All right. Here goes. Mike Trout, baby. Bringin' the thundah!" Mateo said, as he swung and knocked a fastball out of

Yankee Stadium. "That's six out of ten outta the yard. Good luck my friend."

"Yer goin' down, pal," Dave said, grabbing the controller from Mateo, choosing Aaron Judge, and assuming a stance that had his right foot extended in front of his left, hunched down, maybe five feet from the large screen TV showing the pitcher winding up. Dave swung, a tad late, and the ball took a huge arc off the top of the screen, landing in medium right field.

"Not beatin' Trout with that," Mateo said.

The next pitch was sent to dead center, with "510 feet" plastered on the screen. "One for two. Just getting' warmed up here. Aaron Judge!"

"I got next," Chris said, getting a glance from the two competitors.

"It's going to be Trout, so you got me," Mateo said, with a hard fist pound on his chest for emphasis. "You know, just because you're a baseball GOD in real life it doesn't mean it transfers to here, Chris." Chris shrugged.

As the game unfolded, with each pitch becoming even more apparent that Mateo was right and that he'd be facing Trout with his batter Jose Altuve, Chris thought this night was probably going to be pretty cool after all. He really had no intention of dancing, but the food he saw at the stands as they entered, the video games, and the company would be enough to keep him occupied for a couple of hours. After that he'd probably go back and play some D and D with his "other" friends, the ones who didn't play sports and were probably geniuses because of it. Mom could have her "appearances," but he'd still have a good time.

"Mommy. Why can't I go to the dance tonight? I'll just sit and watch. I promise." Nessa asked her mother, who was putting the finishing touches on their Fettucine Alfredo meal for tonight. Her mother smiled at her and squirted some hand soap on her hands and turned on the water.

"Sweetie, we've already been through this. Anabel is the only one who can go because she's a sixth grader and it's the end of the year celebration for her."

Nessa nodded quickly, her brown bangs falling in her eyes. "Like Allie had three years ago, right Mom?"

"Yes. Now you know we've already been through this, Ness. You and Mommy and Daddy are going to watch a movie tonight, right? Your choice."

"Ariel," Nessa said, her eyes widening.

"That's right, squirt. Ariel. For the seven thousandth time. Can you maybe not sing so loudly this time so I can hear the actual singer singing?" Mom tousled Nessa's hair and turned off the burner. Just then Allie walked into the kitchen, opening the fridge.

"And what do you have planned tonight, Allie?" her mother asked, giving her probably too showy outfit the once-over.

Allie saw the appraisal and said, "What?"

"I didn't say anything," Mom said, nose in the air, her face pregnant with meaning.

"Mom. I'm fine," she said. "We're only hanging at Christy's tonight. Maybe watch Dexter or a movie or something."

"Okay, I guess that attire is appropriate for being with your best friends, but maybe ONLY for that."

"You act like I dress differently than any other 15-year-old out there, Mom. I'm usually dressed MORE modest than who I'm with."

"ModestLY."

"Whatever!" Anabel said.

Anabel's mother attempted to pull down her half shirt and expose only a quarter maybe of her back rather than half.

"MOMMMM!" came a screech from the back of the house.

"What the hell is going on?" Allie said.

"Language!" said her mother, while Nessa snickered.

"Can you come help, please?"

"Oh, that's right. Anabel's got the big Fire and Ice dance tonight. Gotta look her best," Allie said, smacking her lips toward Nessa.

"Just a second," their mother said, quickly dumping the fettucine into the colander in the sink and heading toward her current most needy daughter.

"Allie, what's it like?" Nessa asked. "Is it really awesome?"

"Just wait'll you get to middle school, Ness. EVERYTHING will be awesome. Everything is like life or death."

At that, Nessa launched into a spirited rendition of "Everything is Awesome" from the first Lego movie, and Allie joined in, the two spinning in circles.

"Alexa, play 'Everything is Awesome'," Nessa said.

"'Everything is Awesome' is only available through Amazon Prime Music. Would you like me to start your trial subscription now?" the AI voice said.

The girls looked at each other, and, as they had done so many times, Allie counted to three on her fingers and they said in unison, "ALEXA YOU SUCK!" as loud as they could. There was no reply.

Back in her bedroom, Anabel was, well, flustered is too weak of a word. Her mom had to stifle a laugh upon seeing the myriad problems her middle child was having, but also rushing through her mind were the times when she was in a similar predicament, so she chose her mom/concerned face.

"Just look at this. Look at this."

Anabel was holding up a heel that had apparently broken off her shoe. There was a brown smear of some kind on her light blue dress, and that a part of her hair looked singed from the hair straightener she'd probably used for too long.

"It's okay. Everything is fixable. Don't freak. We got this."

Anabel looked in the mirror, and beyond the usual chubbiness and almost-pretty-but-not-quite face that always stared back at her, these current disasters made her just want to crawl in bed with a pint of Ben and Jerry's Cookie Dough ice cream and watch Mean Girls.

"How. Is. This. Fixable?" she shrieked, and fell back on her bed, causing her cat Sylvester to spring across her and bound out of the room.

"Calm down, Sweetie. We can do this."

"We can do . . . what, Mom? There's only so much we've got to work with here," she said, patting her stomach, which was noticeably pooching out from the dress.

"That is SO not true, Annie. You are a beautiful girl. You will make quite an impression at the party, I assure you."

"Yeah, the absolute WRONG impression, Mom. Like, people-will-never-forget-the-disaster-that-was-Anabel-Donan-at-the-dance kind of impression."

"Deep breaths. Deep breaths. Come on. Give me five."

Her mother had taught all the girls this simple technique that all three of them fought just about every time but nearly always worked. Anabel closed her eyes, and at breath two her mother had sat down beside her, lightly stroking her brown hair, splayed out behind her on the bed.

"Better?"

Anabel reluctantly nodded her head and breathed, and as breath five went out in a huge exhale. "Yeah. Okay. So what fire do we put out first?"

"You've gotta get the dress off, hon, so I can see what needs to be done with that. The heel is an easy fix. The hair." She stopped to appraise for a few seconds. "Ah, not a real problem either. Some re-straightening is all it needs. We got this."

Anabel smiled and unzipped the too-tight dress and let it fall to the floor.

"Annie, what is this?" her mom asked, pointing to the light brown smear across the front.

"I have no idea."

"Well, then, how did it get there?"

"Mom. Why always the third degree? I don't know. I had the dress on my bed when I went to school, and I came home and it was like that."

"On your bed. Where the cat and dog lay. All day. That bed?"

Anabel glumly shook her head.

"Mistake, honey. I really hope that's not what I think it is." Anabel grimaced and slowly shook her head. "But even if it IS, I got this." She held up the dress so the stain was at eye level, assessing the damage. "But the hair, that's all you. You can take care of that." She picked up the heel and the shoe and left the room.

Anabel called after her. "But you know we gotta leave in half an hour, Mom. It's almost 6:30."

From across the house, fading, Anabel heard her mom say, "I am aware of what time we have to leave. I am the school secretary, you know. The person who made most of the arrangements for the dance and HAS to be there to chaperone?"

Anabel rose from her bed and went to face her demon. The scale. Again. For the third time today. Like it was going to be any different. It was always there, glaring at her from the threshold like Charon, the guardian of the River Styx, holding out his hand for payment before crossing. Maybe it mocked her as she sat on her bed, on her floor, stuffing sugar-filled crap down her throat. Maybe she should move it, take away its vantagepoint and hence a good deal of its power? She reached down and picked it up, looking for a spot to blind its evil gaze. Even though her bathroom was attached to her bedroom it was really small, and she could see no place to put it where she wouldn't trip on it. Nothing. She sighed.

She carefully placed the glass scale down in its forever spot, even though she in her heart of hearts wanted to smash it, throwing it at the mirror, destroying that enemy too. A quinella. She took off her underwear and leggings just in case she could squeeze an extra ounce out of those. She took a deep breath and stepped on. The numbers flew far faster than they had any right to, always that lightning leap between two digits and three, and what settled, glaring at her, burning through her, was this: 127.4. That was a full pound more than she weighed this morning. Oh my God. Of course I can't fit into the dress.

Anabel's goal weight was 122 for this dance, and she had failed, miserably. She started two months before, at 126 pounds, and really thought more exercise and eating fewer sweets was her path to success. Or would at least bring her close to it. But not to EXCEED it for God's sake.

"Okay honey," her mom said as he entered the room, cutting through Anabel's self-pity and making her almost jump off the demon scale. She took a step toward the bedroom and stopped in the doorway. "The heel is easy. It's on the kitchen counter. Should be dry in five minutes. Just don't put on your shoes until you get to the dance. The stain, a little tougher. I actually think it was a chew bone that the dog brushed across it or something. I just used a damp cloth and it came off really quickly." She looked up at her daughter, who somehow was now smiling. "You're good, girl."

Anabel ran up and hugged her mom. "I love you, Mom. You're the best."

Her mother accepted getting one of the increasingly fewer hugs from her daughter and squeezed hard back.

Anabel groaned, sucked in her stomach, then said, "Hey, if you squeeze a little harder, maybe I can get down to my goal weight!"

Mom released her grip and stepped back from Anabel. "You . . . are a beautiful girl, and I'm sure you're going to have a great time at your dance. No one's going to notice your weight because they'll be dazzled by your smile." Anabel lit up over this. "See? Your smile is radiant."

"Thanks Mom. I'll be ready in about fifteen minutes."

Her mom now having exited the room, Anabel tried to push back her nearly ever-present obsession with her weight by trying to focus on the dance as she put on her dress. Sixth grade was now over, and her last chance to gain even a smattering, even a brush, of popularity was tonight. After tonight her summer would be a series of summer camps, or being with her sisters 24/7, which, although not horrible, was pretty far from her wish of being visible, of being seen, as someone other than Allison's sister or the kid whose mother works at the school, or just another nameless face in a summer program. Tonight has got to be special, she thought. I've got to get beyond the first rung of the popularity ladder. It's either that or another two plus months of anonymity. Of not being invited to the right parties. Of not having a chance to be around the cute guys. She ticked off the list of possible accomplishments for her night, realizing that she would just settle for one or two of them.

She walked over to the mirror and strained to see that beautiful girl that would attract a guy. To see that thin girl that would keep all their eyes on her longer than a second. To see that assertive girl who was taking steps to better her lot in life.

When Anabel arrived at the dance, she felt like a painter imagining what color and brush strokes to use to paint her masterpiece. Her first goal was to check out the decorations and how these changed the layout of the gym. Mom had taught her to be very observant, to notice your surroundings and who populated them, for safety and other reasons. Her mother had been secretary to the principal since even before Anabel was born, so the gym was a comfortable place for her. Well, more than comfortable. A haven at times really when her gymnastics gym was closed or she needed to be alone. Her mother had a key to the school and knew the alarm code, so many a time she'd take Anabel and let her pull out the mats and tumble, away from others' eyes.

The baskets were up, of course, so no fools would attempt to jump up and grab the net or the rim during the dance. The stage with the crowns was in the middle, as her mother told her was the tradition. There were several food stands set up with interesting names around the perimeter, many tables forming a second perimeter and more, a video game section in the back, and space for kids to "dance." As if anyone would in sixth grade. She could hear her sister's voice saying, "Annie, you should be the one to start the dance. If you do it others will join." After Anabel would protest and make a face, Allie said, "Hey, you're the one that wants to be popular, right? How is it gonna HURT if you go out and dance with a cute boy?" The final modification Anabel noticed was the table in the back center, where her mom would sit. She took a deep breath. Might tonight the gym become her Mona Lisa?

With that done, her second task was to find Isobel. Isobel was her bridge. Isobel was known and liked by just about everybody, probably because she was genuine and real and free of snark. She was one of those rare kids that, rather than talk about you behind your back, would find a way to have a two-sided conversation WITH you about it. Regardless of what information she got or didn't get out of it, she made the other person feel heard and accepted. All this made her the bridge, the conduit to bring Anabel closer to some of the in-crowd that otherwise wouldn't notice her. Anabel would in her head sometimes think of her in terms of one of the bridges in town, the Dames Point Bridge, and when she worked out scenarios in her head involving her she'd just substitute Dame's Point for the girl's name.

She spotted Isobel at a table--a table full of Anime kids. Not exactly the direction she wanted to go. It wouldn't look natural to try to draw her away from that crowd, so she decided to wait that situation out and to find her usual friend group. That didn't take long, as she spied Claire anxiously waving her over and pointing to the empty seat next to her. Anabel waved back her acceptance and smiled, joining the table.

"Oh, Annie I love your dress, and your hair," Claire said, awkwardly raising her hand, moving toward Anabel's hair. It was all she could do to not flinch back in wonder of just what she was trying to do here. Claire's hand contacted her hair, and Anabel gave her a WHY look, which Claire of course failed to recognize. She had straightened her hair. That was it. Nothing really special—just took the natural curl out.

"You're so pretty," said Natasha, and this simultaneously cut through the weirdness and made her feel good. Is it possible that underneath all this flab I really am pretty?

"Thanks. You too Tash." Her more flamboyant friend had of course eschewed the whole dress idea and did look really good in baby blue shorts and darker blue top.

"I went two-tone today," she said, standing and twirling around, her dreads spinning like a mop spun in a centrifuge. Natasha was the hippest of her crowd to be sure but had no crossover, no "in" to the crowd she desired. She was still a lot of fun.

"So. We dancin' tonight?" Amelia asked, snapping her fingers to what was currently playing.

Anabel glanced back at the table where Isobel was, and she was gone.

"In a little while," Anabel said. "I'm going to browse some."

The girls waited a beat and then laughed. They were used to their friend attempting to climb the social ladder, and then failing, and then falling back down so to speak to them.

As Anabel was leaving the table, she heard Amelia say, "That girl will never accept who she is, will she?"

And then Natasha added, "And that's too bad because who she is is FINE."

After hunting for a few minutes, Anabel again found Isobel, who was standing talking to Alan Counts. Alan. Counts. The best athlete in the sixth grade. A straight "A" student. The subject of more than a few of her swoons in third period math. She tried to quickly think of a question to ask Isobel, a question open enough that just maybe Alan might like to weigh in on said question also. She got it.

"So, who do you think might win the Vulcan and Ice Queen crowns tonight?" She tried to just look at Isobel so as not to give away her naked ambition. She saw Isobel's face and realized it was the wrong question to ask . . . Isobel, who cared not a whit for such things.

"They give away crowns at this thing, do they? For what?" Leave it to good old Isobel to crap all over her perfect "in" question.

"Maybe Alan and me?" said a voice beside Alan. A voice belonging to Courtney Carson, Alan's girlfriend. Anabel was speechless and shattered. Alan shrugged, probably completely unaware that such things existed. Courtney is the radiant one, Anabel thought, not me, MOM. Her bleached blonde hair seemed to shimmer in the blue light she had so conveniently walked into, also making the sequins on her dress sparkle. And her waist. God. Did she have a waist? And then, to make the tragedy complete, she asked Alan to dance in a voice that was impossibly high. He accepted. They left.

"Hiya, Anabel. What's happening?" Isobel said, curious why Anabel had to this point said nothing to her.

"Nothing much, Isobel. Just the usual. Trying to meet and greet." Anabel was sure her disappointment showed, if not in her voice then in her slumped shoulders.

"Who? Alan? Now you know that boy has a girlfriend. Has HAD a girlfriend for half the year at least."

"Well, not ESPECIALLY Alan," she said, then appended, "You know."

"Annie, you always try too hard. People see that coming a mile away. It's fake. You need to try being yourself around new people. Just be honest and open up to them."

"Not everyone is you, okay Isobel? Miss Effortless," Anabel said, perking up her face.

"So you'd rather keep trying your method and turning boys off?"

"Well, NO, not really."

"Okayyyy," Isobel said, "Then why don'cha TRY being real then? What's it gonna hurt?"

"I'll make a deal with you. Get me into a conversation with someone I want and I'll do my best to be real. And then afterward you can critique me on my degree of realness, or reality, or whatever. Deal?"

"Good Lord, girl. Okay. Who you got your eyes set on tonight?"

Anabel scoured the scene, assessing potential targets and then dismissing them for various reasons as she went. Finally she found someone.

"You got someone?"

"Yep."

"And?"

"You want his name?"

"Well, yeah I want his name. Or do you just want me to pick someone randomly?"

"Because you know everyone."

"Hey, you gonna insult me this isn't gonna work."

"Okay. Okay. How about . . . Peter Roundtree?"

"Peter. Okay."

"What? You think he's outta my league, don't you?"

"Girl, I have no idea what your league is. Damn. Calm down."

"Okay. Sorry. Okay, so how does this work?"

"I'm going to walk up to Peter and introduce you."

"No! What are you talking about? Like he WANTS to talk to me? Like he would have anything to say to me? A thousand times no." Isobel put her hands on her hips, waiting to be told just how this introduction thing would work. "Okay. How about this? You think of a question to ask Peter, and just walk up, with me, and ask him. And then when he responds, I'll respond. And then you'll be all like 'Have you met my friend Anabel?' And he will start talking to me, and then you'll say 'Excuse me, I've gotta go because, I don't know, fill in the blank' and then we'll be there. Talking. Together."

"You are a trip, girl. That same sad strategy you just tried with Alan you want me to try with Peter?"

"Yes, but you're good at it. You'll be way HAPPIER than my SAD, wouldn't you say?"

"Okay. Imma do this for you, but you owe me. You owe me big time."

"You. Are. The. Best," Anabel heard herself saying for the second time in an hour, then hugged her.

Isobel gave her a quick hug back. "Okay, let's go."

Peter at that point happened to be walking towards them. Isobel asked her question. Peter answered. Anabel looked at Peter and responded. Peter responded back. Anabel responded to that. Peter answered again. Isobel made her excuse and walked away. Somewhere in her mind Anabel was thinking that this is not the way things usually go for her, but she went right on talking, and he went on responding, and soon they were smiling at each other, and laughing. It seemed, almost normal.

"Brendan, I want you to know that I really enjoyed your report on Castillo de San Marcos. I haven't been there in years, but your descriptions of firing the cannon and the texture of those coquina walls brought me back to my childhood. My parents used to take me there once a year when I was little. I love St. Augustine!"

Brendan was never very good talking with teachers, and not being in the classroom made it even more awkward for him. He had gotten a Coke and gotten snagged just as he turned to make his getaway.

"Thanks, Mrs. Wilson," was what he managed.

"And you know, there's about a fifty-fifty chance that I'll have you next year in Civics because I'll be teaching both sixth and seventh grades next year. I'd look forward to that." Mrs. Wilson had to be seventy if she was a day, and she was wearing that old lady perfume, and too much of it. What was it? His mom said that Brendan's grandmother wore it all the time.

"I'd like that, Mrs. Wilson."

"Okay Brendan, so you have a good time at the dance and have a great summer."

"Thank you, ma'am. I will."

Turning away from the teacher and back toward the desserts stand, Brendan pondered the hazards of random small talk that awaited him if he continued to mingle rather than just wait for Caitlyn, but then decided that he would stick to his plan of moving about and trying to talk to people other than just Caitlyn. Well, it wasn't exactly his plan. His mother had drilled this in his head for the last week.

Just as he grabbed a small plate full of "Chilly Willy Brownie Bites," as the sign read, he was accosted by Kristen.

"Bren. Hey! How's it going? I see you found the dessert stand. Can I get a picture of you holding that brownie?"

"Kristen, really, no," he said, turning from her.

She snapped the picture anyway, its flash illuminating him forever against a blue background of sparkles. "Well, that wasn't really the best picture, Brendan," she said, showing him his backside in the viewing screen of the camera.

"Don't you have REAL work to do now, Kristen, rather than bothering me?" His smile, though, disarmed the words. Kristen was the one girl that he always felt comfortable with, like a sister without the fights, he supposed, so this teasing between them was natural.

"Candid photos are my real work, Bren. You know that. Hey, hey," she said, excitement growing in her voice and animation intensifying in her face. Brendan stared back at her, hunching his shoulders to convey "What?"

"You and Caitlyn. How's it going? She tells me everything is really good. You two are so cute together. I've been telling her this for over a week now. Ever since---"

Kristen could fill a room and carry on both ends of a conversation very easily, and Brendan let her prattle on a bit as he thought of her role in getting them together. Her role as not-so-innocuous note-passer had kicked it into gear; rather moreover she was the matchmaker, or at least partial matchmaker. Of course she was. How had he not seen that? Because he'd just thought how little they'd talked since he and Caitlyn got together. Brendan dropped his façade at this point.

"Hey---"he said, cutting her off in mid-pontification, "Yeah. You're right. It's been going really well with us. You know I've never really had a girlfriend before . . ."

"She hasn't either Bren. She was 'with' some guy in her school in like Ohio or something, FOR A DAY! It's not like she's a pro at this either." She paused and let this sink in to Brendan. "But she REALLY likes you, Bren. I think, more than she thought she would."

"What is that supposed to mean?"

"No. It's not that. It's just that I think she sent that note because it's just kind of what you do when you like a guy. But she never thought you guys would get this tight this quick."

Brendan couldn't hide his smile, and this caused Kristen to beam also. He and Caitlyn had been spending a lot of time together in the last week, from library study time to bike rides to the movie that her mother chaperoned last Saturday. Any girl that could make him forget at times when the next Rays game was and who was pitching had to be something special.

"Well, yeah. That's true. But I don't want to jinx it by talking about it too much. We're just in sixth grade. This could end anytime."

"I would say we're in seventh now, Bren, and Caitlyn is not just any sixth-grade girl. You know that." She was right. Even Brendan's mother agreed that "That girl is pretty well put together for a 12-year-old," meaning "mature" in Momspeak. "And, hey, you've both got ME on your side." Here she thrust her thumbs at her chest in complete Kristen style. "I mean, really, what else could you want?"

Brendan threw his arms up and opened his mouth in mockery. She slapped his hand. At this Brendan surprised himself by opening his arms and hugging his childhood friend. Kristen swung her camera away from her body so it wouldn't get crushed and hugged him back.

"Okay, so lemme work here, okay?" she said, backing away and repositioning the camera square on her chest. She quickly snapped a shot of him.

"Really Kristen?" he protested.

"Just doing my job!"

"Sure. Hey, where's Caitlyn?"

"Last I saw her she was taking pictures of the shimmery ones near the field entrance," Kristen said, and left him.

This encounter and encouragement left him feeling magnanimous, if he was using that word correctly, and over the course of the next fifteen minutes he had met and talked to several different friends and partial friends of his, both surface-level and some deeper, and, yes, even occasionally allowed (or forced) the conversation to come to him and Caitlyn.

As he was just finishing a conversation with his hockey teammates Brian and Cole, he spotted Caitlyn close by. She was looking for him also, so he gestured to their table, and they sat down together again. It was getting loud in the gym, so it might require him to get closer to her so she could hear him. Maybe he'd have to speak really closely in her ear, closer than normal, to express himself. So his head would be maybe, what, two inches from hers, just to be heard.

Damn.

This was a conflicted evening for Caitlyn. Delightfully conflicted, but yes, conflicted for sure. She knew on the one hand that she must take excellent photos for Miss Thorssen and the yearbook, and that this would require a fair amount of time to find shots beyond the staid and stagnant kids-just-standing-around variety of pictures that she was taught never to take. She'd have to get close to groups, trying to focus on those kids who were the most animated or were most likely to do something crazy, something picture worthy. Being told repeatedly by her teacher (in confidence) that she was the best photographer on the staff, including the eighth grader who had been doing it for three years now, had the effect of making her want to be even better. Her classmates would sometimes make fun of her rabid determination to get pictures of kids everywhere and throughout the school day on campus, but they'd marveled just four days ago when they got their books. Her "C. Patterson" photo byline was throughout the book, and even middle school kids noticed who was getting these best shots. All the teasing they did of her throughout the school year was washed away in ten minutes when they all got their books and saw what she had been doing, piece by piece, moment by moment, all year. How many lunches had she given up, and soccer and football and basketball games she'd seen, and opportunities missed in the mornings to hang out with her friends and talk? But she'd created something lasting, something she could be proud of. Caitlyn longed to make a difference in the world, and yearbook was just a small part of what she could do.

But, to the conflict. Caitlyn knew that her boyfriend was both the lonely and semi-jealous sort, and she also knew that this kind of event, so open, so many possibilities, would be tough for him, and that she couldn't assuage this feeling much because of her responsibilities. So she'd told herself to not get lost in the moment and zone out with her job, or else he wouldn't be happy; or at least not comfortable. They'd discussed his need to find some friends and talk, friends beyond her, but he wasn't a good conversation starter. He could more than hold up his end if you got him going, but the getting him going part wasn't easy. He was even more sensitive than her, and that was saying something. But Brendan was worth it. That night they spent talking, star gazing, and sharing hopes and fears proved that he was not just your sports-driven boy, even if he was that too.

"Hiya," she said to him, sitting down back at their seats.

He mouthed "What?" as if he couldn't hear her. She repeated her line. He just shook his head. So she got really close to his ear and screamed "HIYA!" almost as loud as she could. He jerked back, feigning injury, and she pushed him further in that direction, causing his chair to wobble and Brendan to have to steady himself before he went backwards. He laughed and moved closer to her. His sense of humor. Yeah, I like that too, she thought.

"So, ace photographer, gettin' some good shots out there, tonight?" Brendan said. "They're not worried about Elsa trying to capture their soul in that box?"

"Wrong Disney flick there, pal. You're thinking of Ursula. Little Mermaid."

"Same difference," Brendan replied.

"So to answer your original question . . . Sure. I guess I'm getting the usual shots. Most kids are pretty awkward, but it's early. Probably my best shots have been of those video playing goons scrunching up their faces beating each other to death, or whatever they're doing."

"Not everyone is an Animal Crossing person though you know Cait?"

"You leave Animal Crossing alone!" she said, slapping his wrist. "There is nothing wrong with a game where no one gets hurt, no one dies, nothing gets destroyed, and your objective is to raise pets in harmony."

"Did the manufacturer just pay you for that statement, or did you steal it from the website?"

"Neither," Caitlyn replied, in mock anger. Brendan laughed. "Hey, listen. Have you voted for the Fire King and Ice Queen yet? I think the results are coming in pretty soon."

"You must be kidding. Why would I do such a stupid thing?" Brendan replied

"Yeah. I know. It's pretty silly. But they do it every year. It's a school tradition for generations now, and of course I have to take mucho snaps of it when it happens."

"I think I'm gonna pass on voting for the biggest nose in the air creeps. No thanks."

"Okay, but you can't complain if your choices don't win," she said.

"I got no dog in this race, Cait. Those people can all sail off on their yacht and drown in the ocean for all I care."

"YOU will not be winning the School Spirit award this year, my friend."

"Yeah. I already lost that, remember? You took the picture of Maria Furtado. Photo credit 'C. Patterson.'"

"Hey, that was a great picture."

"Sure it was. Of one of the most popular kids in the school, with her face painted, ribbons in her hair, dressed in some cheerleader uniform. One of my personal favorites."

"You are just jealous of my fame, aren't you?"

"That's it. You got me. Case closed."

"Okay, so I'm going to go vote. And no, don't ask. I'm not telling you for who."

"Oh please, please tell me," Brendan said, his hands clasped together in prayer, falling from the chair to his knees.

"Oh, okay. That's it. I might just vote for you and me for the crowns. How'd you like that?"

"That'll be one vote each for us. Don't think that'll put us on the Titanic though with the rest of them."

"Okay, so you just stay here at our table, happily anonymous."

"Damn straight. I'll be waiting for you, though." He smiled at her.

"I know. I'm sorry. I'll try to hurry. But I've gotta cover the crown thing."

"Can't Kristen do it?" he asked, half pleadingly.

Caitlyn looked at him. She did really want to spend time with him tonight. More time. And she had worked her butt off all year for journalism. And the year was really over, wasn't it? "Okay, I'll ask her to do it."

"Awesome," Brendan said, as Caitlyn moved into the ever-thickening throng of kids in groups of anywhere from two to ten that filled the gym's brown hardwood floor.

"Hello, students," principal Grayson said. "There are only ten minutes left to vote on tonight's Fire and Ice King and Queen. Ten minutes." Anabel looked from the principal back to her . . . friends. Well, if they weren't her friends, some cache was rubbing off on her for sure by hanging out with them for the past half hour or more. If her near-hysterical self of two hours ago could see what this night had become, that girl would have been way calmer. But how could she have predicted . . . this? Her goal here had been to have a few conversations with some of these girls, and the best phrase she could think of for the reality of the situation was that she had been "swept under their wings."

As she was musing on her good fortune, Anabel snapped back to reality when Alyssa Turner said, "Hey. Let's go get the boys in a Tik Tok," to which the others heartily agreed, and the group made its way across the floor.

"So, who would you dance with, if, you know, you HAD to dance with a girl tonight?" asked Tim Waters of Chris's group of boys, seated now at a table.

There were a few titters and one teeth suck among the six boys at the table, but then Mark Randolph said, "I guess Aria. I mean if I really had to." A few boys nodded their assent. Chris thought Aria was out of their league, but this was just a game, so he nodded as well.

"Aria ain't gonna dance with you, boy," said Rafael Ramirez. "Remember in fourth grade when you cut her hair in math?"

To which Mark replied, "Dude, this isn't reality."

"Yeah. Your reality is watching babes in Grand Theft," John replied, causing the table to break up.

"Okay, John. So who's your pick?"

"Lydia Gunter," John said, causing the table to explode with laughter.

"Look who's talking. Wasn't Lydia your partner in that group in Taylor's class? You probably even picked her, right?" A few chuckles were brought.

Gary Bellhorn, Chris's best friend, offered, "Definitely Cassandra Meyer. Love those blue eyes."

Mark turned to Chris, seated at his right, and asked, "So. Who's your pick, Christopher?"

Chris was always slightly uncomfortable talking about girls, but he usually chimed in with the rest when the subject came up. He brought his hand up under his chin and rubbed it, deep in faux concentration.

"Oh. It's that hard?" Mark replied.

"I mean, if I HAD to, I guess I'd pick---"

At that moment Anabel's group had rushed up to the table, and Christy Winter chirped, "Phone Pass Tik Tok, guys?" They looked at each other around the table, a few shrugging, a few just staring.

"Sure," John said, and the boys amidst a few grumbles gradually rose to join the girls.

Anabel's nervousness now doubled as the boys came to them. Getting in with the girls was her priority, but if there were cute boys along for the ride as well? More the better. As Christy was explaining the boy/girl order to everyone, Anabel looked onstage and saw her mother, setting up the microphone. She had told her that she'd have to leave the dance briefly to let the custodians in, that tonight they would come in later so they could clean up the dance mess. She wondered if her mother was thinking of her and how she was doing tonight.

"Okay, ready?" Christy was saying. "Anabel, you're fourth. Here." She pointed to the spot between Chris and Darius Anderson. Anabel assumed her position and Mark nodded that he was ready.

He started with, "I'm gonna pass the phone to a girl who has like five hundred cats." Mark passed the phone to Christy.

"I'm gonna pass the phone to a guy who can eat five hamburgers at once," Christy said.

Anabel's nervousness was increasing, and she had to think of something to say that wouldn't stand out, at least not in a negative way. Regardless of what she thought of her fifteen minutes of fame here, the other girls would be judging what she did for sure.

"I'm gonna pass the phone to a girl who fell in the mud on the second-grade art museum trip," Chris said, momentarily stunning Anabel and making her forget her line. She glanced around quickly, and, miraculously, no one was laughing. Or at least not laughing AT her. She relaxed and accepted the phone from Chris.

"I'm gonna pass the phone to a boy who puked chocolate milk all over the table in lunch last year," she said, bringing richer laughter than before from the assembled. Score!

As Jake accepted the phone from her, Anabel saw that her mother was gone from the stage. After the Tik Tok was finished she told Christy she needed to use the bathroom and left the table.

As Caitlyn left her table to find Kristen, six girls came to it, and one asked, "Are these seats taken?"

Brendan said, gesturing, "You can have all of them except this one."

"Is that Caitlyn's seat, Brendan?" one said, and Brendan now realized it was Rachel Murrow. Ugh. His first "girlfriend." For a minute. In second grade. Okay, not just a minute but a day and a half. Then she had dumped him. Caitlyn had gotten wind of this and teased him about it one night last week when they were sitting in his yard.

"Could be," Brendan said evasively.

"Brendan, come on. We just saw her leave."

"Okay, well yeah then. So why'd you ask?"

"And did you notice what she left you there, lover boy?" Rachel replied, her full lips fully accenting the "b" in "boy." Brendan had known Rachel for a few years, but each year it seemed she got cuter. It was probably the red hair, he thought. But her personality? The opposite.

Brendan looked down to see a small, wrapped gift by Caitlyn's place at the table, its rainbow-colored paper in stark contrast with the white tablecloth. He had been busy watching her disappear into the crowd and hadn't noticed. He picked it up and felt that it was nearly weightless. It was roughly in the shape of a playing card.

"Nope. Didn't see it," he replied.

"Well, it's pretty cool," she said. "I'd love to get a gift from a guy. Wonder what it is?"

"No idea, Rachel," Chris said, trying to elaborate little so the conversation would end.

"You know, if I had a girlfriend that gave me a gift after like two days of being together, I would think it's pretty serious. Whaddaya you think, Brendan?"

"We've been together two weeks, Rachel, and no, it's probably just something small."

"Brendan, how many other guys you see here tonight gettin' gifts?" Brendan shrugged. "Zero. That's how many."

"Okay, so?" he said.

"So . . . that tells me that you guys are pretty seer-e-us."

"Well, okay. I like her, sure. We're good friends."

Rachel turned to the girl seated at her left, Cassandra Meyer, and laughed. The other girls followed her lead. Chris turned away from them and once again looked toward the raised platform of the stage where he could see the principal looking for something. He heard Rachel say, "Look at Jaqueline's dress, ya'll," and the other girls begin to buzz like a hive.

Brendan then realized that his nervousness and the half three glasses of soda he had drank at home during dinner had caught up to him. He wanted to be at the table to see Caitlyn's face when he pulled out the box, but he really had to go. At that point a scheme came into his mind. He would set the box down on the table, go use the bathroom quickly, then watch over it from a safe distance as he waited for her to return. He wanted to see her true reaction, apart from him, when she first saw it. Noticing that the focus of the girls was cattiness to all in their radius and away from him, he slipped it from his pants pocket onto his spot at the table, less noticeably because it was right at the edge and its whiteness blended in with the tablecloth, and headed for the boys' bathroom, well, locker room actually, connected to the gym through double doors.

Ever on the alert, and despite the principal's announcement of the impending coronation, Caitlyn in the midst of searching for Kristen saw a great picture possibility and just couldn't resist. The voting table, one of the more impressive decorating accomplishments of the night, was now bathed in a really cool shade of blue, maybe Cerulean, and she found a spot that was unencumbered with kids to take the shot. But as she framed it, she realized that the principal's secretary was seated at the voting table, and also just then four girls rushed up to the table clutching the white ballots that they were given at the door. Spoiled, she realized, as the kids blotted out the table and ruined the lighting. Maybe after she found Kristen she'd retry.

Just then a goofy boy named Adam started doing the worst breakdance Caitlyn had ever seen just a few feet from her. He had in a matter of seconds amassed a sizeable crowd of gawkers. This time she wouldn't miss. She framed quickly and shot. Her screen showed him in an impossibly perfect angle, his feet up in the air like a dead cockroach, his hands splayed to his side like he was trying to stop a fast-spinning ride, and his face just adorably, sixth-gradably perfect. A teacher/chaperone quickly stepped in to stop the shenanigans, and the delicious ruckus stopped as quickly as it started.

Caitlyn tried to imagine this shot on a big screen of dance memories at their eighth-grade graduation and knew it would be a hit. Wildwood Middle for two years now commemorated the leaving eighth graders with a ceremony that included awards, dinner, superlatives, music, and a slideshow of pictures of the kids from sixth to eighth grade, with a special highlight on major events like the dance. Caitlyn knew this because she had covered this year's graduation on Wednesday night. The audience might lose it at that point upon seeing this picture twenty feet high on the gym's walls. Miss Thorssen had told them many a time that their pictures had multiple purposes beyond the yearbook, including the school's Facebook page, the morning show, and of course the slideshow.

The sight of Kristen shattered her photographer's dream reverie, and she said, "Hey! Kris!" as loudly as she could manage, barely cutting through the wall of sound from the speakers and making her friend's head turn.

"Hey there, girl," Kristen responded. "How ya doin' tonight?"

"Oh, I just got the best shot of Adam attempting to breakdance. This is a bomb shot!"

"Okay, I meant how are you and BRENDAN doing, Cait?"

"Well, now that you mention it, I have come to ask a favor."

"Whaddaya got?"

"I know I was assigned to take the pictures of the crown ceremony, but could you maybe please-you're-the-best-I-owe-you-one do it for me?"

"Sure! You wantin' more time with Brendan?" she said, raising her eyebrows.

"Yes. And fortunately the feeling is mutual."

"Yeah. I got it. No worries. You go back to your man."

Caitlyn hugged her, their cameras clattering together between them, forbidding a close hug.

"I owe you," Caitlyn replied.

"You mean you owe me more than you did before, which is already like, UNCALCULABLE?"

"That's Incalculable, and sure, whatever you say," Caitlyn said, ending the encounter and sending her back toward Brendan. Well, almost toward Brendan. She had to slide a few steps to her right to get a clear view of the stage. It was empty! The secretary must be on a bathroom break. Caitlyn then moved a couple steps toward the stage, lessening the possibility of anyone coming between her camera and the shot, a key Thorssen rule. Just as she was going to press the button, someone jostled her from behind, and the resulting shot was a bit blurry and shaded. She looked to see who the offending party was and the culprit had vanished. She quickly lined up again for another shot and now there were half a dozen kids in the shot. She chalked that up to happenstance, and as she had done many times before was left with the photographer's fleeting sense of loss.

She turned and scouted out the quickest path back to Brendan and saw an opening in the crowd to her left. After a few steps she saw a group of five girls checking out a picture on a phone, which was held up almost in reverence to its glory. Not being able to resist a good shot, Caitlyn took one of the scene. The girl holding the phone whirled around.

"Hey, Caitlyn," Mia offered. "You've gotta see this picture. You'll love it."

This was not unusual, this showing to her of quality snaps that others had taken. Being known as Picture Girl did have its perks. As the phone got closer, Caitlyn could appreciate the quality of the Insta post. A girl's chest, neck, and half her smile, with the "Fiery Foods!" neon sign cutting through her neck area in the background. She was jealous. "And check out that necklace!" Mia said. "I wonder who gave that to her, or if she bought it herself?" Somehow Caitlyn had missed the probably one-inch gold heart charm on a gold necklace perfectly centered on her chest. It was tinged blue because of the blue lights from the "cold" side of the gym. The necklace radiated happiness. This girl was proud of this. Someone had definitely bought it for her. Jealousy couldn't be helped in the photography trade. She sighed.

"You're right. Great pic. Thanks Mia," Caitlyn said, and stepped away from the group and toward Chris.

When Caitlyn arrived back at the table it didn't take her long to know something had gone down between Brendan and the girls. Brendan was staring intently at the center of the table like a cat ready to pounce on its prey, and Rachel and the other girls were busily gossiping about something. She sat and looked between he and Rachel. Rachel's face turned from a smirk to a bright, fake smile. Caitlyn narrowed her eyes at her.

"Hey Bren. You okay?" she asked. He nodded. "What happened?" He shook his head. She looked back at Rachel, who rolled her eyes. Caitlyn took his hand and overcame his resistance to let her hold it in her lap. She looked at him and waited for him to say something. He finally spoke, barely above a whisper.

"It's nothing. Just Rachel being an idiot. Pretty much the usual."

Caitlyn saw Rachel leaning forward, straining to hear their conversation.

"Can you just butt out?" Caitlyn said to her.

Rachel sat back in her chair. Caitlyn saw that Brendan was desperately trying to regain control and squeezed his hand.

"Hey. I'm here. It's okay."

He finally turned to look at her. "I know." He smiled. He let out a deep breath. "I'm okay now." He reached into his pocket and pulled out a small white velvet jewelry box. Rachel, following their every move, of course saw this.

"Wow. Look at that, Caitlyn. He must really lllooovvveee you."

Caitlyn did her best to burn a laser-induced hole through Rachel's skull, to no avail.

"What, you don't want it? I'll take it," she said, reaching her hand across the table in a mock attempt to grab the box.

Brendan's glare stopped her motion. "Don't. You. Dare." Brendan said. Rachel withdrew her hand.

"Come on, Caitlyn. You've got a really cute boyfriend. You should be happy."

"Can you just drop it?!" Caitlyn said, her voice raised.

"And look, Brendan. Look what Caitlyn got you. A tiny little present that looks like a rainbow. And hey, you got her something back? Wonder what's in there?" Rachel said. The smirk returned.

"Could you just NOT?" Brendan said, wanting to cut this off as soon as possible.

"Brendan, why?" she said. "Aren't you happy she got you something?"

Brendan thought of ignoring her but realized this wasn't going to be easy because of her audience.

"Rachel, why do you have to be a pain in the ass to everyone?" Brendan asked, his mouth giving voice to his previous thought.

Rachel, feasting on the bait being taken, replied, "Now why would you say that Brendan? Are you afraid to talk about your girlfriend? Afraid I'll scare her away?" Caitlyn turned away from the girls, focusing on a spot on the gym's ceiling and hoping that this would end soon.

"Of all the people you could have set your sights on tonight, Rachel, why us? Can't you find bigger game somewhere else?" asked Brendan.

"No particular reason. This is just where there were empty seats," she said casually, waving her hand at him in dismissal.

Brendan could feel his anger rising again, the kind of anger usually reserved to punish someone on the boards in hockey. His face was getting flushed. Caitlyn reached out to touch his arm, and this had a slightly stabilizing effect.

"Come on, open your presents you guys. We want to see your reactions," Rachel said, bringing a few snickers from the assembled.

"Can. You. Just. LEAVE!" Brendan said, spittle coming from his mouth.

The previously unflappable Rachel was taken aback by this, and her girls even more so. She pushed back her chair, said "FINE!" and she and her lackeys skulked away.

Brendan, seeing Caitlyn was shaken, tried to lighten things up. "Gee, is that what it takes to get some privacy in this joint?"

"Yeah, maybe," she said, seeing that Brendan's three shades of red were down to two and cooling quickly. He shrugged. "So, what's this?" She pointed to the box.

"Just a little something," Brendan replied coyly.

"And what is THIS?" Brendan asked back.

"Same," she said, lifting her shoulders to accent the supposed normality of the situation.

"All right, then," he said, feigning disinterest.

"Hey, have you heard the music they're playing tonight? It's a lot of eighties and nineties stuff, but more indie and underground." She looked at his blank expression. "Okay, so you don't know any of it, right?"

"We've had this conversation before, Cait. I know maybe ten percent of the bands that you're into. Most I have no clue about. Like, who's this playing now?"

"This is 'I Will Follow.' U2. Off their first record, 'Boy.'" She started singing to the track.

"How can you possibly know all that?" Brendan said, exasperated.

"Are you kidding? My dad LOVES U2. They're like his favorite band or something. I've been hearing their songs since I was born. Before probably."

"Yeah, but to know what record it's off? That's crazy. And they've been around fifty years or more and probably have thirty albums!"

"My dad gave me a lot of his records when he decided that those and the CD's needed to go in favor of Spotify. I used to play them as a kid in my room."

"So that's the origin of Cait's limitless knowledge of music. Her father."

She forced a smile. "My dad's pretty cool, I guess?"

"Yet another thing I like about you. You LIKE your parents."

"Well . . . yeah," she replied, getting Brendan's hands thrown in the air in response.

Realizing he was hopelessly outclassed on the subject of music and getting increasingly nervous, Brendan switched gears. "So, who goes first?"

"Oh, definitely you," was the response.

"All right then," Caitlyn replied, taking her gift and exchanging places with Brendan's.

As Brendan was getting ready to open the small package, Principal Grayson's voice once again boomed through the gym. "Excuse me. Attention please. Attention students."

Brendan turned the gift over to open it, and Caitlyn covered his hand with hers. "Bren. Not now. This is the crowning ceremony." Brendan screwed his face up in mock-terror and Caitlyn smacked his hand and withdrew her gift. "Just wait a coupla minutes." When she started to reply, she shushed him.

"You're just a sucker for this stuff, aren't you?" Brendan asked. Caitlyn smiled dimly.

They both turned to the dais in the middle of the court. Nearly all the lights in the gym went off, leaving the stage's left half illuminated by a blue spotlight and the right a red one, with Principal Grayson centered in a white beam. About 50 feet from the dais, Anabel's group, now seated, went dead silent, one girl stopping the momentum of the cheese-slathered Dorito on the way to her mouth and lowering it in respect back to her plate. Anabel quickly reassumed her seat.

"Those of you who can sit, please do," Grayson announced, pushing her hands down to indicate seating. "And everyone be quiet."

When one of the gaming boys screamed "What???" at top volume, she turned to stare that way, and a teacher flicked the switch on the power strip and the games went dark.

Across the gym from Anabel's group, Chris's throng, now waiting their turn at the video game station, started to make fun of the coming announcement. "Do we really have to be quiet for this." "Blah blah blah." "Here you go Mark. Your big moment!" Then a lone, loud "Hey, why'd you turn off my game?" which was met with stony silence from the principal.

Caitlyn wondered if Kristen was in position to take the shots she needed, and then thought, of course she is. Kristen took her job as seriously as Caitlyn.

"As you all know," the principal's voice began again as the crowd was settling down. "Each year we award the Vulcan crown, symbolizing fire, from the Roman god Vulcan, to one boy, and to the girl goes the Ice Queen crown, from the White Witch Jodi in *The Chronicles of Narnia*." Here she paused for effect, and pointed to the crowns, being displayed on purple pillows by a seventh-grade girl and boy along either side of her. With the crowns held aloft, the gold metal of the boys' crown and the sparkling glass of the girls' hit their respective blue and red spotlights, sending scattered light onto the gym's ceiling. "This is the sixty-fifth year that crowns will be given out here at Wildwood." Some polite applause followed.

"Wow. That's pretty cool," Anabel mused, getting a quick nod from the other girls at the table, each of them thinking how it would fit and look on her head.

"And you also should know that last year's winners, be they still at Wildwood, have the duty of crowning this year's victors. So let me present to you once again Colton Wood and Lara Miller, the fire and ice king and queen from last year." There was a smattering of applause here, the principal's face showing only slight disdain at those who were overexuberant. She regained her regal composure. There was a slight titter in the audience. "And so, the votes have been counted. And it was a close contest, as always. We have so many fine young people at Wildwood. I'm sure if I were voting it would be tough for me to choose also."

"Is this ever gonna end?" Mark said to Chris, who was, as they all were, staring at the stage because it was pretty much the only thing you could see in the darkness.

"So, students, parents, teachers, and administrators, as you should know, while the origins of the crowns stay the same, our fine art department headed by Ms. Adams designs new versions of each crown each year. The winners will wear a first edition crown, unique and original. Now, I am pleased to announce this year's winners, who will first come to the stage and be crowned before they dance their traditional first dance together." She paused, trying to build up the room's tension. She looked out and scanned the audience, front, back, and sides, like she always did in an attempt to get their attention and respect at lunch, in the hallways, etc. After five seconds, she began again.

"I am proud to announce that this year's winner for a girl, who gets to wear the ice queen crown and keep it for two years, is Anabel Donan."

The crowd began to murmur, clearly not anticipating this upset. Anabel's mouth was open, her eyes were wide, and her palms were flat on the table. Everyone around her, including the stunned girls at the table, each having realized the crown was theirs for the taking and that they were robbed, turned to gape at the winner/imposter at their table.

Anabel froze, feeling for the first time in her life the center of this many peoples' attention. She tried to compose herself by closing her mouth and planting a huge smile on her face, but anyone looking beyond her face would see her hands, still flat on the white tablecloth, shaking.

"Anabel, if you'll stand."

Anabel, willing her hands to calm, slowly rose but stood still for the announcement of the winning boy. A blue spotlight shone on her, coming from the direction of the stage, blinding her. She put her hand up to block the beam, and the attentive spotlight operator lowered it slightly, making it possible for her to drop the smile and in the darkness rather wear briefly the more honest look of surprise and maybe even terror.

Brendan said, "Who's she?"

Caitlyn replied, "Brendan, you have at least one class with her. I think it's PE. I've seen her in your class! And she's the girl that we saw in the middle of the road last week yelling for help when that eighth-grade girl crashed her bike and was bleeding. Remember?" Brendan nodded. "Later Georgia told me that this girl had flamed her on Insta just days earlier."

"Wow. That's pretty amazing," Brendan said.

"I know, right."

"Well anyway, we dress out separately. How would I know if she's in a class of 70?" Caitlyn then turned back to the principal in anticipation of the second announcement.

Chris looked from boy to boy at his table and saw that his friends were confused also. He of course knew Anabel and had been around her a fair amount outside of school because their parents were tight. This girl, the one who once dared him to eat dirt in Pre-K, is the ice queen?

The principal raised and lowered her hands, signifying that she wanted quiet.

"Okay, everyone. Quiet. One more to go!"

The auditorium was quickly quiet, more because of the Anabel surprise than the principal's direction.

"All right. Here we go," Mrs. Grayson continued. "The winner of the Vulcan crown, our king of fire, is Chris Lawson."

The boys at Chris's table exploded with "Yeah!" and "There it is!" and "Let's go!" The red spotlight found Chris and his dumbfounded expression. Jake stood up and pounded him on the back so hard that Chris had to steady himself on the table to remain upright. "Go get your girl!" someone said, and Chris's legs moved almost involuntarily toward the stage. His thoughts were pretty much: What is happening? There's gotta be a mistake here. Sure, he didn't have any real enemies that he knew of. Sure, he tried not to stand out negatively when he spoke and acted. Sure, he had plenty of friends. But he wasn't sure and never thought that enough people knew and liked him . . . to this extent? Looking up, he saw Anabel making her way towards the stage, nearly reaching her stairs well before he was halfway.

Seeing her bathed in the blue spotlight that was following her in the dark gym (as the red one was annoyingly following him) made him reappraise her. Her hair was a pretty brown, and it was cut even in the back, the way he liked it. Although he couldn't see her face, he remembered that it was always pretty. Even the slight bulge of her stomach didn't matter so much. And she had always been kind to him, so yeah, there could have been way worse choices here, if he had to pick. But wait: Does this even matter?

Anabel, nearing the steps, turned to look back at Chris and saw that his face looked half-confused and half-contemplative. Not the reaction she would have hoped for had she scripted this, but she wondered what her own face was showing now. She felt it appropriate to wait until he met her at his bottom step so they could ascend together, so she did. She saw his pace quicken and his face gain more purpose.

When they were together, they each took the first step on the way to the dais. Anabel noticed the principal with her arms outstretched one to each student and thought that Mrs. Grayson's background had to be in the theater.

Chris noticed Colton Wood, a hockey opponent/friend of his holding the beckoning crown, smirking as he moved closer to the top.

Anabel noticed Lara's smile, as fake as and as really amazing as ever, and her flowing raven hair, as she waited her arrival.

"Now the new king and queen will be crowned," said the principal.

Back at Caitlyn's table, Brendan said, "How obvious is this lady? Like she has to narrate every moment of this farce," bringing once again a shush from the rapt Caitlyn.

Chris looked out of place, but after a quick resettling of her crown, its "icy" spikes probably a foot and a half above her head, Anabel looked completely in her element, like she had been born for this.

"I give you, ladies and gentlemen, boys and girls, our new king and queen," Grayson announced while holding her hands up for affect and possibly applause.

The gym responded with more applause than she expected, causing Grayson to drop her hands and nod her head. She then looked at the kids.

"The tradition here at Wildwood Middle is for the past queen to choose the first song that our couple will dance to, so I'll turn it over to Lara."

Before Lara moved to the mic, Anabel turned around to see if her mother was watching. She was, meeting Anabel's gaze with her hands to either side of her head and maybe the biggest smile Anabel had ever seen. Anabel mouthed, "I love you" at her mom and turned back around. Lara moved from her place by Anabel and adjusted the mike before she spoke, her voice impossibly bubbly.

"I thought long and hard about this one. Music is so important to me," she began.

Caitlyn said to Brendan, "Yeah, right. I bet she chooses some Whitney Houston or Journey song here."

"So there's the sarcasm I've been waiting for," Brendan said, clapping once. Which of course brought another shush from his girlfriend.

"So," Lara continued," I chose a song that I only heard for the first time last week. It was coming from my brother's room. Usually I have no idea what he's listening to."

"She's so fake," Caitlyn said, with Brendan laughing at her, happy that she was finally sharing his mood.

"But this song, this song really hit me. It's really why we're all here."

She paused for effect, and someone coughed and said, "Let's go." Brendan thought: she's practicing for her Miss Teen U.S.A. pageant.

Her smile drooped for a half second, then came the kicker. "Here's 'Forever' by Death Rattle." She gestured to the DJ stand, and the spotlight hit the surprised DJ, who scrambled to find the song on his laptop, a job made more difficult by the spotlight's glare.

Chris noticed Anabel shaking and mouthed "Are you okay?" to her, which brought a return smile.

Brendan, noticing Caitlyn mouthing "No way," said, "What is THAT song?"

Caitlyn shook her head. "I'm gonna make you the playlist to end all playlists to make you hipper." Brendan shrugged. "But Bren, it's a GREAT song. By Death Rattle." He again looked blank. "William Jones?"

"William Jones? That's about the most generic name I've ever heard. That guy is famous? With THAT name?"

"There's not a lot common about him," Caitlyn responded. "He's probably responsible more for the origin of modern 'goth' than anyone." There was a pause. "Bren, you wanna dance?"

Brendan quickly shook his head.

"C'mon! It'll be fun."

"Caitlyn. This is their dance, meaning no one else dances. Not that I would want to anyway."

Considering this, she replied, "You are both right and NO FUN," she said, turning to watch the pair on the dais descend, this time with solo white spots trained on them rather than red and blue ones.

All Anabel could think was, over and over, don't trip don't trip don't trip. Chris was thinking: Dance? How?

Just then Rachel and her girls returned to Brendan's table, giving him the idea to completely ignore them by ostensibly staring at the royals as they came together on the dance floor. Their spotlights merged together and became one. How cute, Brendan thought.

When the couple met in the floor's middle, the instrumental portion began, the organ playing over the top of a basic beat before the guitar kicked in after a short while. Neither Chris nor Anabel had heard the song before, but each liked the beat and melody right away. Chris, his mind scanning the ways he remembered seeing couples dance and coming up with nothing that fit here, looked at his partner for some cue to get this thing started. He was even more conscious now of his red pants, he of course being the only boy clad as such in the entire gym. Anabel had thought of this moment before, this first dance with a guy, and imagined it being a slow dance, just the two of them at the fringe of the room's energy. Clearly this was not that, so she tried to think of a way to just get through this, with only about a couple hundred people watching her and a partner who clearly looked both helpless and pleading to her for assistance.

Not really finding a solution, Anabel slowly started moving, her body sliding from side to side and her fingers snapping to the beat. Chris affected a poor imitation of even this, but hey, she thought, and least it's begun. The vocals began:

> "When we first met
> I was at a loss
> To describe how I felt
> But now I think of forever"

While Chris was struggling to not look completely inept, Anabel listened to the lyrics in hopes of diverting her nervousness and imagined and hoped a guy someday would say this to her and mean it. Chris looked up at her as if to say, "Am I okay?" and she nodded back and smiled at him.

"Oh, God, I love this song!" Caitlyn said.

"I admit, it sounds good," Brendan replied. At the next instrumental break, he said, "So. You ready to do gifts?"

Caitlyn nodded, never breaking the rhythm her body had found in the song. Brendan turned his gift over and found a seam to pry it open. Almost immediately he noticed it was a sports card, and a beat later he saw that it was a Gretzky card. Not just A Gretzky card, but THE Gretzky card. His rookie card. Holy crap! What is happening?

"So, you like it," Caitlyn stated flatly in response to the puzzled look on Brendan's face.

Just then Brendan realized this could not be the original rookie card, the one that had just sold for $3.75 million at auction. This card was so hardwired into his brain as the Holy Grail of hockey cards, Brendan having drawn it over and over after Grandpa George told him about it to the point where he could almost explain the lighting and shading pictured on the ice, even before he printed out a copy and pasted it on his bedroom wall, that he somehow even for a moment thought it could be the real thing.

Brendan looked at her. "Oh my God, Caitlyn. It's awesome."

"You know it's not the first printing, right?"

"Yeah, I do. But still," Brendan's face glazed over and he stared at the card again.

"You talk about him so much; I figured he was your favorite player."

Brendan reached out and took her hands into his. "This is perfect." Caitlyn beamed.

Anabel sensed that something must happen at this point, some progression, but wasn't sure how to accomplish this. Chris was still dancing, his body more in her rhythm now than before. She had to move close to him because he wasn't even looking at her. After starting maybe four feet apart, Anabel closed this distance by half, causing Chris to look up at her in surprise. She looked at him and smiled, and he returned the smile. He's starting to get into this, she thought, and he noticed that the difference in their height was probably five inches.

Caitlyn, still beaming, mouthed the words "You've become my forever" as Mr. Jones was singing them and looked at Brendan, who initially tried to deflect her gaze by looking above her head. When it became apparent that she wasn't going to break her stare, he looked back at her to hear and see her mouth again, "You've become my forever." He smiled.

Brendan said, "Okay. Your turn," gesturing at the white box in front of Caitlyn.

On the floor, Anabel had again halved the distance between them, at first noticing Chris back away slightly, then looking up and nodding at her. He wouldn't have been her first choice, but here she was, dancing with a cute, athletic boy in front of most of the sixth grade, the spotlight encasing them together. They were maybe a foot apart, and Chris could now smell her perfume and see her glowing face. His doubt and defenses were both now coming down, and he found his hands doing something he never could have imagined them doing. They reached out and took hers for a moment, surprising her. Anabel took his back, and after a few seconds pushed away a bit and twirled around, causing her dress to whirl about her. Chris had no idea how to respond to that, so he repeated grabbing her hands, and she pushed and twirled again. Someone in the audience said, "Whooo!" Anabel's head spun in that direction, but she was blinded again by the spotlight. This is pretty great, she thought. I almost couldn't have planned this any better, she thought.

Caitlyn looked at Rachel and the other girls and turned away from them slightly. She saw the small box in front of her and braced for both the chill she'd feel from the fabric and whatever was in there.

"Wait," Brendan said. "Close your eyes." Trying to blot out the snickers at the table, Caitlyn did as instructed. This is pretty cheesy, Brendan thought. This is not the way I would have chosen to do this, had not Kristen not only come up with the idea and told me that it would be twice as special actually AT the dance as opposed to what I think would be a more appropriate time and place, like in front of my house when we watched the stars for example.

Brendan took the box and made the necklace easily accessible to her blinded fingers. "Okay, so in just a second you're going to open the box, take out what's in it, and hand it to me." Caitlyn giggled slightly, then nodded. She opened the box and took out the object, which her fingers told her was a necklace with a charm on it. "Okay, hand it to me. Keep your eyes closed."

"This is SO adorable," Rachel said, seemingly free of sarcasm.

Brendan took the necklace from her and, as he had practiced more than a few times, undid the clasp and was careful to center the charm along it. He got up and walked behind her, easily able to drape it around her neck and re-do the clasp.

"Okay. Open them."

Caitlyn felt the necklace with her fingers and said, "Oh, Brendan. I love it."

"But you can't even see it yet," he replied.

"I don't care. I still love it."

Rachel and two of the other girls murmured "oooohh." Brendan was too happy right now to even attempt to assess sincerity. "Wait," Rachel said. "I've got a mirror," and reached into her purse, withdrew it, and handed it to Caitlyn.

In the center of the dance floor and not wanting to close their distance any further, Anabel had settled Chris into an easier rhythm, and the pair continued to dance close together. Chris thought that this was way more fun than he ever would have imagined and tried to think of ways to counter the ribbing his friends would give him. He then decided that it didn't matter. Anabel at this point wondered what was going to happen after the dance. Would they return to their separate tables and later pretend that this never happened? Probably. Just brace for it, Annie. But oh, she now didn't want that. She wanted more. Let's just see what happens, she thought.

Caitlyn grabbed the mirror as Death Rattle was going into the song's finale and raised it to chest level. The thoughts of "I love it" and "Oh my God no" flew simultaneously in and out of her mind, her face betraying the thoughts in turn. Brendan's anticipation turned to concern. He had asked around, checked the internet, asked his MOM even, for the right charm. Was the heart too much? Too soon?

Caitlyn's face now blank, she turned to look at Rachel, seeing behind her the "Fiery Foods" neon sign she had seen in the Insta post, on the phone. And Rachel's neck, and chin, and smile. And then somehow the necklace even briefly appeared on Rachel's chest before the cursed image dissolved in her mind.

Brendan was now completely bewildered, asking himself, "Why was she looking at Rachel instead of me?" Caitlyn slammed down the mirror, face up, causing its surface to spiderweb shatter but remain intact.

Rachel said, "What the---"and stared at the remnants of her mirror. As William Jones sang the song's coda, "That's when I knew we were forever," Caitlyn slowly rose, shock and horror on her face. When upright, she clutched at the necklace, and, finding it, ripped it violently from her neck and held it in her hand. Brendan stood, too stunned to speak. "It looks better on her!" she said, throwing it at Brendan and hitting him square in the face. He bent down and picked it off the floor where it rested. His face pleaded to her for understanding, and he took a step in her direction. "DON'T FOLLOW ME!!!" she screamed and ran toward the gym door's exit.

Brendan tried to compose himself despite what felt like electric shocks running through his body. He looked up at the other girls at the table. "What was she talking about?" he demanded of them. No answer. So he repeated it at twice the volume, spitting it at Rachel. "WHAT WAS SHE TALKING ABOUT?"

Rachel's face was alarmed yet questioning, but she said nothing. He looked at the other girls. None met his gaze longer than a second. Brendan looked down at the table. Rachel blew out air.

"I don't know, Brendan. She just freaked out," she said.

"Shut. Up," he said, in equal turns maniacal and measured.

Rachel put up her hands in a giving up gesture. Brendan put his head in his hands, trying to ascertain how this had gone so wrong. The girls then left the table as they had before, and Brendan started to quietly sob. Not even he could have conjured this worst-case scenario.

The song having ended, the audience in some sections applauded while others started to murmur, having been freed of their ordered quiet. Anabel looked at Chris, trying to say "Well?" with her face and body. He returned her gesture. She then stepped toward him, taking his hand in hers. He allowed this, and then Anabel lifted them up in a show of appreciation to the audience, to the voters perhaps, or the few, mainly adults, who applauded. At that moment the lights came back on and the video games started to boot up again.

Their hands still aloft, Anabel slowly lowered them but didn't right away let go of Chris's. She both nodded and gestured that he come join her at her table, and Chris went, yieldingly. This is so not happening, she thought, realizing that her star would probably never shine brighter than this, but hoping someday that it might.

TWO YEARS LATER

Saturday, May 23, 2021: Six days before graduation

Saturday, May 23

So glad I have to do this every day to explain how stupid my life is. Stupid and getting stupider. By the minute. So in today's game (we were tied one all with four minutes left to go in the third) I took a hard hit from the Whaler's Steve Hill on a backcheck and slammed my shoulder into the boards. It was on fire and I limped to the bench as the referee blew the whistle. This league always confuses me. They say they don't want 14-year-olds getting hurt and they'll call penalties pretty quickly for hard hits, but then they don't all the time. It's not like I don't dish out my share though.

So anyway, I'm on the bench, and the coach checks me out. Even though my shoulder is screaming at me otherwise, I lie and say I'm okay. He knows he's got to put me back in. I'm the only one who can guard Hill. Four minutes left. He scores. We lose. Not gonna happen. So coach calls time out to give me a breather. My shoulder barely feels like it's there, so I'm lifting that shoulder, my left—not my main stick shoulder--and rotate it as much as I can to get some feeling back. The coach is calling a play and I'm half listening, half thinking how no matter what play is called I'm going to knock the crap out of Hill first chance I get. I look over at the Whaler bench and he SMILES at me.

The ref blows the whistle and we start again. We win the face-off at neutral ice and Kevin starts the play by getting the puck and passing to Alex. I'm on the left wing and I'm open. Alex threads the needle between two defenders and the puck hits my blade perfectly and I'm in full stride. Alex is well-covered, so I have two options. Pass to Kevin in the middle for a shot full on by the goalie (he's the best on the team in head-on shots, especially five-hole ones) or deke the middle defender and shoot from a 45-degree angle. Then I see Hill in front of me, coming from a shot on the boards against my crumpled teammate Brian, and I knew my plan.

I look at the goalie, pull my stick back like I'm going to shoot, then send a no-look pass to Kevin, who works his magic, going top shelf left just past the goalie's glove. The puck clangs against the bar and goes in. We're up two one. I can hear a quick roar from the crowd.

But that's not the story.

This is the story.

As soon as I released the puck, Hill skated in front of me. He was off balance still from Brian's hit. So, easy prey. I raised my stick and hit him with a full power thrust in the chest. In that moment I was already forming my argument that he was coming at me and it was self-defense. Yeah. Right. You should have seen the look on his face as he flew backwards, hit the ice and then thudded against the wall. And then he didn't move. At all. I skated away to join my celebrating teammates, and a hush cut off the temporary roar of the crowd and filled the arena.

At that point and without turning around I just skated back to the bench, but their faces were filled with concern if not out and out horror. I forced myself to turn around when I hit the board. Coach McCloskey was between me and the goal, and he looked at me like I was Satan. He was just stunned. And that's hard to do to McCloskey, who had played minor-league hockey in his day. All Hill's teammates, his coach, all the refs, were there at Hill's crumpled body. Again, dude wasn't moving. Well, that's what he deserved, I thought. Shouldn't have cheap-shotted me earlier. Seconds turned into minutes and he still wasn't moving. And then it hit me. Coach turned from that scene again to me.

"What did you do?" he asked, as if scolding a dog.

"What?" I replied. "You saw what he did to me on the boards."

"Brendan, this is way beyond that. Come on." McCloskey's mouth was open, and he rubbed his hand down his face, almost like in a movie. "You're going to get suspended by the league. I'M going to suspend you." Brendan opened his mouth but nothing came out. "You better hope he's okay," he said, before joining the gathered throng near the Whaler's goal. I turned and saw frantic parents, scared siblings, and heard a woman screaming directions to 9-1-1. At that point, I knew what I had done. As Grandpa George often said: **truth will out.**

But I still didn't feel much either way about it.

-Brendan

Chris thought it was convenient that the coaches on his travel team found a hotel right across from the baseball complex where the 14U state championships were being held. He'd left his room two minutes ago and waved at his parents sitting in the bleachers as he entered the dugout. His team was on the field taking grounders and fly balls being hit by the assistant coach.

"You here today?" This was from the head coach, Coach Bryson.

Even though Chris knew what he meant, he replied, "Standing right here in front of you, Coach."

Coach Bryson narrowed his eyes at Chris. "In body? No doubt. In mind? Only you can tell me that."

Chris had been told that he'd be pitching today, and clearly the coach was trying to figure out whether this was a good idea. This was the semi-final game of the tournament, and if they lost they were out. A win would mean advancing to tomorrow's championship game on the main field with some state TV coverage and "exposure," as the coaches liked to say. His last start was fairly a disaster. Five earned runs in two innings. Last night Chris had hit a three-run-shot in the bottom of the seventh to put his team ahead. They won 6-4. But last night he really felt like playing, felt like being there. Tonight . . .

"Sure, coach. I'm ready to go."

Silence.

"You know, if you're not, if you're in whatever head space you get into at times where it seems like you'd just as soon be someplace else, then you're just pissing all over the efforts of the, the other coaches, your teammates, all the parents. Hell, even the other team in a way."

Silence.

"What do you want me to say, coach? It's your decision. Start me or not."

Chris looked down to see another pitcher, Joshua, warming up with a catcher. He'd go if Chris didn't.

"Well, I'd get four-five solid out of Joshua. Three-four earned. We'd have to score some to win, and we're facing a tough southpaw today. You. Who knows? You might walk four in the first or no-hit them five." The coach sat down took off his cap. He looked at Chris. "You gonna make a fool of me today, boy?"

"I don't plan on it, sir. I'll do my best."

The coach, having heard this before, looked out at Joshua warming up.

"Joshua. Come on in. Get the gear on. You're catching Lawson today. He needs to warm up."

Chris saw the boy's face fall slightly as he started back in and picked up the catcher's shin guards. The coach leaned in closer to Chris.

"Okay. We'll ride our season on you today. Don't make me regret the decision."

He walked over to his bag and handed Chris the two shiny game balls. Chris put one in his glove and turned the other over in his fingers, already starting to practice his different grips for his different pitches. Chris walked out onto the field as his team was coming in to start stretching. As the coach started on his pre-game pep talk with the team Chris turned to ostensibly listen, but his head was elsewhere.

He began to notice other players at times casting looks at him. They're probably trying to figure out the same thing coach is, he thought. He decided to look over their heads, like he was concentrating. I won't really know what version of me is here today until I hit the mound. That'll have to be good enough for all of them.

So, where to go next? I can always get them into the depths of despair—that's the easy part—but bringing them out? Not so easy. Jodi's been kicked out of her band. Broken up with her girlfriend. Weed has so consumed her life and reason for being that she can't see much past her next high. Relationships with her parents, her friends, her bandmates—all gone. So, where do I go from here?

Caitlyn stared at her blank computer screen and its chapter title: Despair. So, do I have her bring herself out of this, by herself? Or have one person, multiple people, help? But to what degree do they not trust her, or to what degree do they reach out to help her. She's screwed up so many times now. Who would trust her? But then again, she was a basically good person before all this, so on the other hand, who wouldn't? How far do you go with someone before you give up on them? Or, if not completely give up, how many layers of insulation or protection do you need so they won't hurt you again? And when you let someone through those layers, those walls, you are definitely risking once again.

So many possibilities, she thought. I wish life had such a palette of possibilities as this that I could just dip my brush in and paint my story. She looked at the clock on her laptop. 6:00. Dad said we'd be going out to dinner at 6:30. Hardly any time. But I've showered and dressed and I'm pretty much ready. Maybe this last 30 minutes, just a burst of brilliance here, is what I need to feel better about the direction of the book? Hearing her brother Luis have an argument with their mom made the decision of putting in her earbuds easy.

She did this and chose her favorite "reading music" file on You Tube, which was a storm on a dark night near the seashore, turned up the volume just to the point where the voices of Luis and her mom were drowned out, lowered her shoulders, and looked down at the keyboard. She had it!

Just as her fingers found the home keys her door opened in front of her and Kristen was standing there. Caitlyn froze at the seeming apparition before her, then quickly ripped her earbuds out of her ear, letting them clatter to her desktop.

Kristen looked like a kid getting ready to open the big present on Christmas Day. "Cait!" she screamed, running to her friend and with a tremendous hug almost knocking her just arisen form back down in her chair. Caitlyn willed herself to speak, but just a stammer came out. Kristen pulled out of the embrace and looked at her. "My girl," she managed, tears starting to brim her eyes.

"Wait. What? I thought you, I thought you weren't--"

"Yeah. I know. I lied to you. I'm sorry! Your parents thought it would be cool if we just came over and surprised you a day early," Kristen said.

With not having seen her best friend outside of a four-inch screen in two years, Caitlyn trembled with excitement. "So," she said, somewhat hyperventilating, "Are you guys going out to eat with us?"

"Lie. I admit. My parents are in on this too. They're here, and mom made your favorite, that lasagna with heavy Ricotta cheese and mushrooms."

"I so missed you," Caitlyn said, gripping her friend like a vise until Kristen squeaked a bit and Caitlyn realized the pressure she'd exerted and released her.

"Me too. But it's not like we didn't Facetime EVERY DAY the whole time you were gone."

"We missed five days, Kristen. Five. Days. That's really inexcusable!"

"That's what I miss through the phone. Your delivery. Your body language. Being in the same room with you." Kristen hugged her again. "Oh my God. This is the best." The girls held this embrace for a beat longer than normal, then released.

"Come on out and see my folks. And you won't believe how tall Joaquin is." She took Caitlyn's hand and led her through the hallway, much narrowed by the moving boxes lining each side, and into the living room, where they found both families sitting and talking.

Kristen's mother rose. "Caitlyn," she said, smiling, and threw her arms open for a hug. "Kristen has so missed you." Caitlyn accepted the embrace willingly.

"Hi Mr. Rothstein," she said to Kristen's father, the much more stoic of the two. He slightly waved back, smiling. Caitlyn could never figure out how he was married to Kristen's mother, who on the spectrum was just a slight notch less enthusiastic than her daughter, with her husband anchoring the opposite pole.

"You girls are fourteen now. I think you can call us Nancy and Richard. Think that's okay, dear?" she asked of her husband. He nodded his assent.

Caitlyn looked to Mr. Rothstein's right and saw what she first thought was a stranger, then recognized Kristen's brother Joaquin, who had to be 6'4". "Hi Cait," he said a bit uncomfortably. He was probably roped into the families' get together, she thought, although he was a really sweet kid--well, MAN now.

"How tall are you now, Joaquin?" Caitlyn asked.

"Six five," he replied, this time his voice sounding deeper.

"Joaquin's the center for the Lakewood High team, Cait," Kristen's mother returned.

"That I DO not doubt," she replied, noticing this time the sheer length of his legs, scrunched up between the sofa and coffee table.

"And how have you been, Kristen?" Caitlyn's mother asked.

"Really good Mrs. Patterson. Nearly end of the year. Graduation coming up. High school really close. Another successful yearbook in the can. And my best friend—home!"

Caitlyn's mother adored Kristen and Kristen's mother felt the same for Caitlyn, which made their friendship so much easier, Caitlyn thought.

"All right, well I'm sure you girls have a lot you want to catch up on. We were thinking of eating at around 7. Did Kristen tell you her mother made lasagna for you tonight?"

"Yes. She's awesome," Caitlyn said, smiling at Mrs. Rothstein.

"Okay, so we'll plan on about an hour from now," Caitlyn's mother said.

Caitlyn's brother Luis, who was now 12, said, "Yeah, boyyy. Lasagna," and got up and patted his stomach.

Caitlyn explained, "Flavor Flav is his hero."

Joaquin stood up as well. "Hey, squirt. Play me in some one on one?"

Luis stared up at Joaquin, clearly a foot or more taller than him. "Wutchu gonna spot me, dude?"

"16."

"16, going to 21?" Joaquin nodded. "Bet. Let's go. You haven't seen my three-point shot in a while, man. You goin' down!"

Joaquin stretched his right arm to its upper height, then mimicked a shot blocking motion. "And you haven't seen me blocking shots, little man." Luis crouched and sprang and was just able to hit the larger kid's wrist. "Vertical baby," he said.

"Dude, you barely hit my wrist," Joaquin said, laughing.

"Enough talk. It's time for action," Luis replied, patting the older kid's back on his way out the door.

Later, sitting on one end of her bed with Kristen on the other, Caitlyn said, "Wow. This move was our strangest--moving BACK to somewhere, but I'm sooooo happy now to be back in Jax."

"Let's talk, girl. What's up with youuuuuuu?" Caitlyn had missed her friend's silliness and spontaneity.

"We got in two days ago."

"Yeah, right when our trip to St. Augustine started. Boo!" Kristen howled.

"Like I planned it! And you can see the chaos of the house. 95% of my stuff is still packed away."

"Yeah, but I see you've got your laptop out. How's the book coming?"

"I hesitate to call myself a writer, but--"

"That is SO not true, Caitlyn. I've read, what, the first 50 pages or so and it's really good."

"Well, at least you think so."

"But it's going to be hard for you to finish it now because YOU'RE BACK and we've got school next week and so much to see and do."

"Yeah, about that," Caitlyn started.

"What?" Kristen said. "It's like the coolest thing ever that you can shadow me for the last week, Cait. AND that you can go to graduation. And you wouldn't BELIEVE how hot some of these guys have gotten . . . "

"Good old mom," Caitlyn said with a thin smile. Kristen's mother was the PTSA Vice President and therefore had some sway at the school. "I can't imagine the boys I knew in sixth grade being 'hot,' and even if they are, have they matured at all?"

Kristen smiled thinly, closed one eye and threw up her hands. Both girls lost it.

"Come on Cait. How do you NOT think that this is awesome?"

"Kristen. I've been gone for two years. TWO YEARS. It's gonna be really weird."

"No it won't. You've kept up with people on Insta and Snap, right?" Caitlyn nodded. "And we're not really doing anything. Just a few finals, but they're not actually teaching this last week. You can just hang out and get used to things again."

"You know I was all virtual in Guam, right? I've only been with a few other kids besides my bandmates for most of that time. And pretty much just on the base. The Navy was so freaked that they didn't let any of us off base for a long time after COVID hit, and then just my dad for business. I am SO not used to people right now."

Kristen blew out air. "Yeah, I get it. More than half our 8th grade was all virtual all year, though. I haven't seen those kids in a year. It's awkward for everybody. Wonder what they'll look like IF they even show for the graduation."

"Yeah, but at least you had 7th grade with them."

"For ¾ of a year."

"Well, sure, still, that's more than I've had."

"But Cait, everybody loves you. They're gonna welcome you back. You know it."

"Kristen, we were in sixth grade then. Look at us then and now. No one's even gonna recognize me."

Kristen looked at her in mock-appraisal. "You know, you really don't look that much different from then to now."

"Oh thanks. Is that your way of telling me that I'm still flat chested?"

Kristen snorted and fell backwards and almost off the bed. Caitlyn joined her laughter.

"Like I'm a 32D myself, right?" Kristen said, scrunching up her breasts as much as possible.

When the laughter had subsided, Kristen said, "What's it like, living in Guam? I looked it up, and you were in the middle of NOWHERE."

"Yeah, that's pretty much it. The middle of nowhere. Okay, so the first thing I noticed is that if it isn't grown on the island, your chances of getting it fresh are slim to none."

"Oh man. Must've been hard for you."

"Absolutely! I ate a lot of soy and bean-related things. But as far as friends--my bandmates were all cool. And I got a lot closer with Luis during COVID."

"Your bro's dope," Kristen said, narrowing her eyes slightly, "But little man ain't so little anymore."

Caitlyn nodded. "But the worst thing is we were just getting ready for our first real concert, you know, beyond just a couple dozen people, because we were going to open for really the only other band on the island, these sad adult '80's hair metal guys, when my dad got the call."

"I don't see how you can ever get used to that," Kristen said, shaking her head.

"You don't. It's only happened a few times, but it still really sucks when it does. But hey, at least I'm back here. With you."

"Yeah, true that. Hey, how's Mike?"

Kristen paused to consider. "We're good."

"That's not a ringing endorsement."

"Well, yeah, okay. We're OKAY. How's that?"

"I thought you guys were doing fine," Caitlyn said.

"I guess we are."

"So what's the problem?"

"It's just, I don't know, he doesn't have that much energy. Doesn't like to go out and do things as much as me."

"Kristen, WHO has your energy?" Kristen shrugged. "But that's never been a problem before. You have your friends (namely ME!) for that. He's just more of a homebody."

"Sure. I get that. I guess we're more than fine. It's just, sometimes . . . "

"You want more."

"Yeah. I want more. I want different. I'm just a not do the same things every day in the same way kind of person."

"Of course you're not," Caitlyn said, accenting the "of course" with a sharp head nod. "That's why we get along so well."

"And now, YOU'RE HERE. AGAIN!!! Ah!!!" Kristen opened her arms and hugged Caitlyn again. Just then, the door opened, and her mom was in the doorway. She stepped into the room and smiled.

"Somehow I knew you two would just get right back into your groove," Mom said. The girls broke and looked at her. "Okay. Time for dinner," Mom said, leaving.

"Give me a second, Kristen," Caitlyn said. "I need to save here." She gestured to the file, as of now blank but titled "Rebirth" open on her computer.

"Okay," Kristen said as she got up, straightened her shirt, wiped a tear from her eye, and walked out.

Caitlyn chose SAVE from the file menu and closed her laptop. Staring at the wall in front of her, she thought that this was going to be okay, that she could do this. There were a lot of people she still knew, and kept in contact with, and most people liked her. But still, going back to Wildwood for just a week, with people knowing I'm just a lame duck tagging along to Kristen? And then the weirdness of graduation. And herself being already done with all that back in Guam, and Kristen being there with Mike, and she being alone. Transitions suck, she thought, but she could do it.

But what if she sees Brendan again?

When Mr. Lawson stood, that was the cue for the tables to stop their eating, drinking, and hobnobbing. And, Chris thought, the wait might finally be over.

"It's about time this nonsense came to an end. At least for us," Chris said, looking at Anabel, who looked stunning in a new gold dress that showed off her tiny waist even more than usual.

"Shhh! Chris, this is important. 25 years is a long time to be married to someone," she replied. Chris shrugged. "And you know how close our parents are to the Attler family." Chris sighed. Anabel was enjoying this moment in the Grand Dining Hall of the

Wildwood Yacht Club. Even though her family had been members for years and she'd been to her share of celebrations, nothing matched its current grandeur. I guess this could double for prom as well, she thought. She ticked off in her head some proms that she knew of in the last couple of weeks and decided they had probably ended. But why change the décor if you had a few more recent events scheduled? Maybe just tweak it a bit? This dress wouldn't quite work for prom were she in high school, but she knew she looked awesome in it.

"Well," Chris continued, "At least we're gonna be free soon." This brought a furrowed brow from Anabel.

"Thank you. Thank you," Chris's father continued. "We are all so happy to be here to celebrate Kay and John's 25th wedding anniversary. My wife and I went to high school with them, and we've been so happy to have maintained that friendship and to have watched our families grow together."

Here he paused, clearly hoping for some effect, Anabel thought. She had dared to think of a life with Chris, just as any girl does for a boyfriend. Well, a real boyfriend. Not just a middle school boyfriend. Which to be honest Chris started out as, but, two years later, they were still together, so at least there was some chance that it might last.

"So let's raise a toast to 25 MOSTLY (a pause that brought a few chuckles) happy years of marriage, with the hope of 50 more." Anabel's father Demetrius rose first, to Mr. Lawson's right, and this rippled through the crowd, with all of them standing in seconds. Glasses were then clinked together, and a few elder gents said, "Here here" to accentuate theirs, and then some kind of spirit or Coke or tea was drunk by all.

Chris chugged the rest of his Sprite, begin to get up and whispered "Let's go" to Anabel, who pulled him back down, to avoid embarrassment. "What?" he almost hissed at her. She put her index finger to her lips.

At that point John/Mr. Attler stood and the crowd quieted again. Chris saw him puff up his already-too-prominent chest and really hoped this wouldn't be him in 35 years or whatever.

"I'd like to do another toast to my beautiful wife, Kay, who looks as good today as on that late Fall day in 1996 when she made me the happiest guy in the world." Glass clinked. He held his up again and waited. "And," here he paused and reached into his jacket, withdrawing a small box, "I'd like to give her something to commemorate those 25 years together." He handed it to his wife. Her look of surprise was genuine, Chris thought, maybe one of the few real things tonight so far. She took it and looked back at her husband. "Well, honey, open it," he said, and she opened it to reveal . . . something that made her even more surprised. Her other hand covered her mouth. "Can you turn it around for our guests?" he asked. After gawking at it another few seconds, Kay turned it around so the room could at least see something beyond a box, and at that point the lights went out, save for one that centered the two of them. "It's three and a half carats," John said, and the room's ceiling and walls were filled with the diamond's sparkle. More than a few women gasped, and the lights held that way for another ten seconds before they all turned on again.

"John," stammered Kay. "It's beautiful."

Chris felt like gagging but resisted the urge to fake gag aloud because he knew it would bring a blow from Anabel and certainly piss off his parents. John let the murmurs continue for a second before taking Kay by the shoulders and kissing her. The couple sat down.

Mr. Lawson continued. "Wow, that was really special," he said, looking John's way. "Okay, so now folks, go ahead and finish your dinner. There will be dancing in the ballroom in 20 minutes if you're interested. If not, you're welcome to sit and chat further." There was a pause. Chris looked imploringly at his father, who nodded gently in his direction. "And of course you young people are free to explore the game room. Or the library."

Chris laughed. "The LIBRARY," he emphasized. Anabel poked him. At that point the conversation returned and Chris, Anabel, and several other kids got up from the table. Anabel mouthed "dock" at him and then to a few of their other friends.

"I want to play a couple games of pool first with Gary and the guys. Okay?" Chris told her.

"That's fine. Just meet me out there when you're done." Chris nodded toward the game room to a few friends across the room, and they followed him in that direction. Anabel stood and walked through the double doors onto the porch that led to the dock. Coming from the other direction was Alan Counts.

"Hey Anabel," he started. "Lovin' that gold dress."

She looked down at her dress and the way it made her breasts stand out. "Thanks Alan."

"Hey, you headin' towards the dock?"

The look in his eyes and face were something that she had gotten used to in the last two years. Well, it wasn't just one look, but more of a spectrum, from appreciation to . . . hunger. This one was somewhere in between, but if she were forced to pick one . . . hunger.

"Sure."

"Can I walk with you?" he said, offering his turned-up palm.

"Of course," she said, hoping it was a touch playful.

"Where's Chris?"

"Playing pool."

"Oh, but he's here, right?"

"Of course he's here, Alan. His dad made the toast."

"Oh, I was in the bathroom for that."

This was the same Alan who never gave her the time of day in sixth grade. Who had at one time had the best-looking girl in the school, Courtney Carson, as his girlfriend. Who was the best athlete at Wildwood Middle, starring in track, football, and basketball. Who, even after she and Chris got together, and for half of seventh grade really, still had nothing to do with her. But, when she turned her corner, I mean fully turned it, sometime around Christmas break of that year, they all stared at her. Wanted to talk to her. Maybe wanted to be her. There was still of course inside her that fat girl looking from her prison, dying to get to out into the fresh air, that girl who denied her looks, who had little self-confidence. Every day she battled that girl, then had to remember what she did look like, and the effect she did have, on almost everyone who met her. On most days that first look reminded her of what she'd become and then the world was bright and fat Anabel remained locked in her cell.

As soon as she cleared the hurdle of her bathroom scale in the morning, that is.

She took Alan's offered hand and he led her down the stone steps and onto the walkway that was lined with something. Tulips? It was kind of hard to see, but something expensive, that's for sure.

"So, you looking forward to graduation?" Alan offered.

"You know it."

Alan glanced backward over his shoulder to the porch where they'd started their walk down the dock.

"And what's that deal with your crowns that you guys won back in sixth grade? They're out of the display case. You're like, decorating them or something?"

"They gave us back the crowns two weeks again and told us to decorate them, showing how we've changed since then," Anabel replied.

"How you've . . . changed? Okay, so how do you show that? On a crown? I mean, that crown was on display, sitting in the glass case in the hallway, for a long time. But it still looks awesome, with those like icicles shooting up from it. I still remember that night when you won it."

I bet you do, Anabel thought. "I really haven't given it much thought yet, but I will." Lie. Of course she'd thought about it, just as she thought about most things, obsessively. They reached the end of the walkway and stepped out onto the wide dock. Expensive boats lined either side before it ended in a brightly lit gazebo.

When they reached the end, Anabel sat facing the club while Alan sat opposite her on a bench that went around a tree that formed the gazebo's middle.

"So, what's up with you, Alan? Who you taking to graduation?"

"Oh, I'm not sure yet. I--"he started.

"You're . . . not sure. Alan, it's in six days!" Anabel returned, throwing up her hands in disbelief.

"Yeah, I know. I'm working on it." Pause. "I was thinking of asking Marcy McConnell". He looked at her, trying to get a read on whether it was possible for Marcy to say yes.

Okay, so I'll play his game. She put on an a somewhat exaggerated "thinking" expression. "Okay. Marcy. Okay." She held this look a few seconds and uncrossed and recrossed her legs, with Alan's eyes following. "So Marcy. . . broke up with Marco a few weeks ago. Don't think she's seeing anyone. Or has her sights really set on anyone."

"But someone's probably already asked her out."

"Not sure about that. Could be," Anabel said.

"Could you, you know, check?" he asked.

Anabel knew this was coming. Maybe this was the reason he wanted to talk to her on the dock. Well, not the ONLY reason, but she was as connected with what was going on in the eighth grade as anyone.

"Okay, lemme Insta her." Anabel sent the message.

"Thanks," he said. "Hey," he said, pulling out his phone. "Have you heard that new Tyler the Creator song?"

"He's got a new one? Nope. Haven't heard it." At that, she noticed Chris and some others starting down the steps toward the dock.

"Gimme a second and I'll pull it up," Alan said, and she could see a Spotify playlist on his phone. "Here it is," he continued, pressing the play button. The song ("Wusyaname") began and now Chris was starting the long walk on the dock. He was with a few other people, but she couldn't make out who they were.

After about 15 seconds, he asked, "Whaddaya think?"

"I like it," she replied distractedly.

Alan looked at her. "Hey, listen," he began, then faltered. This got her attention. "I know you and Chris are together and are like really tight, but . . ." Here he took her hand. "You know, somewhere later, maybe even in high school." Pause. "I mean, I'd like to go out with you, you know, when you're single again."

All Chris heard was ". . . when you're single again," but he had been watching Anabel and wondering who she was talking to for a good 100 feet now. He was even more interested when he got close enough to see that she was holding hands with someone, or at least someone was holding her hand? This should be interesting.

"Hi there. Who we got here?" he said, arriving at the round tree bench and peering exaggeratedly around the corner. Alan, still facing the lake and completely caught off guard, released Anabel's hand and looked sheepish. "Oh, hey Alan. How're you doin'?" With this Chris clapped Alan on the back with a beyond-friendly blow.

"Hey Chris. Didn't see you coming there," he managed. Anabel looked imploringly at Chris.

"No, I guess you didn't," Chris replied, sitting next to Anabel and taking her hand firmly in his. She noticed the others at a safe distance down the dock, wary of possible fireworks here. "So. What were you two on about? You seemed pretty chummy here."

Alan looked helplessly at Anabel in hopes of being bailed out. Nothing. "We were just talking about graduation and who I might ask out." Chris stared intently at Alan. Neither athlete has the size advantage here, Anabel thought, but Chris lifted weights a lot for baseball, whereas Alan swam.

Anabel knew she had to intervene. "He wants to ask Marcy McConnell out," she came up with.

"Marcy? Good pick my man. She's cute. And she broke up with Marco what, a couple months ago?" Chris couldn't give a rat's ass about who was dating who but because of Anabel's constant updates to him he couldn't escape them either.

"And he wanted me to see if she's going with anyone yet," Anabel added, hopefully plausibly explaining the half-truth of the situation.

Chris wasn't buying it. "Oh, so that's what you were talking about." He looked at her.

"Well, and then, you heard that song he was playing. It's the new Tyler the Creator."

"Yes, I did hear something," he said dismissively. "But I heard something else too. Something about you being single again?"

Alan looked at Chris, searching for avenues of either oratory or physical escape.

Anabel to the rescue. "Okay, so yeah, he mentioned about, in the future, later, maybe in high school, IF I was single . . . "

"If you were single . . . what?" Chris released her hand and looked at her. Then at Alan. "Oh," he said with an exaggerated head tilt and then knee slap. "Oh, he wants to go out with . . . with you? If you were single?"

Alan was clearly flustered, and while he didn't think Chris would actually punch him could never have guessed what his next lines would be.

"So, I tell you what," Chris started, his voice full of import. "Why don't we make the future . . . now? You two want to go out together? Go ahead. You have my blessing."

Anabel noticed the others take a further step back. "Chris. Come on. You know, he was just talking."

Taking the bone she threw him, Alan said, "Yeah, man. Just talking. And Anabel said nothing to me back. She just heard me out. Seriously, man, she did nothing." Here Alan stood. Chris was still seated.

"She did nothing. Okay." He scratched his head exaggeratedly. "Wait . . . is holding your hand nothing?"

Alan, both bracing himself and getting defensive at this point, said, "Okay, so yes. I held her hand. Just for a few seconds. But she didn't hold mine."

Chris, knowing this to be true, or at least what he gathered from the positions of their hands and the bewildered look on Anabel's face when he encountered them, and completely regardless of this understanding, showed Alan a puzzled expression. Then his face changed, showing a hint of menace.

Alan sensed this. "Come on, man. This is pretty harmless stuff here, Chris. Everybody knows you guys are together. I wouldn't do anything with you guys together."

Chris rose and halved the distance between them, which wasn't much to begin with. Alan's face was now only a foot from Chris's. Chris began, "No. No problem. No harm no foul. But I'm serious." Here he turned to face the now-risen Anabel, her face stricken. "You guys wanna go out, be my guest." He looked again to Anabel, who was shaking her head fervently. He took Anabel's hand and put it once again into Chris's, who withdrew his just as quickly.

Chris then walked away from the pair and started talking with the people that he had come with, his back to the former situation. Anabel looked angrily at Alan and turned her palms up pleadingly for him to diffuse the situation, to beg, to grovel, to just make things go back to normal. Alan sighed audibly, and after a few seconds moved toward Chris.

Chris sensed him coming and whirled around. Alan instinctively flinched and threw his right arm up to block a blow. Chris's face was stern, but then it fell, and he calmly took Alan's blocking arm down even though it took some force, then smiled. Chris looked past him to Anabel and said this to Alan while continuing to stare at her. "It's okay man. I'm just fooling with you." Alan stared at him uncomprehendingly, then slowly smiled himself. "Yeah, man, I was just shittin' you. You and her both". He jerked a thumb at Anabel, then looked at Alan. "You're good, man." Alan was still dumbstruck.

"Hey Annie, come on. Jess and Tre wanna hang. On the porch," he said to Anabel.

She noticed Alan's bafflement and quickly glanced at him and then at her boyfriend, who held his hand out beckoningly for hers. Before she could take it, Alan asked, "So, did Marcy reply yet?" This brought a smile from Chris.

Anabel pressed the power button and scrolled through her notifications. "Nothing yet," she told him. He shrugged and sat back down. "I'll let you know."

Anabel smiled dimly and moved toward Chris and the others. She then took his still-offered hand and they started toward the club together.

That night Anabel was lying on her bed, thinking of the events that transpired, and trying to figure out what Chris was aiming at on the dock. He'd never done anything like that before. And he'd noticed other guys flirting with her, quite a bit, and did nothing. He did nothing because he's got nothing to worry about and he knows it. That's why. But then, why tonight? What point was he making? And was he making it to those other kids, or to Alan? Or to her? She again checked out her Insta post showing her in the dress, taken by Molly, at the front of the club, and saw 234 likes with her dress picture. Scrolling down, she saw a couple dozen comments. She vowed to read them later and set down her phone. So, the night was a success. Well at least, given the weird Chris thing, a qualified success.

She looked across the room and saw the Ice Queen crown on her desk. I've thought about this and have some ideas. There were six spikes coming out of the crown. Anabel had determined to decorate one spike per day starting today and ending on graduation morning. She got up and moved to the desk, stepped over the dozing cat Lupin, and sat down. She had four finalist pictures arrayed for the first spike. They were all of her and Chris. She touched the first, of them at the dance in sixth grade. Awkward but still cute. But it really doesn't fit the "how you've changed" idea, so with it she started her discard pile. The second one was of them at the beach, probably in seventh grade. This was probably in the Fall or Winter of that year when the water was just turning colder. She was clearly cold in this picture because it showed her covered by her favorite light-blue wrap with Chris was hugging her. Ooh, that's a finalist for sure. Picture three showed the two of them, maybe a few months ago, on Chris's father's boat, sitting close together as the sun went down behind them. Another finalist. But wait, maybe I should show some kind of progression in time too, for each spike? Like where we started and where we are now? That would rule out this one. Number four, upon closer inspection, was blurry, but a great moment, at her 13th birthday party, surrounded by their friends. Blurry, you gone.

So the winner was the beach pic. She looked at it again. We're so happy here. And we're so young. Look at us. She still had some of the weight that she later shed, which sullied it somewhat, but their expressions trumped this. As she had as yet not really decided how logistically this decorative thing was supposed to happen on the crown she set it on the top shelf. Anyway, that was a good start. And Chris will like it.

Sunday, May 24, 2021: Five days before graduation

It really hasn't changed. Not so much as I would have thought. Well, it's only two years. But this neighborhood was well-established. Caitlyn's morning runs were grounding for her. Beyond exercise, they tied her to a place and a time in a way car rides never did.

There's where that old man lived, the one who waved at her every time she went by. At first she didn't notice his front porch chair with him in it but when she was in front of the house she did, coffee mug in one hand and the other raised in greeting. She waved and smiled back. The more things change, the more they stay the same.

She was listening to her Spotify "Running Mix," which was composed mainly of punk and high-energy stuff, with the Buzzcocks' "Ever Fallen in Love (With Someone You Shouldn't Have)" currently playing. At this point she was halfway through the run and mused that she should start seeing even more familiar sights on this part.

After a minute the YMCA came up on her left. Only a few cars were there now, the hardcore every-day-before-work swimmers, but in a week it would be hopping with campers being dropped off about now and parents driving away smiling. On the right was the park and field where she had played soccer and hung out with Kristen and others so many times. At the park she saw the swings she'd cried on when her Guinea pig Rascal died.

Needing to see if it was still there, she swerved into the empty park and made a beeline to the basketball court and found its backboards, rims, and nets still pretty pristine after, what, five years? When she hit the first corner, she saw it: Kristen and Caitlyn BFF! Of course it was still there, emblazoned in concrete. What, like they were going to cut it out? Satisfied, she U-turned back onto the sidewalk of Evergreen Avenue and continued on.

A little further ahead she saw Kristen's red brick with white trim that was kept spotless by her parents. She noticed the paper in the driveway and remembered it was Sunday. Not a stir came from that direction. She soldiered on.

Ahead was the Kristen-named "Small Forest," which was just maybe two acres of thick, old trees that jutted high above anything else in the neighborhood. But these trees were dense, always with undergrowth, so they made for hideouts and great cover in the scorching Florida summers.

Just as she was passing it, she heard a rustle and spotted a small deer right on the edge, busily chewing from a bush. Startled, it raised its head and paused, staring at her. She stopped dead and was still. Five seconds passed. Ten. Caitlyn knew if she took a step, it would bolt. To where, she didn't know. Probably to hide and then scamper out to the thicker woods beyond their neighborhood. Not wanting that to happen, she hit pause on her phone, slowly took out her earbuds and let a few more seconds pass.

The deer knew she wasn't an immediate threat, but still slowly turned and moved to greater safety through the trees. Caitlyn smiled and continued her journey.

Almost home now after nearly three miles of running, she noticed her breathing was heavier than normal and chocked that up to two weeks of first crying, then moping, then writing, then packing, then moving, then unpacking, etc. All of which kept her from running. Possibly.

As she hit the home stretch, she knew what was next. Brendan's house. If she continued straight, her path for hundreds of runs, she would pass it. If she turned right and made a detour around his block, she'd miss it. Perhaps buoyed by the deer spotting she continued straight.

After half a minute it appeared on her right. Like the rest, little seemed altered. Although it had been two years ago, she remembered swinging on the rope swing there, dangling from the oak tree in the dead center of the yard there, and Brendan pushing her too hard but seeming to enjoy her cries as she hit the top, her feet seeming to touch the sky. And there, the front steps where they'd shared their first hug, and sat and watched the stars, his beagle Stamkos at their feet, looking up at them. And finally there, in front of the garage, where she'd last seen him on that May night in sixth grade, in his jeans and red shirt, right before the dance. The dance. It had been a lifetime ago. Would he even remember her now? Would he care? Maybe he was even DATING Rachel at this point. Again. No. Kristen would have told me if that was happening.

The pain of that moment of realization that Brendan was after Rachel even while WITH her flooded back across the years. Sure, Brendan had told Kristen that he had nothing to do with that picture, that she must have taken the necklace when he was gone from the table. Sure. Who would leave a piece of jewelry, obviously in a jewelry box, unguarded at a table with a group of non-friendly girls that included your ex-girlfriend? She had never bought that idea. It was just all too coincidental, that she just happened to sit down at his table, and supposedly take the necklace meant for me.

Also, Kristen had said that she and Brendan had a class together, which with her following Kristen around for a week meant that she would at least be in the same room with him if not SEE him or TALK to him, which didn't make her happy. Caitlyn knew she was resilient, but still this was a painful part of her past that she didn't want to revisit. She wondered if her not having dated anyone since him was because of how scarred she was or just a lack of available guys in Guam and decided on the latter.

Passing his house, with only a block to go (how convenient back then she thought while simultaneously willing her brain to drop the subject of Brendan) she kicked it into high gear and the Clash's "Janie Jones" just pumped her up more. She finished with a flourish, her upward momentum and speed stifled by the hill in her front yard, and she crashed to the grass in relief.

God, I LOVE this movie, Anabel thought. Even in a theater only a quarter filled during opening week, this is awesome. On the screen the song "96,000" was on, with maybe two hundred people around a New York pool on a hot summer's day, singing about how their lives would change with that many dollars. She looked over at Chris, and he was fidgeting, still. She had to beg him to go, and when he saw on the marquee inside the mall that it was over two hours he just moaned.

"Seriously? Why does this movie have to be that long? It's a musical, right? Can't they just SPEAK the words so it'll go quicker."

"You are NO FUN," Anabel said. "And yes, there is dialogue, too."

"Well then why is it over two hours long?" he asked.

"Look, I sat through that boring hockey game with you a couple nights ago so you said you'd go with me to the movie. Fulfill your end of the bargain!"

"I'm here, right?" Chris said flatly.

"You might actually like it. Grace said it was really good."

"So what does she know?"

"Chris, come on," she had said, and he reluctantly bought the tickets and they had gotten a large Diet Coke and popcorn before finding their seats.

He got up and said, too loudly, "I've gotta go to the bathroom."

"Again?" she said. "That's your third time already."

"And?" Chris replied.

"AND the movie is less than an hour in."

"Blame it on the big Coke," he said, and left.

While he was gone, Anabel resolved to just shut him out as much as possible and enjoy the movie. I wish I would have gone with Grace. She said she'd see it again. But no, for some reason I chose Chris. Well, of course I chose Chris. But maybe not of course. I don't have to do everything with him. She decided that she didn't do everything with him, but that maybe she'd have to be more selective in the future.

When Chris returned, he suffered another five minutes and finally shut his eyes, soon slumping onto her. Good, Anabel thought. I don't have to deal with him anymore, and I can focus.

Later that afternoon, Caitlyn and Kristen were thrifting at three downtown shops after pizza at Bruno's Famous. Caitlyn was buried in the middle of a thickly packed dress rack, so much so that she had to almost grunt to withdraw a dress to fully check out. Kristen moved from the row they were busily scanning to the next opposite her and leaned against the bar, then set her head on top of her hands for full Kristen affect. Caitlyn looked questioningly at her.

"What?" she said. "You done already? Or are you tired of these awesome stores because you go to them every weekend even though my thrifting-starved butt wasn't within 3,000 miles of one for two years?" Kristen continued to stare at her, her face a puzzle. "Dude? What?"

Kristen raised her head, tittered, then said, very deliberately, "Okay." She clasped her hands together on top of the rack and continued. "So, are you going to address the elephant in the room, or am I?"

Caitlyn stared back blankly, then got it, but said, "Oh, you mean are you going to buy that $100 green flapper dress with the hella sequins in the front of the store?" which brought a frown from her friend.

"Cait, seriously."

"What?"

"Come on. You know . . . "

"What?"

"Well, I was hoping you'd start it, but I guess I can."

"Start what?"

Exasperated, Kristen threw up her hands. "Really?" Caitlyn raised her eyebrows. "Okay. Brendan. BRENDAN. B-R-E-N-D-A-N. Brendan."

"Old news. Not interested," Caitlyn said.

Kristen now walked around to her, took the dress Caitlyn was looking at and laid it on top, and took her by both shoulders. "Cait. You always don't want to talk about it. But now you've gotta. You're back. I told you he's in my math class. We're going to see him. Tomorrow."

Caitlyn took Kristen's hands and gently lowered them. "Yes. I'm aware," she said. There was a silence. Awaiting a response, Kristen heavily blinked at her a few times. "What else do you want? That was a long time ago. I'm done."

"Caittttttttt! You know the story. Rachel must have taken it from the box and tried it on, somehow, while you guys were gone from the table. Brendan told me that night that he had NOTHING to do with that picture that she posted. Come on!"

"You know, even IF I believed that story, it's water under the bridge. Gone. Half a lifetime ago. Why should I care now? And even if I did, you told me about that hockey incident. THEN I could always see his anger, just below the surface. But THAT. Knocking that kid out and giving him a concussion. That's just brutal."

"But that was never directed to you, Cait. If anything you kept that in check."

"So what? If he'd do that to some random kid in hockey who's to say he wouldn't do it to someone else outside of that?"

"You know he wouldn't, Cait. Seriously."

"No, YOU know I just don't want to bring all that back up. Just let it go, Kristen. I'm done." Caitlyn felt her face getting flushed.

"But . . . you guys were so good together. Remember?"

"Kristen, we were together two weeks. TWO WEEKS. How is that even a relationship? And I was 12. 12! Just drop it, okay?"

"But wouldn't you even--"Kristen began.

"DROP! IT!" Caitlyn turned and stormed out of the store, her violent push to the door making it clatter against the frame and bringing the stare of the cashier.

Caitlyn knew her strategy of getting over things was predicated more on denial than anything else, but hey it worked for her she thought as she sat down on the bench in front of Lilly's Second-Hand Boutique, the last thrift shop they were going to. She hoped Kristen would give her a minute to gather herself and calm down, but this was not the way her friend was built, and right on cue Kristen turned the corner and stormed toward her.

Caitlyn turned her back and tried to will herself back to the tranquil images of the deer, and the forest, and the old man, and the park. In vain.

May 24

It feels like the only time I can lose my pain and general disappointment in my life is when I'm playing online. In Call of Duty you really don't care about satisfying other people or their emotions if you say or do the wrong thing. I play with mostly idiots, faceless entities scattered over the world, and who cares about those guys? This world is where I'd want to live. If you die, you just start another game. No lingering pain. Or resentment. Or loss. What was that line from that book he had read this year in Mr. Gowson's language arts class? "Fire was bright and fire was clean." And "It was a pleasure to burn." *Fahrenheit 451.* That's one dude's world that is more messed up than mine. But if I could just have fire to burn away my memories, what lingered inside me. . . that would be great.

So today I was playing the "Shock and Awe" challenge. The guys online have always gone nuts about how wild that is, so I intentionally saved it a time when I could spend mega time on it. And I'm thinking hockey suspension time is just about perfect. Anyway, you're Sgt. Paul Jackson, and he's trying to capture or kill Khaled Al-Asad, who was a fictional dude, but Brendan still liked the meaning of his name when he looked it up: the eternal lion. So he was on a quest to kill The Lion. As I got deeper into it, the whole city was evacuated because of a nuke threat. So I figure I'm playing the hero, getting in and out, killing The Lion in the process. Just as

I'm in the middle of it, the bomb detonates, killing me and 30K other marines. Damn! I spent like four intense hours on it (pissing off my mom, who wanted me to go shopping or something. Okay, I had previously told her I would) just to have that happen. So that was a pretty stupid part of my day.

So while I was playing, I knew I had to finish because the Bolts were playing later that night, so maybe I screwed up or something with the mission, missed something I should have done, because I was rushing, who knows, but anyway the Bolts were playing Montreal with the series tied two all. As always, I performed the Grandpa George pre-game ritual of touching the signed picture of Gretzky that's on our den's wall showing him holding up one of the Cups he won in Montreal, then fixing a turkey and cheese sandwich with mustard, then pouring a tall glass of iced tea. It's late in the game, and it's looking like OT, but I never worry about that because Vasy is the best goalie in the league. So I figure we've got the advantage. Then Victor Hedman, with a minute left, throws one of those 2/3 ice passes, aiming for Point, but the Canadian's Suzuki steps in, steals the pass, and sends a slap shot over the diving Hedman's stick and just under Vasy's glove for the game winner. Now we're down 3-2. That sucks. And to lose at home too. So now we've gotta win AT Montreal to stay alive, which would set up a game 7 at home. Game 7 would be Friday. Friday is the day of the "graduation." No way I'm going to that lameness and miss game 7 if that happens.

Judging from our conversation between the first and second period, Mom would definitely be pissed, but so what? What is she NOT pissed off at me about lately? Let me see if I can quickly recap. You're going to the graduation. No I'm not. Yes you are. No I'm not. Then you won't be playing hockey anytime soon. You mean like two weeks soon, cause that's the length of my suspension. No I'm talking beyond not. Really, like what. Like the rest of the season. The rest of the season. You must be joking. You wouldn't do that to me. Yes I would. Mom why. Because graduation is important. But why. No one graduates from eighth grade. Well in your school they do.. But for what purpose. Because you need to get out more and see people. Why. Because you're either at that rink or have your nose buried in your computer playing those violent games all the time and that's not good for you. What is good for me mom, getting my heart stomped on repeatedly. Brendan you know this has nothing to do with that. Mom it has everything to do with that. How are you getting your heart stomped on by going to graduation?   I don't know but it happened last year. Last year was COVID Brendan there was none. Okay so the year before or whatever, I don't care. That's even more reason COVID hasn't been good for you, Bren. Mom COVID hasn't been good for anybody. I don't care you're going and that's final. Good Luck with that Mom. Okay you make your decision and I'll make mine. And besides, I hear that girl has moved back with her family maybe you can see her again. Yeah I know Kristen has informed me of that useless fact so what? So what is that you two were so nice together. Sure mom for like five days and that was two years ago like it even matters anymore.

That was pretty much that, and then she folded her arms in her chair and motionlessly stared at the game for the second period. I forgot to write that her boyfriend Mike was there for the game, and he pretty much just sat there and ignored our whole argument. Mike's actually a pretty good guy. Definitely a better guy than Dad. I get along with him pretty well, except when he jumps in sometimes in my mom's defense. Which he does less of now when he sees it because he knows it just pisses me off more. He knows hockey, having played at during high school, and he's a huge Lightning fan too, and he knows the history of the NHL and players also. So he's useful to have around.

So, between that period and the next, between the crappy Lightning playing and the hassle from Mom, I pummeled my pillow for a minute or so to work off some steam. Grandpa George's words of **harness your anger** flitted through his head between blows and had some effect of ending them.

So, that's it. Another stupid day in the life of Brendan Ellison. Til tomorrow, signing off.

-Brendan

As Anabel opened the doors to Performance Gymnastics and stepped inside, she felt the familiar feeling of comfort. This was her safe place. Her haven. Where she could drop her pretenses and just be herself. Such was not always the feeling with her, and as always she turned to see the team picture from two years ago, when she was in sixth grade, the year she and Chris got together. It showed two rows of tall or tallish girls, mostly thin, long-legged girls, except for the girl in front left, who was short, and dumpy, and had stringy brown hair and an expression to mirror all of that.

That was her. The OLD her. The one she vowed never to return to. Ever. The one who served as a warning, a flashing beacon of caution to what her life could become again, if she let herself go, dropped her guard, fumbled the ball. And other poor metaphors.

And after this, she walked confidently down the entryway to the gym floor, seeing her current self-reflected in the full-length mirror, the self that for almost a year and a half now had slain the BEFORE Anabel in the team picture every time she did this ritual. Blonde, wavy hair, now in a high ponytail. Slim waist. Firm butt. The leotards that were definitely NOT too revealing. HERE was the one place she didn't want to have to maintain and guard her image. She didn't want to attract attention. She wasn't on the team anymore, and really was just a hanger-on when she was. Her weight disallowed her from being able to do anything that would have made her better, like for example stay on the beam for longer than ten seconds without flailing and falling.

As she walked to the mat where she was going to begin her routine, she noticed two girls struggling to reach the overhead bars. First they tried jumping, then stacking a couple of cushy blocks underneath, but they still couldn't reach. They looked longingly to their mothers, but they were busily chatting and couldn't see their daughters' struggles. Anabel walked in their direction, and one spotted her coming and moved out of the way.

One of the girls, who was wearing pink tights with a pink ribbon in her hair, said to Anabel, "We can't get up." The other one looked too sheepish to speak.

"Yeah. I saw you struggling," Anabel said.

"Can you help us?" the same girl asked.

"Of course. It looks like you just need a boost up, right?" The other girl, in yellow tights, nodded her head.

"Yeah. That'd be great. Thanks. My name's Julia, and my friend is Ginger."

"Well it's very nice to meet you. I'm Anabel." The girls smiled. Anabel lifted Julia up until her small hands grabbed the bar. Julia adjusted her grip some. "Do you want me to help you get started swinging?" Anabel moved toward her.

"Well, I don't know. Let me see." Anabel backed away. Julia started swinging, slowly, and her smile grew wider the higher she went.

"Wow, you're doing great!" Anabel said and noticed that Ginger was smiling too.

After swinging for maybe 30 seconds, Julia announced "Dismount!" and landed perfectly about five feet from the bar.

"My turn," Ginger said, and looked expectantly at Anabel. She lifted the smaller girl onto the bar, and Ginger indicated that he she wanted Anabel to stay there. She started swinging a bit, and Anabel was ready to catch her lest she fall. After ten seconds she said, "Okay. All done. Can you get me down?" Anabel complied.

"Wow. You two are really good."

"Thanks Anabel," Julia said, and the two girls smiled widely at her. As Anabel turned she missed both of the girls' mothers in rapt attention, apparently having watched the whole affair.

Arriving back at the mat, she pulled up "Tranquility mix" on Spotify and turned the volume up high. She then adjusted her earbuds and stepped onto the soft mat of one of the tumbling floors. This late in the day on Saturday the high-level girls were gone, either at a competition or just done for the day, so Anabel noticed only a handful of other gymnasts in her field of vision, including the kid who used to be and probably still is the best male athlete in the gym, Brian Yorker, working out hard on the rings in the back.

Before she struck her pose to begin a few practice runs to prep for tumbling, she ticked off one by one the failures she had experienced in this gym. The fall off the beam in her first competition, landing hard on her arm. Embarrassing. The time she was warming up and collided head-on with Amber Nestor, who cried for ten minutes while her mom frantically ran around trying to get her ice. Anabel's fault. And the scariest for her, her head hitting the edge of the ball pit hard after a vault, her mother gone shopping, her head bleeding, and some girls actually GIGGLING at her lack of finesse and downright ineptitude. She had overcome all of these. To be here. Free of demons. Free of worry. Expectations lowered. Defenses lowered. Calm.

One last thought flitted through her head before starting the initial run: I'm done with crown decoration for tonight too. On the way home from the movie, when Chris turned on his rock station too loudly for comfortable conversation, she had thought of the exact picture she wanted for tonight. Predetermining that this was to be a families picture, as in hers and Chris's families, together, she knew she wanted the one in front of Williams's Lobster House from Christmas of last year, the one where they were hiding their COVID masks behind their backs before going into the 25% capacity-at-the-time restaurant. She had worn the green thrift store dress, the one that cost $50, but worth every penny. EVERYONE looked good in this picture. She'd already printed a copy on her computer and it was sitting on her desk.

As she flung her arm into position, raised her fingertips to point to the ceiling, thrust her chin toward there as well, one foot forward and one flat, she fleetingly wondered what ideas Chris had for his crown.

Later that afternoon, Chris was finishing up an episode of The Office with his brother Liam, who was 10, when Liam suggested, "Wanna shoot some hoops?"

"Dude," Chris replied. "It's dark out there. And it's late." He looked at his curly brown-haired brother, who at times was REALLY hard to say No to.

"Come ooooonnnn," Liam whined. "We have a light you know." Chris didn't answer. "Come on, Chris. Ten minutes."

"Sure," Chris replied. The boys then moved through the den to the garage, where Liam grabbed his new Wilson basketball. Chris pushed the garage door opener and they moved onto their driveway.

"Okay, you got me for ten. After that I have to start decorating my crown."

"Doing what? Did you just make that up?" Liam said, laughing. "What crown?"

"The stupid crown that I won at the end of sixth grade. Remember?" Liam shook his head. "Well anyway, They gave it back to me like a week ago, and Anabel and I are supposed to decorate our crowns to show how we've changed since then."

"Oh, okay, cool. So you're doing it for her?"

"Yeah, sure, I guess."

Liam missed a ten-footer, then stopped and looked at his brother. "Man, if I had a girlfriend like Anabel, I'd do stuff for her, too."

"What do you mean?" Chris asked.

"Well, she's really . . . hot."

Chris immediately started cracking up. "Wait. Did you just call Anabel 'hot'? Dude that's awesome." His continued laughter brought a point-blank throw to his chest from Liam, with the ball bouncing away almost to the street. "Okay, just for that, now I'm gonna tell her what you said."

After retrieving the ball, Liam, ball raised in menace toward his brother, said, "You better not," and mimicked hitting him with it again.

"What? I think that's cute," Chris said, flinching slightly.

"Great. So I'm cute."

"No, man, really. I love that you guys get along well."

"She's so nice. She always talks to me. She plays games with me. She helps me with my homework. She's like a sister."

"Yeah, that's true."

"What's it like, having a girlfriend?" Liam asked.

"It's fine, I guess."

"Fine. Come on. What's it like . . . kissing?" Liam's small face was upturned to Chris. He couldn't joke here. This was serious to little dude.

But then he did. "It's like kissing Mom."

Liam made a disgusting face. "Stop lying! No it's not. I've seen you guys before. That is nothing like kissing Mom." Chris shrugged. "So come on. What's it like?"

"It's pretty cool."

"Yeah . . .?"

How much could he really explain this to Liam, without going too far?

"Well," Chris began. Imagine someone that you like, and then wanting to do more than just touch or hold hands with that person." Liam, wanting more, was in rapt attention. "Yeah, so then you kiss. You press your lips against hers and you kiss." Liam nodded. "That's pretty much it, dude."

"Okay, so I guess I get that. But what's it like having a GIRLFRIEND? You know, someone to always be with."

"Not so different than being with friends. It's someone you like, a lot, and you spend a lot of time together and do things together."

"That's it?" Liam asked.

"Well, no, there's more," Chris said.

"So . . ."

"MORE that I'm not going to tell you because you're too young."

Liam again held the ball up in mock-menace to Chris.

"Okay, look, when you get older you'll have a girlfriend and you'll know what's it's like and we can talk about it then. I'll be your advisor. It's not that hard."

"And until now, Anabel will be my friend and keep doing things with me."

"Yeah Liam. Sure."

"But she's my HOT friend."

Chris laughed again. "Yeah, okay, you're hot friend."

"And YOUR hot girlfriend."

At that point Chris stole the ball from him, ran out to the three-point arc their father had meticulously painted on the driveway, and swished the shot. They played for another not ten but thirty minutes, as thoughts of Anabel and decorating the crown went in and out of Chris's mind. Sure, she was special. And she was definitely hot. But after two years of being together, sometimes it starts to feel like the same thing over and over. Definitely not gonna try to explain that to the runt. It was just . . . the expectation. The expectation that X amount of any given day would be spent with her. Not that it was exactly a chore, but . . . well, sometimes it was. Like watching that crappy movie earlier today. But there are so many other good times. He thought of them at other movies, darker movies, movies she was less interested in really, movies both in theaters and in their living rooms, and the feel of her in his arms . . .

Later that night, Caitlyn sat at her computer and once again thought of where to begin in her novel. I'll have Jodi wallowing in her room for a couple days and thinking about all that she had and lost. She wondered how to successfully revisit scenes she'd already written but add more detail. Wait, hadn't she already planned for that? She had! She had, by at the time leaving some things vague for the reader to fill in herself, so even if she went back, the details would be new. Yes! Nothing better than to see in fiction what you would never want to happen to you in real life. She decided that she'd start with the scene of the horrific performance onstage which led to her being booted from the band. She began to visualize then scribble down notes of just how wrong it went, how Jodi went from on top of the world, from star to pariah, from insider to outcast, from happy to sad.

How much of this is me and how much is fiction?

Sunday, May 24, 2021: Five days before graduation

It really hasn't changed. Not so much as I would have thought. Well, it's only two years. But this neighborhood was well-established. Caitlyn's morning runs were grounding for her. Beyond exercise, they tied her to a place and a time in a way car rides never did.

There's where that old man lived, the one who waved at her every time she went by. At first she didn't notice his front porch chair with him in it but when she was in front of the house she did, coffee mug in one hand and the other raised in greeting. She waved and smiled back. The more things change, the more they stay the same.

She was listening to her Spotify "Running Mix," which was composed mainly of punk and high-energy stuff, with the Buzzcocks' "Ever Fallen in Love (With Someone You Shouldn't Have)" currently playing. At this point she was halfway through the run and mused that she should start seeing even more familiar sights on this part.

After a minute the YMCA came up on her left. Only a few cars were there now, the hardcore every-day-before-work swimmers, but in a week it would be hopping with campers being dropped off about now and parents driving away smiling. On the right was the park and field where she had played soccer and hung out with Kristen and others so many times. At the park she saw the swings she'd cried on when her Guinea pig Rascal died.

Needing to see if it was still there, she swerved into the empty park and made a beeline to the basketball court and found its backboards, rims, and nets still pretty pristine after, what, five years? When she hit the first corner, she saw it: Kristen and Caitlyn BFF! Of course it was still there, emblazoned in concrete. What, like they were going to cut it out? Satisfied, she U-turned back onto the sidewalk of Evergreen Avenue and continued on.

A little further ahead she saw Kristen's red brick with white trim that was kept spotless by her parents. She noticed the paper in the driveway and remembered it was Sunday. Not a stir came from that direction. She soldiered on.

Ahead was the Kristen-named "Small Forest," which was just maybe two acres of thick, old trees that jutted high above anything else in the neighborhood. But these trees were dense, always with undergrowth, so they made for hideouts and great cover in the scorching Florida summers.

Just as she was passing it, she heard a rustle and spotted a small deer right on the edge, busily chewing from a bush. Startled, it raised its head and paused, staring at her. She stopped dead and was still. Five seconds passed. Ten. Caitlyn knew if she took a step, it would bolt. To where, she didn't know. Probably to hide and then scamper out to the thicker woods beyond their neighborhood. Not wanting that to happen, she hit pause on her phone, slowly took out her earbuds and let a few more seconds pass.

The deer knew she wasn't an immediate threat, but still slowly turned and moved to greater safety through the trees. Caitlyn smiled and continued her journey.

Almost home now after nearly three miles of running, she noticed her breathing was heavier than normal and chocked that up to two weeks of first crying, then moping, then writing, then packing, then moving, then unpacking, etc. All of which kept her from running. Possibly.

As she hit the home stretch, she knew what was next. Brendan's house. If she continued straight, her path for hundreds of runs, she would pass it. If she turned right and made a detour around his block, she'd miss it. Perhaps buoyed by the deer spotting she continued straight.

After half a minute it appeared on her right. Like the rest, little seemed altered. Although it had been two years ago, she remembered swinging on the rope swing there, dangling from the oak tree in the dead center of the yard there, and Brendan pushing her too hard but seeming to enjoy her cries as she hit the top, her feet seeming to touch the sky. And there, the front steps where they'd shared their first hug, and sat and watched the stars, his beagle Stamkos at their feet, looking up at them. And finally there, in front of the garage, where she'd last seen him on that May night in sixth grade, in his jeans and red shirt, right before the dance. The dance. It had been a lifetime ago. Would he even remember her now? Would he care? Maybe he was even DATING Rachel at this point. Again. No. Kristen would have told me if that was happening.

The pain of that moment of realization that Brendan was after Rachel even while WITH her flooded back across the years. Sure, Brendan had told Kristen that he had nothing to do with that picture, that she must have taken the necklace when he was gone from the table. Sure. Who would leave a piece of jewelry, obviously in a jewelry box, unguarded at a table with a group of non-friendly girls that included your ex-girlfriend? She had never bought that idea. It was just all too coincidental, that she just happened to sit down at his table, and supposedly take the necklace meant for me.

Also, Kristen had said that she and Brendan had a class together, which with her following Kristen around for a week meant that she would at least be in the same room with him if not SEE him or TALK to him, which didn't make her happy. Caitlyn knew she was resilient, but still this was a painful part of her past that she didn't want to revisit. She wondered if her not having dated anyone since him was because of how scarred she was or just a lack of available guys in Guam and decided on the latter.

Passing his house, with only a block to go (how convenient back then she thought while simultaneously willing her brain to drop the subject of Brendan) she kicked it into high gear and the Clash's "Janie Jones" just pumped her up more. She finished with a flourish, her upward momentum and speed stifled by the hill in her front yard, and she crashed to the grass in relief.

God, I LOVE this movie, Anabel thought. Even in a theater only a quarter filled during opening week, this is awesome. On the screen the song "96,000" was on, with maybe two hundred people around a New York pool on a hot summer's day, singing about how their lives would change with that many dollars. She looked over at Chris, and he was fidgeting, still. She had to beg him to go, and when he saw on the marquee inside the mall that it was over two hours he just moaned.

"Seriously? Why does this movie have to be that long? It's a musical, right? Can't they just SPEAK the words so it'll go quicker."

"You are NO FUN," Anabel said. "And yes, there is dialogue, too."

"Well then why is it over two hours long?" he asked.

"Look, I sat through that boring hockey game with you a couple nights ago so you said you'd go with me to the movie. Fulfill your end of the bargain!"

"I'm here, right?" Chris said flatly.

"You might actually like it. Grace said it was really good."

"So what does she know?"

"Chris, come on," she had said, and he reluctantly bought the tickets and they had gotten a large Diet Coke and popcorn before finding their seats.

He got up and said, too loudly, "I've gotta go to the bathroom."

"Again?" she said. "That's your third time already."

"And?" Chris replied.

"AND the movie is less than an hour in."

"Blame it on the big Coke," he said, and left.

While he was gone, Anabel resolved to just shut him out as much as possible and enjoy the movie. I wish I would have gone with Grace. She said she'd see it again. But no, for some reason I chose Chris. Well, of course I chose Chris. But maybe not of course. I don't have to do everything with him. She decided that she didn't do everything with him, but that maybe she'd have to be more selective in the future.

When Chris returned, he suffered another five minutes and finally shut his eyes, soon slumping onto her. Good, Anabel thought. I don't have to deal with him anymore, and I can focus.

Later that afternoon, Caitlyn and Kristen were thrifting at three downtown shops after pizza at Bruno's Famous. Caitlyn was buried in the middle of a thickly packed dress rack, so much so that she had to almost grunt to withdraw a dress to fully check out. Kristen moved from the row they were busily scanning to the next opposite her and leaned against the bar, then set her head on top of her hands for full Kristen affect. Caitlyn looked questioningly at her.

"What?" she said. "You done already? Or are you tired of these awesome stores because you go to them every weekend even though my thrifting-starved butt wasn't within 3,000 miles of one for two years?" Kristen continued to stare at her, her face a puzzle. "Dude? What?"

Kristen raised her head, tittered, then said, very deliberately, "Okay." She clasped her hands together on top of the rack and continued. "So, are you going to address the elephant in the room, or am I?"

Caitlyn stared back blankly, then got it, but said, "Oh, you mean are you going to buy that $100 green flapper dress with the hella sequins in the front of the store?" which brought a frown from her friend.

"Cait, seriously."

"What?"

"Come on. You know . . . "

"What?"

"Well, I was hoping you'd start it, but I guess I can."

"Start what?"

Exasperated, Kristen threw up her hands. "Really?" Caitlyn raised her eyebrows. "Okay. Brendan. BRENDAN. B-R-E-N-D-A-N. Brendan."

"Old news. Not interested," Caitlyn said.

Kristen now walked around to her, took the dress Caitlyn was looking at and laid it on top, and took her by both shoulders. "Cait. You always don't want to talk about it. But now you've gotta. You're back. I told you he's in my math class. We're going to see him. Tomorrow."

Caitlyn took Kristen's hands and gently lowered them. "Yes. I'm aware," she said. There was a silence. Awaiting a response, Kristen heavily blinked at her a few times. "What else do you want? That was a long time ago. I'm done."

"Caitttttttt! You know the story. Rachel must have taken it from the box and tried it on, somehow, while you guys were gone from the table. Brendan told me that night that he had NOTHING to do with that picture that she posted. Come on!"

"You know, even IF I believed that story, it's water under the bridge. Gone. Half a lifetime ago. Why should I care now? And even if I did, you told me about that hockey incident. THEN I could always see his anger, just below the surface. But THAT. Knocking that kid out and giving him a concussion. That's just brutal."

"But that was never directed to you, Cait. If anything you kept that in check."

"So what? If he'd do that to some random kid in hockey who's to say he wouldn't do it to someone else outside of that?"

"You know he wouldn't, Cait. Seriously."

"No, YOU know I just don't want to bring all that back up. Just let it go, Kristen. I'm done." Caitlyn felt her face getting flushed.

"But . . . you guys were so good together. Remember?"

"Kristen, we were together two weeks. TWO WEEKS. How is that even a relationship? And I was 12. 12! Just drop it, okay?"

"But wouldn't you even--"Kristen began.

"DROP! IT!" Caitlyn turned and stormed out of the store, her violent push to the door making it clatter against the frame and bringing the stare of the cashier.

Caitlyn knew her strategy of getting over things was predicated more on denial than anything else, but hey it worked for her she thought as she sat down on the bench in front of Lilly's Second-Hand Boutique, the last thrift shop they were going to. She hoped Kristen would give her a minute to gather herself and calm down, but this was not the way her friend was built, and right on cue Kristen turned the corner and stormed toward her.

Caitlyn turned her back and tried to will herself back to the tranquil images of the deer, and the forest, and the old man, and the park. In vain.

May 24

It feels like the only time I can lose my pain and general disappointment in my life is when I'm playing online. In Call of Duty you really don't care about satisfying other people or their emotions if you say or do the wrong thing. I play with mostly idiots, faceless entities scattered over the world, and who cares about those guys? This world is where I'd want to live. If you die, you just start another game. No lingering pain. Or resentment. Or loss. What was that line from that book he had read this year in Mr. Gowson's language arts class? "Fire was bright and fire was clean." And "It was a pleasure to burn." *Fahrenheit 451*. That's one dude's world that is more messed up than mine. But if I could just have fire to burn away my memories, what lingered inside me. . . that would be great.

So today I was playing the "Shock and Awe" challenge. The guys online have always gone nuts about how wild that is, so I intentionally saved it a time when I could spend mega time on it. And I'm thinking hockey suspension time is just about perfect. Anyway, you're Sgt. Paul Jackson, and he's trying to capture or kill Khaled Al-Asad, who was a fictional dude, but Brendan still liked the meaning of his name when he looked it up: the eternal lion. So he was on a quest to kill The Lion. As I got deeper into it, the whole city was evacuated because of a nuke threat. So I figure I'm playing the hero, getting in and out, killing The Lion in the process. Just as I'm in the middle of it, the bomb detonates, killing me and 30K other marines. Damn! I spent like four intense hours on it (pissing off my mom, who wanted me to go shopping or something. Okay, I had previously told her I would) just to have that happen. So that was a pretty stupid part of my day.

So while I was playing, I knew I had to finish because the Bolts were playing later that night, so maybe I screwed up or something with the mission, missed something I should have done, because I was rushing, who knows, but anyway the Bolts were playing Montreal with the series tied two all. As always, I performed the Grandpa George pre-game ritual of touching the signed picture of Gretzky that's on our den's wall showing him holding up one of the Cups he won in Montreal, then fixing a turkey and cheese sandwich with mustard, then pouring a tall glass of iced tea. It's late in the game, and it's looking like OT, but I never worry about that because Vasy is the best goalie in the league. So I figure we've got the advantage. Then Victor Hedman, with a minute left, throws one of those 2/3 ice passes, aiming for Point, but the Canadian's Suzuki steps in, steals the pass, and sends a slap shot over the diving Hedman's stick and just under Vasy's glove for the game winner. Now we're down 3-2. That sucks. And to lose at home too. So now we've gotta win AT Montreal to stay alive, which would set up a game 7 at home. Game 7 would be Friday. Friday is the day of the "graduation." No way I'm going to that lameness and miss game 7 if that happens.

Judging from our conversation between the first and second period, Mom would definitely be pissed, but so what? What is she NOT pissed off at me about lately? Let me see if I can quickly recap. You're going to the graduation. No I'm not. Yes you are. No I'm not. Then you won't be playing hockey anytime soon. You mean like two weeks soon, cause that's the length of my suspension. No I'm talking beyond not. Really, like what. Like the rest of the season. The rest of the season. You must be joking. You wouldn't do that to me. Yes I would. Mom why. Because graduation is important. But why. No one graduates from eighth grade. Well in your school they do. But for what purpose. Because you need to get out more and see people. Why. Because you're either at that rink or have your nose buried in your computer playing those violent games all the time and that's not good for you. What is good for me mom, getting my heart stomped on repeatedly. Brendan you know this has nothing to do with that. Mom it has everything to do with that. How are you getting your heart stomped on by going to graduation? I don't know but it happened last year. Last year was COVID Brendan there was none. Okay so the year before or whatever, I don't care. That's even more reason COVID hasn't been good for you, Bren. Mom COVID hasn't been good for anybody. I don't care you're going and that's final. Good Luck with that Mom. Okay you make your decision and I'll make mine. And besides, I hear that girl has moved back with her family maybe you can see her again. Yeah I know Kristen has informed me of that useless fact so what? So what is that you two were so nice together. Sure mom for like five days and that was two years ago like it even matters anymore.

That was pretty much that, and then she folded her arms in her chair and motionlessly stared at the game for the second period. I forgot to write that her boyfriend Mike was there for the game, and he pretty much just sat there and ignored our whole argument. Mike's actually a pretty good guy. Definitely a better guy than Dad. I get along with him pretty well, except when he jumps in sometimes in my mom's defense. Which he does less of now when he sees it because he knows it just pisses me off more. He knows hockey, having played at during high school, and he's a huge Lightning fan too, and he knows the history of the NHL and players also. So he's useful to have around.

So, between that period and the next, between the crappy Lightning playing and the hassle from Mom, I pummeled my pillow for a minute or so to work off some steam. Grandpa George's words of **harness your anger** flitted through his head between blows and had some effect of ending them.

So, that's it. Another stupid day in the life of Brendan Ellison. Til tomorrow, signing off.

-Brendan

As Anabel opened the doors to Performance Gymnastics and stepped inside, she felt the familiar feeling of comfort. This was her safe place. Her haven. Where she could drop her pretenses and just be herself. Such was not always the feeling with her, and as always she turned to see the team picture from two years ago, when she was in sixth grade, the year she and Chris got together. It showed two rows of tall or tallish girls, mostly thin, long-legged girls, except for the girl in front left, who was short, and dumpy, and had stringy brown hair and an expression to mirror all of that.

That was her. The OLD her. The one she vowed never to return to. Ever. The one who served as a warning, a flashing beacon of caution to what her life could become again, if she let herself go, dropped her guard, fumbled the ball. And other poor metaphors.

And after this, she walked confidently down the entryway to the gym floor, seeing her current self-reflected in the full-length mirror, the self that for almost a year and a half now had slain the BEFORE Anabel in the team picture every time she did this ritual. Blonde, wavy hair, now in a high ponytail. Slim waist. Firm butt. The leotards that were definitely NOT too revealing. HERE was the one place she didn't want to have to maintain and guard her image. She didn't want to attract attention. She wasn't on the team anymore, and really was just a hanger-on when she was. Her weight disallowed her from being able to do anything that would have made her better, like for example stay on the beam for longer than ten seconds without flailing and falling.

As she walked to the mat where she was going to begin her routine, she noticed two girls struggling to reach the overhead bars. First they tried jumping, then stacking a couple of cushy blocks underneath, but they still couldn't reach. They looked longingly to their mothers, but they were busily chatting and couldn't see their daughters' struggles. Anabel walked in their direction, and one spotted her coming and moved out of the way.

One of the girls, who was wearing pink tights with a pink ribbon in her hair, said to Anabel, "We can't get up." The other one looked too sheepish to speak.

"Yeah. I saw you struggling," Anabel said.

"Can you help us?" the same girl asked.

"Of course. It looks like you just need a boost up, right?" The other girl, in yellow tights, nodded her head.

"Yeah. That'd be great. Thanks. My name's Julia, and my friend is Ginger."

"Well it's very nice to meet you. I'm Anabel." The girls smiled. Anabel lifted Julia up until her small hands grabbed the bar. Julia adjusted her grip some. "Do you want me to help you get started swinging?" Anabel moved toward her.

"Well, I don't know. Let me see." Anabel backed away. Julia started swinging, slowly, and her smile grew wider the higher she went.

"Wow, you're doing great!" Anabel said and noticed that Ginger was smiling too.

After swinging for maybe 30 seconds, Julia announced "Dismount!" and landed perfectly about five feet from the bar.

"My turn," Ginger said, and looked expectantly at Anabel. She lifted the smaller girl onto the bar, and Ginger indicated that he she wanted Anabel to stay there. She started swinging a bit, and Anabel was ready to catch her lest she fall. After ten seconds she said, "Okay. All done. Can you get me down?" Anabel complied.

"Wow. You two are really good."

"Thanks Anabel," Julia said, and the two girls smiled widely at her. As Anabel turned she missed both of the girls' mothers in rapt attention, apparently having watched the whole affair.

Arriving back at the mat, she pulled up "Tranquility mix" on Spotify and turned the volume up high. She then adjusted her earbuds and stepped onto the soft mat of one of the tumbling floors. This late in the day on Saturday the high-level girls were gone, either at a competition or just done for the day, so Anabel noticed only a handful of other gymnasts in her field of vision, including the kid who used to be and probably still is the best male athlete in the gym, Brian Yorker, working out hard on the rings in the back.

Before she struck her pose to begin a few practice runs to prep for tumbling, she ticked off one by one the failures she had experienced in this gym. The fall off the beam in her first competition, landing hard on her arm. Embarrassing. The time she was warming up and collided head-on with Amber Nestor, who cried for ten minutes while her mom frantically ran around trying to get her ice. Anabel's fault. And the scariest for her, her head hitting the edge of the ball pit hard after a vault, her mother gone shopping, her head bleeding, and some girls actually GIGGLING at her lack of finesse and downright ineptitude. She had overcome all of these. To be here. Free of demons. Free of worry. Expectations lowered. Defenses lowered. Calm.

One last thought flitted through her head before starting the initial run: I'm done with crown decoration for tonight too. On the way home from the movie, when Chris turned on his rock station too loudly for comfortable conversation, she had thought of the exact picture she wanted for tonight. Predetermining that this was to be a families picture, as in hers and Chris's families, together, she knew she wanted the one in front of Williams's Lobster House from Christmas of last year, the one where they were hiding their COVID masks behind their backs before going into the 25% capacity-at-the-time restaurant. She had worn the green thrift store dress, the one that cost $50, but worth every penny. EVERYONE looked good in this picture. She'd already printed a copy on her computer and it was sitting on her desk.

As she flung her arm into position, raised her fingertips to point to the ceiling, thrust her chin toward there as well, one foot forward and one flat, she fleetingly wondered what ideas Chris had for his crown.

Later that afternoon, Chris was finishing up an episode of The Office with his brother Liam, who was 10, when Liam suggested, "Wanna shoot some hoops?"

"Dude," Chris replied. "It's dark out there. And it's late." He looked at his curly brown-haired brother, who at times was REALLY hard to say No to.

"Come ooooonnnn," Liam whined. "We have a light you know." Chris didn't answer. "Come on, Chris. Ten minutes."

"Sure," Chris replied. The boys then moved through the den to the garage, where Liam grabbed his new Wilson basketball. Chris pushed the garage door opener and they moved onto their driveway.

"Okay, you got me for ten. After that I have to start decorating my crown."

"Doing what? Did you just make that up?" Liam said, laughing. "What crown?"

"The stupid crown that I won at the end of sixth grade. Remember?" Liam shook his head. "Well anyway, They gave it back to me like a week ago, and Anabel and I are supposed to decorate our crowns to show how we've changed since then."

"Oh, okay, cool. So you're doing it for her?"

"Yeah, sure, I guess."

Liam missed a ten-footer, then stopped and looked at his brother. "Man, if I had a girlfriend like Anabel, I'd do stuff for her, too."

"What do you mean?" Chris asked.

"Well, she's really . . . hot."

Chris immediately started cracking up. "Wait. Did you just call Anabel 'hot'? Dude that's awesome." His continued laughter brought a point-blank throw to his chest from Liam, with the ball bouncing away almost to the street. "Okay, just for that, now I'm gonna tell her what you said."

After retrieving the ball, Liam, ball raised in menace toward his brother, said, "You better not," and mimicked hitting him with it again.

"What? I think that's cute," Chris said, flinching slightly.

"Great. So I'm cute."

"No, man, really. I love that you guys get along well."

"She's so nice. She always talks to me. She plays games with me. She helps me with my homework. She's like a sister."

"Yeah, that's true."

"What's it like, having a girlfriend?" Liam asked.

"It's fine, I guess."

"Fine. Come on. What's it like . . . kissing?" Liam's small face was upturned to Chris. He couldn't joke here. This was serious to little dude.

But then he did. "It's like kissing Mom."

Liam made a disgusting face. "Stop lying! No it's not. I've seen you guys before. That is nothing like kissing Mom." Chris shrugged. "So come on. What's it like?"

"It's pretty cool."

"Yeah . . .?"

How much could he really explain this to Liam, without going too far?

"Well," Chris began. Imagine someone that you like, and then wanting to do more than just touch or hold hands with that person." Liam, wanting more, was in rapt attention. "Yeah, so then you kiss. You press your lips against hers and you kiss." Liam nodded. "That's pretty much it, dude."

"Okay, so I guess I get that. But what's it like having a GIRLFRIEND? You know, someone to always be with."

"Not so different than being with friends. It's someone you like, a lot, and you spend a lot of time together and do things together."

"That's it?" Liam asked.

"Well, no, there's more," Chris said.

"So . . ."

"MORE that I'm not going to tell you because you're too young."

Liam again held the ball up in mock-menace to Chris.

"Okay, look, when you get older you'll have a girlfriend and you'll know what's it's like and we can talk about it then. I'll be your advisor. It's not that hard."

"And until now, Anabel will be my friend and keep doing things with me."

"Yeah Liam. Sure."

"But she's my HOT friend."

Chris laughed again. "Yeah, okay, you're hot friend."

"And YOUR hot girlfriend."

At that point Chris stole the ball from him, ran out to the three-point arc their father had meticulously painted on the driveway, and swished the shot. They played for another not ten but thirty minutes, as thoughts of Anabel and decorating the crown went in and out of Chris's mind. Sure, she was special. And she was definitely hot. But after two years of being together, sometimes it starts to feel like the same thing over and over. Definitely not gonna try to explain that to the runt. It was just . . . the expectation. The expectation that X amount of any given day would be spent with her. Not that it was exactly a chore, but . . . well, sometimes it was. Like watching that crappy movie earlier today. But there are so many other good times. He thought of them at other movies, darker movies, movies she was less interested in really, movies both in theaters and in their living rooms, and the feel of her in his arms . . .

Later that night, Caitlyn sat at her computer and once again thought of where to begin in her novel. I'll have Jodi wallowing in her room for a couple days and thinking about all that she had and lost. She wondered how to successfully revisit scenes she'd already written but add more detail. Wait, hadn't she already planned for that? She had! She had, by at the time leaving some things vague for the reader to fill in herself, so even if she went back, the details would be new. Yes! Nothing better than to see in fiction what you would never want to happen to you in real life. She decided that she'd start with the scene of the horrific performance onstage which led to her being booted from the band. She began to visualize then scribble down notes of just how wrong it went, how Jodi went from on top of the world, from star to pariah, from insider to outcast, from happy to sad.

How much of this is me and how much is fiction?

Monday, May 25, 2021: Four days before graduation

"Isn't my mom the best?" Kristen said, unbuckling her seat belt and loudly smacking as she kissed her mom on the cheek as they sat at the light.

"Yeah she is," Caitlyn added, also making the same smacking sound from the back seat toward Mrs. Rothstein, which brought a chuckle from the driver.

"As hard as I work for that school, for darn little pay, there better be some perks, right?" Kristen's mother said as she slowly accelerated with the light's turning green.

"And we get to spend ALL DAY together!" Kristen happily chirped, turning to look at Caitlyn's half-smile in the back seat.

Kristen's mother saw this in the rear-view mirror. "Cait honey. Your mom said you were nervous about today?"

"It's been two years, Mrs. R," she replied. "Who's even gonna remember me still?"

"Okay, now that's just dumb. Mom, she follows like 50 kids from school still."

"And Caitlyn, you've always had so many friends. You're so vibrant. Who wouldn't want to be friends with you?"

"Yeah. My girl," Kristen said, fist-bumping her.

"I know," Caitlyn semi-whined. "But it's been SO long."

"That doesn't matter, Cait. Come on! You're gonna step into that hallway and peoples' faces are just gonna light up!" Kristen exclaimed.

"Wait. Just checking. This IS still middle school, right? The place where immaturity and judgement reign? Kristen rolled her eyes.

Just then the car turned left and the school came into Caitlyn's view for the first time in two years, with the first building she saw of course having to be the gym, the site of the dance, the last building she had been in, fleeing that May night amidst tears and pain. It hadn't changed at all from what she could tell.

"Look at the banner for graduation we put up, Cait," Mrs. Rothstein said as they sat at the light on the side of the school.

Caitlyn couldn't help but see the enormous banner advertising Friday's main event because it stretched from one side of the building to the other and served as both a goofy goodbye to COVID and celebration of the graduation.

The banner was yellow and green, the Wildwood Middle school colors, of course, but Caitlyn noticed that it told a story, their class's story from left to right. The first picture was a group of smaller kids waving goodbye to elementary school while stepping toward Wildwood Middle, then a second picture of an older, taller girl happily showing her 7th grade report card to her dad, a third picture of the school's closing for COVID for the fourth quarter shown by bars and locks, then a fourth of a classful of now 8th grade-sized masked students and a teacher, then finally a picture of students ripping off their masks and running toward a likeness of the gym, with "2021 Wildwood 8th Grade Graduation!" across its top.

"That is REALLY awesome," Caitlyn said.

"I know, right," said Mrs. Rothstein. "We really weren't expecting the school board to let the kids go maskless for the graduation, but it squeaked through with a 5-4 vote."

"And Friday at the end of school at the same time we're all gonna rip off our masks and throw them away," a gleeful Kristen added.

"That's awesome," Caitlyn replied, as she felt the nervousness rising in her that she had tried so hard to squelch ever since she learned that she'd be shadowing Kristen for the week.

The car moved forward and turned left to enter the car line. Caitlyn could see her favorite sixth grade teacher on duty greeting the kids and parents ahead.

"Miss Johnson is still here?" Caitlyn asked. "I love her."

"YESSS. Isn't she the best?" Kristen responded.

As their car slowly made its way to the drop-off spot, Caitlyn's usual confidence began to flood into her, and the expression of surprise and joy on Miss Johnson's face as she exited the car with Kristen told her that it everything was going to be okay.

As the girls made their way through the breezeway to the 8th grade waiting area, the buzz that Kristen said would happen toward Caitlyn was happening. Before they arrived at their destination Caitlyn had gotten half a dozen hugs and was clearly the topic of the morning. Caitlyn couldn't recognize everyone she saw due to time constraints and the ubiquitous masks, but through her remembered social media connections and Kristen's narration quickly became familiar once again with most of the students she saw.

Her head spinning, Caitlyn had forgotten that homeroom and first period is when they would be in the same class as Brendan, whom she noticed as the students sat silently listening to the morning show. She was seated next to Kristen in the back, and Brendan was in the front row, closest to the door. She tried to catch his eye, and at least smile, but he seemed rigid, focused either on the show or on not seeing her. Later when they broke up into study groups it seemed like again that he consciously had his back to her, which was fine.

Odd, she thought as the period neared its end. I feel more relaxed than he does, and I'm the one that has been gone for two years.

Monday, May 25

Study day today in school. Oh boy. More time to spend not caring about subjects that have little to nothing to do with my future. Last Friday was the day where all the teachers sat down with each student and talked about their average and what they'd need to score on the final exam. So I had to sit through six of those conferences (Coach Williams couldn't give a rat's ass and didn't do his) and THEN had to listen to Mom rant at me again about my grades at night because grades were sent home electronically that day. I was just dreading that talk, and I tensed up from the moment Mom's yellow Rav 4 pulled into the driveway until half an hour later when it was finally finished. I had 4 C's and 2 D's, and she was PISSED. So pissed that I had to talk her into letting me play the game on Saturday, and then I destroyed Hill with that hit and got suspended, which made her more pissed but convinced that I would at that point spend every waking minute studying for the exams this week.

Yeah, right.

She's never going to stop trying to get me back to that all "A" student that I was in elementary before Dad left. Ain't gonna happen. And her telling me that she got scholarships because she was in the top 5% blah blah blah of her class have no effect. Maybe if she thought more about her marriage and less about herself then Dad wouldn't have left.

Anyway, so the only decent part of my day was when the team was at lunch talking about tonight's game vs. the Oilers (which they lost without me 2-1, of course). That loss probably ruined our chances for the playoffs, and I was going to miss the next two games anyway. So yeah, some hope there at lunch, and I tried to fire them up as best as I could, then they lost, and it sucked. Just like everything sucks.

And then probably the worst part of the day was history. SHE came back, just as Kristen said she would. And it really makes no sense, because Kristen said she already completed 8th grade in Guatemala, or whatever the hell country she was in before she moved. But there she was, sitting next to Kristen in class. I did my best to turn my back completely to them, although out of the corner of my eye I saw them looking my way a couple times. I'm not sure what the point of that was. I want nothing to do with her. I want nothing to do with anything that brings me pain.

Then just like 20 minutes ago of course Kristen had to call me and ask me about seeing Caitlyn again and was a pain in the butt about it. She knew I wanted nothing to do with her. I did thank her for not doing something incredibly stupid like coming over to me with her and talking to me. "Brendan, come on. I'm NOT going to do that to you!" was her response. She better not. Then she asked me about going to graduation and I told her I'm not going what's the point and then she did her Kristen thing and of course told me all the fun I'd have and what was going to be there and so on and I told her none of that interested me but she said at least you'll see me and then I said well there's always that which kind of pissed her off. She can't be thinking of some fantasy that she's going to get me and Caitlyn together again, because that's just insane.

Of course she is.

Tonight I guess I studied SOME and Mom dropped a bombshell by asking if I wanted to go to the shelter on Saturday and get another dog. Stamkos just died like two months before. I'm not sure I'm ready for another dog. But then maybe that's just what I need. Something in my life that I don't disappoint. What a concept. I told her I'd think about it.

So yeah, there's my mandatory diary entry for the day. You're welcome Dr. Fuller.

-Brendan

Ask any kid at Wildwood Middle what their favorite time of the school day is and you're liable to get one of two answers, if not both: lunch and PE. The two times in the day where kids could avoid the constant surveillance of their teachers' oppressive eyes. Anabel was fine with PE for the most part because she had several friends in that class and it wasn't too difficult—the coach let you just walk the track if you wanted to rather than actually playing something—even if the Florida sun caused its own problems with maintaining her makeup afterwards.

Pre-COVID, there were 12 possible seats at her lunch table. If for any reason one of those not-assigned-but-you-bet-your-ass-they-were-assigned seats became open, there would have been great cause for discussion as to possible candidates for the open spot amongst her and her friends. And while there weren't necessary applications for said seat, you can bet the jockeying for position started the day someone departed. It was the center table in the cafeteria, with Anabel occupying the most central seat possible.

If any of the girls had a boyfriend and wanted to sit by him on a given day, then her seat was just empty for the day. This of course was a risk, if not really to her place at the table then to the knowledge and gossip that was so essential to maintain her standing in the group. All the girls understood the balance that had to occur here, and rarely was one gone for more than a day a week from the table lest she miss something or some nasty bit of gossip start about her. And for this to happen, she had to fit in with the boyfriend's friend group also. All a tricky balancing act.

And then there were split days, like Anabel wanted for today, when she planned on catching up on the news for part and sitting with Chris for part. Here she could get not only the dirt from the girls but the affirmation of Chris also. And this was a lower self-esteem day, so she needed both.

Although Anabel enjoyed her position at the table, she thought many of these rituals fairly ridiculous. She wondered, though, what she'd do if she actually had to EARN her position with them, as most of them had to do every day.

When she arrived at the girls' table, hers was the only seat empty, and it was clear that they were in the midst of discussing something that happened before school, so she quickly said hi and while trying to catch up with the conversation began to assemble her lunch, which today was half a can of tuna fish, some almonds, and some blueberries. From what she gathered, Courtney had said something derogatory about Megan's outfit, which caused Megan to blurt out that she had caught Courtney's boyfriend with another girl at the mall last week ("I've never seen her before. Maybe she goes to Lincoln?"), which Courtney said was a lie and then explained to everyone gathered in the waiting area before school that at least she had a boyfriend. Pretty much the usual, Anabel thought. Since no one had been with their boyfriend anywhere near as long as Anabel had been with Chris, she was looked at the relationship guru.

Lillian turned to Anabel and said, "So what do you think, Anabel?" Anabel saw the other ten heads turn to look at her. "Well, I saw Megan's outfit, and I thought it was cute," causing several of them to nod their heads. "And the mall thing with Taylor? I'm sure it's true. He's done that before, so why should Courtney be surprised now. She knew what she was getting into." More satisfied nods.

Never very comfortable with the arbiter role, Anabel hoped that was the final word on the subject, or at least all that would be required from her because she didn't feel like playing the game today, which was mentally exhausting, and after spending four hours studying for her coming Geometry final last night she needed a rest.

As the conversation switched several times, Anabel found herself both tuning out and wanting to leave their table and join Chris's table, where she could easily fade into the background. When one of the girls left to use the restroom, and feeling her duty disposed of, Anabel quickly said goodbye and moved herself and her lunch to the boys' table.

She sat down in the seat next to Chris, the one that was always open in case she wanted to join them. They were busily discussing some sporting event, of which she would neither care about nor have any knowledge of. Good.

"Hey," Chris said, his mouth full of some chicken concoction that seemed to involved pasta sauce as well.

"Hey," she replied back, popping a blueberry in her mouth.

"So when CP3 made that fadeaway, that put them 6 ahead, and that was it," Gary, Chris's best friend, said.

"What'd he have for the game?" Chris asked.

Anabel noticed that Chris had some red pasta sauce on the corner of his mouth. She instinctively wetted a napkin and was going to wipe it. Halfway there she froze as he saw her. "What are you doing?" he asked. She opened her mouth halfway and then closed it.

"38," Gary responded.

"Damn. That dude is old but he can turn it on when he needs to," Ricky said.

Although she didn't want to participate, usually one of the guys pulled her into the conversation somehow, and although oftentimes it was about something she didn't know anything about, she enjoyed their attention. She knew they liked to talk to her, flirt with her, and she usually liked it as well, but today it wasn't happening, and although she didn't necessarily want it, the lack of it was felt. Chris's ignoring her was felt more acutely, and she decided to use this time to go over her plan for the rest of the day in her head.

Anabel was giving it her best each period during Study Day, focusing on the class at hand and being attentive to whomever person or group she was in for that period, but everything came crashing down on her during after lunch during Geometry, her demon class.

Today she had eaten a small bowl of strawberries for breakfast and the small lunch and had forgotten to pack the granola bar that usually sustained her through last period Geometry, and as usual was feeling the accompanying lack of energy her meager diet brought. She was trying to remember concepts from the beginning of the year piled onto the difficult new topics that they had not yet been tested on but for some reason still were going to be on the exam and at some point she found herself missing parts of the conversation that her group of four had been having.

"Annie, you okay?" Marlon asked, touching her on the elbow that was propping her up at that point.

"Huh? Yeah, okay. Just tired," she replied.

"You don't look so good," Ellie said.

"I'm okay."

Ellie reached into her backpack and pulled out a small bag of nuts. "Here. You need to eat something."

"Thanks El," Anabel said, and then added, "And I need a bathroom break. See you guys in a minute."

As she shakily got to her feet and walked to sign out for the restroom, she nodded at Mr. Ridgely, who nodded back. Just as she was exiting the room, she heard Ellie say, "That is just too much work. I guess it's worth it to her though . . ."

Anabel exited the room and walked down the deserted hallway, final arriving at the restroom. She was alone, and went into the first stall, sitting down heavily and putting her face in her hands. She didn't need to use the restroom. She just needed to close her eyes for a minute.

She ripped open the nuts and threw them all into her mouth, then close her eyes and chewed slowly. She's right. Being me is a lot of work. And, for what? How much longer am I going to want to play this game? It's utterly exhausting. Next year in high school I'll just be one of many, and it'll be easy to throw this off and just be me again. But what will Chris think of me then, if I stop being me, the it girl, the one to watch? The trophy?

She allowed herself to relax, as much as possible on the toilet and before she knew it the bell ending sixth period sounded.

When she got back to the classroom, all the other students were gone, and Mr. Ridgely looked at her quizzically. She shrugged back, and quickly grabbed her things. Anabel realized she must have been gone for 15 minutes or more of the period. As she turned to leave the teacher spoke.

"Hey. I'll write you pass. Stay a second." Anabel nodded. "You okay?"

"I'm fine Mr. Ridgely. Just tired."

"How're you feeling about the final in here?"

"Not great actually. I really need an 'A' on it."

"I'm sure you've done the packet, right?" She nodded. "Do you have any questions for me?"

She thought a second. "None right now I guess. I've got Chris to help me too."

"That's true. All right." He quickly scribbled her pass. "Just know that you can message me any time and I'll help."

"Thanks. I really appreciate that." She took the offered pass. "I'll see you tomorrow."

"See you then," he said.

That night after dinner Chris had gone on to the computer to try and crack the coding problem he was having with his add-on, "Return From Nowhere." He had been stuck on this one scene where the players encounter the Orc from Hell, which he knew would pretty smoothly fit into the Dungeons and Dragons universe and that he possibly could make some money on. The problem was they've gotta get past the orc to enter the cave. But first they had to get through a wall the orc had put up, and the game would glitch out and kick the players back a few minutes before in the story. He had spent probably 200 hours over the course of the year on the game, and despite trying numerous times and ways to figure this problem out he had just ended up figuratively beating his head against the wall as his players were literally trying that, among other things. Neither was successful.

Next he spent half an hour once again researching on the Internet, then another half hour probably consulting his coding book. No luck. He should have kept a log because he was sure he was now repeating previously failed ideas. He knew what he had to do. He always knew what he had to do. That if he did this thing, it could be solved in probably minutes. But he didn't really want to do it and was unsure of it could really happen.

It was, of course, to just jump into one of their games, play with them, then at some point kind of subtly ask for their help with his problem. These guys were probably geniuses, certainly above Chris's level, and each had designed his own add-ons for D & D and were widely known on the site as clever game designers. Colton, Sebastian, and Enrique.

Chris made sure his "progress" was saved and closed out his program. He clicked on the "D & D" iconic dragon picture on his toolbar and the online site populated. He clicked on "Join a Game" and looked for the one titled "Gonna Kick Ur Ass," the one the trio had decided on years before and was still funny. The game's eight player slots were currently full, which meant both that Chris would have to wait until someone left (he hoped it wasn't one of them, because while one of them could generally solve his problems their brains were like a well-integrated computer together at times) and that he could observe and see what they were doing and more importantly maybe what they were saying.

Chris could see their band was climbing a mountain, going in and out of its caves, fighting creatures, resting, eating, and that clearly the top of the mountain was their goal. He plugged in his headset so he could listen to their chatter.

"So tomorrow we start out before sunset, because if we don't then that village is going to be hopping with activity. No way we get to the throne room in that scenario." This was Sebastian.

"You know it. And let's make sure we've taken an energy serum so that we're at full health before the battle. Galbor's gonna be plenty pissed when we wake his ass up and start shreddin'". The familiar voice of Colton.

"Dude, we HAVE no serum, remember? That wizard in Gondalier was gone when we were in town." Sebastian again.

"Oh, yeah. Damn." Colton.

"I think you guys are both wrong," Enrique opined. "Let's stay up for a while and use our time to make sure our map is right and we're fully ready in terms of weapons and strategy, sleep during the day, then hit them right as they're going to sleep. This will mitigate our lack of health."

Chris heard murmurs of assent from the other two and a few other voices he didn't know and watched as they put their plan in place. Sometime in the middle of the day (a minute of real time was an hour in the game during non-action times) they were sneak-attacked, and Chris, whose mic was on mute, laughed as their avatars scrambled and their owners cursed at the injustice of it all. During the melee, Chris saw someone get killed, which meant his quest was ended. Which meant Chris's could begin.

He quickly pounced on the keyboard, hitting the JOIN button and waiting for the game to recognize him and let him in. Well, it wasn't HIM. It was an alias. If those guys saw that it was Chris himself they'd probably curse him off the game or kill his avatar themselves.

The reason for this current dilemma was of his own making. It used to be the four of them, together, quest after quest, adventure after adventure, spending way too much time virtually conquering kingdoms and rescuing folks. But that was before Anabel. Now if he got an hour to play every other day he was happy. And there of course was more. When he started dating Anabel, and, well, his world changed, he not only stopped playing with them but ignored them in the hallway when they spoke to him.

Then came the breaking point. Chris had always straddled the two worlds of sports and gaming well because he was good in each, and although this brought some strange looks at times when he was hanging out in the lockers or whatever with his gaming buds, he was still Chris, the power-hitting first baseman, one of the best players on his travel team. Or WAS one of the best players, at least. So he had always used this respect to protect his gaming guys, both physically at times and verbally, having the effect of a stop sign to those who would bully them. And then there was that day when Reece Faulkner and half his lacrosse team were walking down the nearly empty school hallway, spotted the trio, and just descended on them. Chris saw what was happening, quickly walked their way, and watched Reece push Enrique hard into the lockers. Enrique slammed backward, hitting his head and causing his backpack to drop at his feet, and looked at Chris pleadingly. Chris looked back, then continued down the hallway. It was an act of 7th grade stupidity, just being a dick, but that was that.

"Hey. Welcome Lothar 2236. Never seen you before. You a newbie. Who you be?" said Colton.

Transitioning from this memory, Chris forgot his mic was on and said, "No newbie here. I'm-" Realizing he was jeopardizing his ruse, he pressed MUTE and waited. Surely one of them would recognize the voice that they had spent maybe a thousand hours with. He waited.

"Whoah. What happened there, Bud?" Colton replied. Silence. "Okay, guess dude lost his mic. Hey, you can still type in the chat, right?"

Chris pulled up the chat box and typed YES.1

"Can you hear us though?" Sebastian asked.

Chris again wrote YES.

"Okay, good. So listen . . ."

Sebastian then filled him in on the details of the mission, of which he mostly knew 75% or more from listening to their pre-attack plan. Chris was good at Dungeons and Dragons. Not as good as them, but good. If he earned their respect, they might help him—whether they knew him or not—so he would look for a smart risk to take to impress them.

Night turned to day and then to night again in the game, with Chris making sure he was contributing well and proposing ideas rather than just reacting to them. They ultimately actually chose HIS battle strategy to use, and this might be the opening he needed.

After a couple of hours (Chris was watching the clock because he had school tomorrow. It said 12:48) they took the throne, ending the game. This was his chance.

Chris typed, "Hey. Any of you guys code? I'm having a problem that I need help with?"

"Yeah, we all do. At least Enrique and Colton and I do. What's happening?"

Chris explained the problem to them, and they began discussing how to solve it, but after a few minutes he heard Enrique say, "Shit dude. It's nearly one. We got EXAMS tomorrow!" This nearly always happened, this wail of disbelief at the time, as time just fast-forwarded whenever Chris was playing.

"Yeah, you right," Colton said. "Hey listen. Here's my email address. Send me what you're working on and I'll send it to the others. Good playing with you Bro. You the man. Great battle plan."

Chris typed OKAY and then THANKS and gave them his information, careful to give not the email address they probably would still recognize but rather one he used sparingly, and afterwards signed off the game and shut down his desktop. Mission accomplished.

Ten minutes later his mom knocked on his door and then entered.

"So Mr. Gamer," she began, "What progress have you made on the slideshow so far?" Hands on hips. "And why are you still up?"

Chris thought of lying but what would really be the point? "Absolutely zero progress mother dear," he said, his right handing forming an "O."

"And why is that?" she returned, hands falling from hips in with impatience.

"Because I have until Friday."

"That's only four days away, Chris. And you do have school you know? And sleep IS a real thing."

"Mom. You know I'm good at Power Point. I'll get to it soon. Promise," Chris said, putting a hand over his heart.

"Yeah. I know what your promises mean. Please don't forget that I AM the president of Blue Key, Christopher," she replied, but now smiling. He nodded. "Okay, Thursday night AT THE LATEST, okay?"

"Will do. Yes ma'am. Got it, Boss. Aye Aye Cap'n," he said, saluting her.

"I've told you there are a lot of pictures there, so it's a lot of sorting you'll be doing."

"What? You got a hundred pictures?"

"No. WAY more than that. Remember that these were taken by all the students AND the journalism kids."

"Okay, okay. I'll get started soon. Finished by Thursday. A lot of sorting. Got it."

Ugh. One more thing that he was obligated to do, Chris thought.

Caitlyn was in the den watching a movie with her brother Luis.

"Yo, Cait. Who's your favorite Avenger?" Luis was clad in his Avengers pajamas and sharing the same blanket with her on the couch.

"Hmmm. I guess Iron Man," she replied, distractedly watching Avengers Endgame with him for probably the tenth time. She knew he wanted the question also, so she obliged. "Who's yours?"

"Gotta be the Hulk," he said, flexing to show off his growing muscles.

"Yeah. The Hulk fits you dude. You rage like him," she said, which brought a yell from the still-flexing boy.

At that point the Hulk came into the scene during some crazy battle where you really couldn't tell what was happening, she thought. Just a bunch of people beating the crap out of one another. Luis was caught up now in the scene, which allowed Caitlyn to continue checking out her sixth-grade yearbook, trying to compare the faces that she'd seen today to those on the page, sometimes covering the lower part of their faces to simulate what she had seen earlier that day. Some kids had hardly changed, and some had done such a makeover that she never would have known it was the same person.

She came to her picture and saw how short and choppy her hair was. She was wearing a shirt from their elementary school. She looked like she was about 8. Of course these were the beginning of the year pictures, so they were closer to three years earlier than two, she remembered. Then she saw Kristen, who totally looked the same to her. But then her best friend who she Face-Timed with every day would I guess. The girls mainly looked the same but the boys had changed so much.

The last face she saw before shutting the book was Brendan's, in the last of the pictures. His of course was the sports club. She could barely remember him being this small. And cute. And outgoing. His face was lit up, and he wore a Fortnite t-shirt. His hair was short. He had freckles. He wasn't so different at the dance, I guess. But this picture must have been taken before his dad left. Something left him when that happened. She remembered even in that brief time they were together their talks about it and how much it had shattered him. He had little self-confidence. She had had to look through that to see the real Brendan.

When she glanced up, Luis was out cold, and the wall clock said 9:30. Caitlyn heard her mom finish a conversation with her dad and enter the kitchen.

"Hey. Who's still awake in there," she asked. "Time for bed."

At this Luis stirred, and looking at the TV said, "But there's only like ten minutes left Mom."

"Okay. Then brush teeth and lights out. School tomorrow," Mom replied.

Caitlyn said "YEAH" to Luis, who kicked at her as she made her escape from the movie that never ends and moved towards her room.

While brushing her teeth, the phone rang. Seeing it was Kristen, Caitlyn pressed the off key to silence the call and quickly texted "Brushing teeth." When she was finished, she called her friend back.

"So," Kristen said, as if bringing this up for the first time even though they had basically talked each class about the kids in it and how much they'd changed. "How was your first day?"

"You are too funny," Caitlyn said, laughing.

"Okay so that's not why I called."

"Yeah?" Caitlyn asked.

"I CALLED because I wanted to tell you that I just got off the phone with Brendan and he SWEARS he's not going to graduation." Caitlyn was silent. "I know. I know. I've tried to talk him into it, but he just doesn't want to go."

"Okay. Is that really surprising?"

"Well . . . No, I guess not," Kristen said. "But I thought, you know, that he might, or at least that his mom would make him go. She's always trying to get him to do things, and he's always fighting her about it."

"That doesn't really sound that different than in sixth grade," Caitlyn said.

"No. I guess not. But I keep trying. You know Cait, he's a really good guy, underneath everything." Again Caitlyn was silent, not knowing what to add. "But Saturday apparently he did something really violent. He told me that he smashed this kid in the chest with his hockey stick and the kid got a concussion."

"What?" Caitlyn managed.

"Yeah. Said the kid had cheap-shotted him earlier and he was getting him back."

"By giving him a concussion?" Caitlyn was aghast.

"He's got a lot of anger, Cait. You know. Because of his dad."

Caitlyn of course knew this.

"Well, I'm sorry to hear that. But listen. I gotta go. Going to write some."

"Yes! Your book. When are you gonna let me read it?"

"When it's done!" Caitlyn said.

"You are NO FUN," Kristen replied.

"Sometimes," she said. "I'll see you tomorrow girl."

"Bye bestie. So glad you're back. Love ya."

"Love ya too," Caitlyn said, and pressed the red circle on her phone that ended the call.

Caitlyn plugged in her phone and sat down, pulling up her favorite writing music on You Tube: Rainstorm in the Mountains. She opened her file (working title "Pool") and started a new chapter.

While she had her character Jodi sitting in her room and thinking just how far she had fallen, she was going to write a series of chapters showing these events in flashback, which should serve to horrify the reader. One that she had in mind in particular involved her putting her two-year-old brother Aiden in danger. This was the scene she was dying to write.

It starts out at Jodi's house, and her parents are out for the night so she's babysitting. What Jodi had done beforehand is to tell her friends that the party was at their house tonight, and that as soon as her parents left she would text them to come over. They were to bring whatever they wanted and they would party both in the house and on the pool deck. But when I write this I have to be clear that Jodi loved and was still planning on watching her little brother. She could show this duality with a scene right before the call doing something with Lil Bro Aiden. Then right after the phone call/scheme/plan is afoot!

Caitlyn focused on bringing the details of the scene to life, dropping hints about the pool deck as she showed the scene of the burgeoning party. And then Jodi getting a little too drunk and starting to lose focus. And then of Aiden waking up and wandering from his room. And having Jodi see him and hold him. And having her friends talk about what a good job she was doing balancing partying and babysitting and ogling Aiden. Until she wasn't, and she had the drink that would put her over the edge and to sleep. And then of one guy who at the last second saw Aiden, after everyone else had left the pool area and come inside, about to jump in the pool, and rush and grab him before he jumped. While Jodi slept. Drunk. Crisis averted. For the time being. Until Jodi's dad saw the footage on the pool's security camera the next morning. And she was in deep shit.

Caitlyn looked at the clock, saw it said "11:49," realized she had to go to school the next day, and then proceeded to start another chapter because she was so in the zone and didn't want to stop.

This chapter ("Rehab") involved Jodi in rehab, doing well, finishing the program and getting out, and her former bandmates who had booted her from the band seeing her progress but still being skeptical. And then another blow. Her girlfriend has another girlfriend, who Jodi sees her kiss in the club before a show. Which shatters her. Caitlyn thought: Should I have her relapse now? Should that be some kind of final blow? Would the reader care even MORE if I did that? Or would that just be too much?

The clock now said "1:13," and she realized these questions could be answered another night. She hit SAVE and then closed her computer, anticipating what intrigue day two of the great Caitlyn Patterson Return to Wildwood Middle After Two Years Show would bring.

Anabel closed her day by realizing that although she had chosen three finalists, she didn't choose the picture of the day to decorate her crown with. Snapping on the light on her bedside table, she walked to her desk and the three pictures neatly arrayed down the left side of it.

One was of her and Chris one time when they went sailing with friends. They were sitting on the front of the boat and the sun was setting behind them. They both wore sunglasses, and although the picture was framed well she decided against it because you really couldn't see their faces. The second was of her and her sister Nessa in a heap after a game of Twister, Nessa's leg covering her stomach and her own legs thrown in the air away from the camera. It was probably earlier in that year. Their expressions were of pure joy. This was definitely a contender. The final one was just of her, downtown, after having dinner at Harry's. She had on a cute red dress, and her hair looked great. It was in profile from her left, and she liked that it didn't show her stomach at all. Tough choice. She went with the second one with her sister, setting it on top of the others she had chosen so far.

Then she picked up the pictures and looked at them. One of her and Chris. One of the families. Then one of her and Nessa. Not what she would have imagined as she started out, as she had chosen a couple dozen great ones of her and Chris before she started, but she was happy with her choices.

Tuesday, May 26, 2021: Three days before graduation

With the graduation event only three days away, Melinda Rothstein's world had doubled in intensity. On top of the normal husband and son and daughter to take care of 24-7 there were times in the year when this school volunteer worked what seemed like 40-hour weeks also. The beginning of the school year was one. Processing the applications was a pain. Some adults just had no idea how to completely fill out a form. And the t-shirt sales hit at that time too. Coordinating and picking up things from the printer. And other little random reasons she found herself at the school for the better part of two weeks at the start.

And the other time was of course the end-of-the-year. She was always instrumental in whatever Kristen's class was doing, and this year was the big one—graduation. The decorations were late.

The caterer totally screwed up their order for food. The bill for the tables and chairs came in and it was SO not what she was quoted. Phone calls. Face to face meetings. Time. Almost dressed, she started ticking off the things that still needed to be done before Friday and felt completely behind the 8-ball. It wasn't yet 9:00 and she already had engaged in a heated discussion with Elegant Catering, which yielded the desired results but hamstrung the trio's current attempt at being on time.

"Mom. Are you coming?" Kristen yelled from the family room where she and Caitlyn were sitting. "We're like fifteen minutes late!"

"Just a second," Melinda yelled back at her daughter.

"We're going to have to get a late pass, Mom. That's me AND Caitlyn you know."

"I think you'll be okay, Kris," she said, slipping on her shoes and checking the mirror once more before walking to the girls. "And Caitlyn's just observing!"

"Hey Mrs. R," Caitlyn chirped.

"Good morning Caitlyn," she returned. And to her daughter said, "At least someone is treating me civilly around here," which brought a sigh from Kristen, who rose with Caitlyn, each grabbing their backpacks and lunchboxes as Melinda swept into the room clutching her purse and what she called her "school bag".

"Yeah, right," Kristen said, and they exited the house and scurried to the car.

Upon arriving at school, the girls dutifully reported to the office and got their late pass, with Melinda explaining to Wildwood Middle Principal Amelia Grayson that the tardiness was her fault. After the girls left to go to homeroom, Melinda talked with Amelia about the results of the catering phone call.

"He wasn't going to give it to me, despite our verbal agreement for $8 a head, but ultimately he said yes, so we won't need the extra $1,200."

"That's good. Every year this event gets pricier, and I really wanted to avoid the scrutiny of Area Director Peters. We got audited and had some problems with last year's numbers at graduation."

"Great. So I'll get with Valerie about the check," Melinda said. The principal waived her out and shut the door before beginning her Principal's Message that came right after the morning show.

Melinda heard her say "Good morning students. This is Principal Grayson. As you know today starts our first day of exams . . ." as she walked in and sat down opposite Valerie Donan, the school secretary.

"Hey Melinda. How's it going?" Valerie asked, reaching for the check that was slotted upright on her desk. "Got it right here," she said and handed her the check.

"Actually, I won't need it. I got them to accept the offer that they quoted me originally."

"Oh," Valerie said, withdrawing the check. "Bet that made Amelia happy."

"Oh yeah. She said the Area Director is carefully watching everything we spend."

"Always. Even though it's OUR money, that WE earn through our fundraising, they still think they need to regulate every cent."

"Bureaucrats. What are you gonna do?"

Valerie shrugged. "Hey, I think Friday is going to be great. We all so appreciate your work on this . . . and everything. Anabel is so excited about it."

"She got her crown from the case, right?" Valerie nodded. "How's the decorating coming?" It was astonishing how much Anabel looked like her mother, she thought. She'd kill for those high cheekbones.

"Oh I'm sure she's knee-deep in it. She said it'll be a great chance to show how she and Chris have changed, together, during that time."

"It really is remarkable that for almost all of middle school they stayed together. I think I had a dozen boyfriends. Some maybe for a day!" Both chuckled.

"Yeah," Valerie said. "I think it helps that Chris's family and ours are so close and that we're often together. The kids just have always gotten along well together. And Chris is wonderful."

"He does seem like a nice kid," Melinda said, and then her phone signaled her that she had received a text. It was from the caterer. Something wrong with the chicken. Good God. "I'm sorry Valerie. Something else from the caterer. Another trip across town!"

"Okay," the secretary said. "We'll see you Friday, if not sooner." Melinda said goodbye and left.

As Caitlyn and Kristen started up the stairs toward first period, Caitlyn knew that she couldn't avoid making eye contact with Brendan as they entered, late, as he would be there, seated right next to the door. And it was right at the point where the teacher would be addressing the class, right at the beginning, so they'd interrupt that and EVERYONE would be staring at her. Including him.

Reaching the door first, Kristen of course threw it open like she was storming the palace, and sure enough almost every eye in the room landed on the pair. Kristen said "Hi ya'll" far louder than she needed to and moved towards their seats in the back. Caitlyn hoped this would provide cover for her so she could scoot past Brendan, but when she looked at Brendan, he was looking right at her. She swallowed and slowed a second. When she smiled and quietly said "Hi" to him his eyes dropped to the study packet on his desk, and her smile diminished and she stared out at the other students, all waiting for her to sit so they could stop listening to the teacher give directions and start working, or at least for some of them act like they were working, because no one liked these state-mandated exams, and the curve was so ridiculous that you'd have to be a moron to do poorly on one—or just not care.

Caitlyn then moved to the back behind her boisterous friend and wondered why after two years Brendan couldn't at least look at her and return a hello. She hadn't done anything to him . . . really.

When she and Kristen were walking into the lunchroom in the middle of the day, Kristen nudged her and pointed to a girl that was crossing in front of them. The blonde-haired girl had on a bright yellow shirt and matching skirt and shoes, with small balls for earrings. Caitlyn mouthed "What?" at Kristen, who ignored her and continued walking to the table where they had sat yesterday.

Kristen intentionally sat with her back to the girl so Caitlyn could have a good view of her, and said, "Guess who that is?" The girl was seated at a table with other popular girls, and Caitlyn could easily identify five or six of them from first glance. She stared at the blonde, who was smiling and saying something to the girl next to her as she unzipped her lunchbox and pulled out a half-sandwich.

Caitlyn said, "Gimme a second," and tried to mentally scan some of the faces she had been looking at last night in the yearbook. Kristen was grinning at her.

"Look at her face. It's still the same, although so much else has changed."

"Oh crap. Is that Anabel? Anabel Donan?" Her mouth was ajar.

"In the flesh," Kristen said.

"She's so much more- "

"Skinny? Yeah?"

"And her boobs are really- "

"Bigger? Yeah?"

"And her hair is- "

"Blonder? Yeah. Isn't that nuts?" Kristen asked.

Caitlyn tried to reconcile the girl in front of her with the yearbook picture that her mind could now conjure and what she remembered of Anabel from sixth grade.

"That's just crazy," Caitlyn said. "What happened to her? She would never have been with the bright and shiny kids before."

"Remember? She's the one that won the crown, at the dance. Her and Chris Lawson."

"Yeah. So?"

"Well, pretty much starting from there, she just did the glow up thing. Lost a lot of weight. Started hanging out with that crowd."

"Bleached her hair," Caitlyn offered.

"That too," said Kristen.

"Well, yeah, but still. Wow." She paused and stared at Anabel. "But, you know, she doesn't look all that comfortable really. She's squirmy." Kristen briefly turned to look at Anabel and then turned around again and shrugged.

"And get this. She and Chris? They're still together!"

"What the--? " Caitlyn offered. "No way. Quit making stuff up."

"I'm serious. You wanna see Chris?" Kristen turned and had to rise slightly out of her seat to scan the cafeteria, spotting Chris at the corner table with his sports friends. "He's over there. In the corner."

Caitlyn turned and saw Chris in profile. He looked the same, just six or eight inches taller than before. "There he is," Caitlyn said.

"This must be kinda cool for you, right?" Kristen said, smiling. "It's like you remember the little kid version of everyone and look at us now . . . "

"Yeah, really great, Kris. Nothing like leaving home for two years and you come back and everyone is a stranger."

"Cait, come on. You know I didn't mean it that way. I just think . . . I don't know, it's like we always used to wonder how we'd look in the future, and now look at us. This is the future." Kristen thrust out her chest and swept her hair back with her hands, getting a laugh and shoulder slap from her friend.

"Whhaaatttt?" Kristen said, resuming her normal position.

Just then a boy with brown hair, acne, and a lunch try full of chicken tenders and fries was standing next to Kristen, who looked at Caitlyn briefly before announcing, "Hey Caitlyn. This is EJ. EJ—Caitlyn."

"Hi," EJ said, taking the empty seat. Caitlyn shot her a "What's up?" look that EJ didn't see. "So, Kristen tells me that you just got back to Jax after being away for two years. That's gotta be weird." Despite what was beginning to seem like a setup/ambush, Caitlyn thought he was cute and friendly.

"Yeah, actually, we were just talking about that," Caitlyn said, stepping on Kristen's toe protruding through her slides under the table, and Kristen shifted in her seat and withdrew her legs and feet from further harm.

"So whattaya think? Have things changed that much?" He popped a curly fry that he had dipped in a massive mound of ketchup in his mouth.

"Actually quite a bit," Caitlyn said.

"Yeah, but Caitlyn knows so many kids still and has kept up with them on Insta and through Snaps, so she's not that out of it," Kristen said.

"Thanks pal," Caitlyn said.

"You probably don't remember me," EJ said. "I only moved here the last month of sixth grade."

"Yeah, that's probably it," Caitlyn said.

"EJ's dad is in the Navy too, Cait, just like your dad," Kristen continued, forging whatever links she could muster between the two.

"That's great," Caitlyn said.

As if she were expecting it, Kristen lifted her head to see her boyfriend Mike coming to their table. "Oh hi, Mike," she said, grabbing his offered hand.

"Hey girl. Hey Caitlyn." Kristen had introduced the two of them yesterday, and Mike's low-energy persona seemed to be the ying to Kristen's overwhelming yang. "EJ," he finished, nodding in the boy's direction. Kristen stared at him an extra second, and Caitlyn at this point knew the ruse was real. "Hey Kris. Mr. Loxler is letting kids eat in her class today and ask him history questions. Wanna come?"

Kristen nodded enthusiastically. "Definitely. Hey Cait. I'll see you in fifth period," she said, and then quickly packed her lunch up and left with Mike. Caitlyn smiled at EJ, who seemed to not be in on it.

"So . . . that happened," EJ said, laughing.

"That would be Kristen," she said, shaking her head. "The eternal matchmaker."

"That's okay," EJ said, picking up his tray and feigning to leave the table, "I can sit over here," he said, taking a few steps toward the open table opposite them. Caitlyn's mouth fell open, and then EJ moved back to his seat. "I was kidding."

Caitlyn closed her mouth and laughed. He has a sense of humor, she thought. Maybe meeting some new boy isn't the worst thing that could happen to me now.

"And finally, walkers are dismissed. Have a wonderful day, Falcons. Study hard for tomorrow's tests. Only two days left of exams. You can do it!" Mrs. Lawson said cheerfully.

Anabel was always the last to leave Spanish, partly because she rode home with her secretary/mother and partly because Senora Gomez didn't follow the school rules of only letting students go when their "group" was dismissed, much to the consternation of the administrators, so the classroom was usually clear by this time. Anabel tried to turn that into a positive for her and frequently used those two minutes to go over something difficult with the always-helpful teacher.

"Bye Senora," she said, rising.

"Goodbye Anabel. How you feelin' about our exam tomorrow?"

"Way better about your class than Geometry."

"Ah . . . math. The Aquiles entero of many a student."

Anabel stared dumbfounded at her teacher. She guessed it was good that Senora spoke in Spanish beyond their understanding at times, but it could be frustrating.

"Achilles' heel," she interpreted.

Anabel nodded. "No doubt that is mine."

"I'm sure you'll do fine. You're such an excellent student."

"Thank you Senora."

As Anabel exited and took the two flights of stairs down to her mother's office, she thought: If only she knew. If only she knew just how hard I had to work at everything to get all A's. It just wasn't fair. Her mom finished in the top five in her graduating class. Her sister Allie is a freakin' genius. Even little Nessa at times sometimes explained things to her that made Anabel feel inferior. To her 11-year-old sister. Not cool.

And then there was Chris. Teachers called boys like him "a typically lazy 8th grade boy," meaning that he did what he needed to get an "A" and nothing beyond, whereas Anabel went far and beyond, sometimes double the work, but miss a concept and do poorly on an assignment. Like she'd get so caught up in writing a story that she'd forget it had to be in first person, like the Holocaust narrative she'd written for Language Arts. Ms. Saunders cut her a break and gave her a "90" but she really shouldn't have as a major rule of the assignment had been broken: BECOME a Holocaust survivor and write it in-the-moment and with feeling. Anabel had done hers in third person.

This feeling morphed into dread over the geometry test and she nearly ran right into the exiting principal as she opened the office door.

"Oop, sorry, Mrs. G."

"Anabel. Always in a hurry!" Anabel smiled at her. "You ready for Friday?" The kids liked Mrs. Lawson because she would frequently stop what she was doing and help them with a problem, or at least go out of her way to say Hi, to everyone. Even the kids who NEVER made eye contact.

"Yes ma'am. Need to start studying for Geometry."

"I remember Geometry was my stumbling block when I took it in high school. You know, it's really extraordinary that you're taking it in 8th grade. I took it in 10th. You students push yourselves so hard. It's so encouraging."

"Yes ma'am we do," Anabel said, smiling thinly.

"All right. Well, good luck, girl. You put in your time and you're going to do fine," the principal replied, patting her on the back as she left the office.

Anabel quickly reached her mom's office, located next to Mrs. Grayson's and plopped down in the blue plush chair opposite her desk and let her backpack hit the carpet. What with exams and stress about the coming graduation, lately the effort to keep up appearances had taken on extra weight—pun intended. Her mom must be in another office, she thought, and pulled out the remainder of her lunch that had she saved to eat away from the other girls. She closed her eyes and began with the half-chicken sandwich and crackers, which tasted amazing at the end of the day, and she washed it down with water.

When finished she packed the remnants up and sunk back into the chair, its cushions enveloping and holding her like the pillows and blankets of her bed on a sleep-in Sunday morning.

"Hey Annie!" her mom cheerfully announced upon returning, startling Anabel, who had been dozing for five minutes.

"Oh, hey Mom."

"How was your day?"

"Fine. Ok, so stressful really."

Her mom narrowed her eyes a bit. "Why stressful?"

"Exams. Geometry especially coming tomorrow."

"I knew you'd say that. But you always pull it out in the end, Sweetie. Hey, how about this?" Invite Chris over for dinner and then you guys can study afterward?"

"Okay, sure, sounds good. But . . . listen, I don't want to talk about exams right now. They're just living in my brain 24-7 at this point."

"Okay, okay. I get it," Mrs. Donan returned. "Change. Of. Subject."

"Graduation," Anabel offered. "How's everything coming?'

"Saw Ms. Rothstein this morning. As usual she's got things in hand. Some minor concerns but she'll take care of them."

"So you said the setup is basically the same for each grade level for each year, right?"

"Yes, they are," her mom offered. "These shindigs are logistically complicated enough, so when we find something that works, we stick with it."

"So there will be some kind of raised stage, just like we had in sixth grade, right?

"Sure Annie, but why are you always so concerned about the details of it?"

"Um, hello. I'm your daughter." Her Mom shrugged. "I just want to know what's coming."

Just then the intercom went off on the desk, and the principal asked her mother to go to her office next door. "Okay, coming," she said.

Anabel stared blankly out of the office window as her mother left. The crossing guard, his shift having ended with the rapid disappearance of 600 children, was taking off his yellow neon vest. It's more than that, Mom. Sure, you made me this way some. But this idea of needing to control . . . everything? That's me. That's my salvation and my demon. When you spend all your life wanting something and then get it you never want to give it up. Hence the effort. Hence the worry. Which usually yields the glory. The basking.

But, at what price?

Later that night after a dinner of spaghetti and meatballs and garlic bread she and Chris were sitting in her room, ostensibly studying. Anabel was really studying and Chris had some notes in front of him in case she needed help but was otherwise engaged with his Dungeons and Dragons world. Such a waste of time, she thought.

"Hey, can you help me please?" she pleaded, briefly covering with her hand the massacre taking place virtually on his monitor.

"After this battle I can take a break. Gimme five," Chris replied.

"Sure," she said, moving toward the bathroom and closing the door. After peeing she washed her hands and went to leave when she looked down at the scale.

"WHAT ARE YOU DOING?" thundered from her bedroom. "You saw he had the Sword of Blindness. Why would you fight him when he has that?" A pause. "How stupid are you?" Another. "Yeah, that's what I thought. Dumb ass!" She then heard her mother's indistinct voice through the mandated-when-Chris-was-in-her-room open door and then her own door. Then another pause. "Oh sorry Mrs. Donan. My bad," Chris replied.

It was crazy how Chris became another person while he played these violent games, cursing and yelling at people he'd never seen before. What the point of that was she would never know.

She looked down again but unfortunately the scale was still there, her silent sentinel. Anabel locked the door and took off her clothes. She exhaled loudly before stepping on the scale. 108.2. That's where it should be. That's fine. Graduation was a formal dress affair, and she knew the waist on the dress she'd bought was pushing it anyway, but God how small it made her look! If she stayed at 108 for the next three days she'd be fine, she thought, and also that the second half of the chicken sandwich from this afternoon should have ended up in her mom's office trashcan rather than her stomach, but also remembered the tiny portion of spaghetti she'd eaten and the garlic bread she'd avoided.

"YEAHHHHH!" sounded from Chris, and she knew something momentous had occurred.

"Hey Annie. I'm ready. Whattaya need?" Chris said.

"Okay, give me a minute," she returned, hastily throwing her t-shirt and shorts back on. She heard Chris leave the room and start a conversation with Nessa in the den. Which gave her a minute to sit down and at least somewhat figure out what specifically she needed help with. She exited the bathroom and plopped on her bed, avoiding her cat and the notes spread across it. It was on page 4, I think. She flipped through the notes until she came to the red stars. She always carefully coded her notes as she learned the material, and RED was her warning color. "Length, Area, and Perimeter of Plane Figures" it read.

Anabel had barely time to read through the formulas and sample problems in this section for the twentieth time before Chris reappeared, sitting back down in his desk chair and pressing a button on the laptop which brought what looked like some kind of camp scene on the monitor. He pressed another button to see the statistics from the battle, and said, "What do you need?" to her.

"Geometry help," she said despondently.

"Of course you need Geometry help Annie, but with what?"

She paused a second. "Perimeter of plane figures."

"Yeah," he said distractedly, appraising his efficiency in battle compared to the other marauders. "What about it?" He had still barely glanced at her since he entered the room.

"I can't figure it out."

"What about it can't you get? It's not that hard." He grabbed his notes and after a few seconds found the section that he needed. "Here," he said, and folded the sheet and threw it toward the bed, which was five feet away. It fluttered and landed a foot short. Anabel made a "ugh" sound and waited for him to pick it up and hand it to her, but he was already seated and choosing a new battle to start.

"Chris!"

"What?"

"I need your help!"

"What?" he said, whirling around to her. "I just gave you the notes. Just follow the sample problem. Perimeter, right? The perimeter is the length of its boundary. And then to get area it's just the surface inside the boundary." He sounded like Mr. Ridgely, who often spoke above her head.

"What? I didn't follow that. Can you come over here please?"

He had turned back around and his avatar was moving across what looked like a field toward a cliff. "I just started a quest. Just follow the sheet."

"If I could just follow the sheet I'd let you play your stupid game and not bother you, but I CAN'T FIGURE IT OUT. I need your help."

Chris mumbled something indistinct, and she realized it was to someone probably halfway across the globe. Her anger rising, Anabel stood up and moved to him, touching him on the shoulder. "We'll need a mage and an elf for this. Know anyone?" he said into the microphone.

After this he turned to her. "WHAT?" he said, also becoming annoyed.

"What do you mean WHAT? I need your help. Like over on the bed with me help."

"Why?" he asked, flummoxed that she was still not getting it.

"What is wrong with you? Turn off your damn game and come help me!"

"Seriously Annie. I just started."

"Yeah 'just' as in like 30 seconds ago 'just'. Gimme a break."

"Hey listen. Gotta bow out of this one. See you soon. Good luck," he told the anonymous player. The headset clattered to the laptop's surface. "Okay, let's go," he said, finding a spot on the bed apart from her notes and by Anabel's striped tiger cat, who he started petting, which produced a half meow and a full yawn.

See picked up his notes and glared at him, but he was still looking at the cat.

"Can you look at me maybe?" she asked, her face starting to flush.

"Sure," he said, and stared at her.

She straightened out the paper. "Okay, so I think I get how to do the perimeter. You just find the boundary and it's like the perimeter of anything else, right?"

"Yeah. That's what I said," he answered. "Not real hard."

"Okay, so in this problem the perimeter is 28 cm. But how do you get the area?"

She looked at her. "Are you serious? I just told you. Find the surface inside the boundary."

Anabel stared at the problem. "Okay, but how do you get the area?"

He pointed to the formula on the page. "It's right there. Use that formula. Just like she did in the sample problem." Anabel stared at the problem as Chris went back to petting the cat. After half a minute he turned back to her. "Pretty easy, right?"

"No, it's not easy. I don't get it!"

"What the hell, Annie? It couldn't be any simpler."

"For you sure. And thanks for being a dick about it and making me feel like shit." Chris shrugged. "Can you maybe REALLY help me understand it?"

"I'm not really sure what else I can do. You know how to add and multiply, right? And then you have the formula. What else do you need?" Chris's face was incredulous.

"Maybe a boyfriend who's not an asshole. That would be a good start!" Anabel threw the paper at him.

"I'M an asshole because you can't figure out an area problem WHEN YOU HAVE THE FORMULA AND SAMPLE PROBLEM RIGHT IN FRONT OF YOU? Sure. Why don't I just take the test for you too?"

"Being an asshole in this case has nothing to do with math and everything with your attitude."

"Sure Annie," he said, rising.

"Look, I get that school comes easy to you but you know it doesn't to me, and all I'm asking is that you spend half an hour with me and not with some random jerk you've never met killing imaginary creatures on a screen!"

Chris slowly shook his head. "You know what? You can just figure it out on your own."

Anabel's father stepped into the doorway. "Everything all right in here?" Anabel tried in vain to appear in control, which of course was all too easy for Chris.

"Sure Mr. D. We were just discussing some math stuff," Chris said, smiling.

"Hmmm. Can you DISCUSS a little quieter maybe?" he asked.

"Sure Dad. I think we were finished. Chris was just leaving."

"Now I didn't say he had to leave, I just--"

"No that's okay Mr. D. I've got studying for another class I need to do."

"Okay. Well, see you next time Chris," her father said and left the door frame.

Anabel thought of a lot of things to say but decided to try to burn a hole through him with her eyes. Chris was oblivious to this as he packed up his laptop and cord and gathered his notes. When he did turn to her and see the stare, he shook his head and shrugged.

"See you tomorrow," he said, and left. She heard him say goodbye to her parents and Nessa before the front door closed. She walked over to the window onto the front yard and watched him as he undid his lock, stored it, and rode away on his bike. Was what she was asking for really that hard to provide? The thought that video games were her equal, or beyond, could not be shaken from her head, so she got up and looked at the pictures she had chosen as possible for today to decorate the crown. Noticing that none of them had Chris, she realized the obvious shift (unconscious or not) that her brain had taken in the selection, and without much thought chose a picture of her and her mom cooking a Thanksgiving meal together in the kitchen, which showed most of Dad's family in the background watching a football game. She put the picture on top of the others. Then for the next hour and a half she lied down on her bed and pored over her math notes continuously until her mother turned off the light, took the cat, told her she loved her, and turned off her sleeping daughter's light.

Back at his house, Chris shot a few three-pointers in the dark until the basketball bounced into the neighbor's yard. His cue to exit. He then entered his house through the garage and walked toward his room.

He encountered his brother Liam brushing his teeth in the bathroom by Chris's room and he nodded at him. Chris unpacked his laptop and plugged it in. Liam popped his head in.

"Yo. Wanna play some Madden?"

"Can't man. Exams tomorrow," Chris told his disappointed brother.

"Yeah but you ain't studyin', right?"

Chris didn't like lying to his brother but really needed to now.

"Yeah. Big math test tomorrow."

"Dude, math is easy!" Liam said. "Come on Chris." He wore a pleading expression.

"Yeah, YOUR math is easy. What're you doing in math now?"

"Word problems. Fractions. Basic stuff," Liam responded. "Come on, just one game. I'll let you be the Bucs."

"Can't little man. Gotta study. Rain check on that."

"You suck dude," Liam said, shutting his door loudly which saved Chris from having to do it.

As he opened the laptop, he again thought how Anabel could be a drag on his free time. How can she not do a problem when the sample problem is right there? Makes no sense. Fortunately, he had MORE free time though because she had to study so much, so that was good. Most of the time. Like now. He went to the D & D website and maneuvered to Neverwinter. He had to see if the guys were online. They hadn't as of yet responded to his plea for help, but maybe if he reminded them again they would. He searched the groups for "Gonna Kick UR Ass" and soon found them.

His plan was to try to join in again and then find an opening to ask them for their help. This proved more difficult than last time. No one had died, they were still in the quest, and it was pretty boring just watching, so after an hour he was about to call it a night and try another time when Sebastian exclaimed the familiar, this differing only slightly by night and the exact time: "Damn. It's 11:43."

Murmurs of acknowledgement buzzed through the group, and Colton said, "Everybody cool with pausing and finishing tomorrow?" One lone voice dissented but was soon overruled and Chris knew he had to act fast before the trio exited completely. If he had to pick one of them to ask it would have to be Sebastian, who had been a gamer the longest and already successfully published a Neverwinter quest and made some royalties off it.

Chris once again knew he couldn't let them hear his voice, so he quickly typed, "Hey this is Lothar2236 from yesterday. Did you get a chance to look at that problem I was having?"

"Still having problems with your mic, dude?" he typed, then laughed. "Can you hear me though?"

"YES," Chris returned.

"Okay, so yeah, we all tried to open it but you had it password protected."

Chris did a faceplant. How stupid! He typed: "Sorry. Yeah. That was dumb. I'll take the protection off and get it over to you now."

"All right, man. We'll see what we can do."

"Thanks so much for any help you can give me," Chris typed, then logged off, opened his module, stripped away the need for a password, then sent it to Sebastian. He then signed off and closed the laptop. What tests did he have tomorrow? Geometry and language arts. No big deal. He'd review the geometry notes in the morning, and everyone knew language arts was always just a multiple-choice reading comprehension test. Even his teacher was unamused by the test.

As he was getting up he noticed the Vulcan crown that he was supposed to be decorating for Friday and thought first that he wasn't going to do it and then that Anabel would kill him if he didn't. But since she wasn't high on his list now of favorite people, he thought that ignoring it for one more night wouldn't hurt. So he did.

Caitlyn looked at both the pile of full moving boxes and the carcasses of the unboxed and sighed. Four done and six, seven, eight, nine, ten, ELEVEN to go! The boxes formed two columns as they leaned to one another in the corner like two drunks that had just stumbled out of a bar. She stared at her laptop, its black screen beckoning to be lit with words, words from her story, then back to the boxes. Okay, I'll do at least one more before writing. At least one more. Then she thought, come on Cait, what do you really want to do now, and sat down in her chair and turned on the computer, its DELL image filling the screen as the computer whirred to life.

She once again pressed the folder "NOVEL" and saw its chapters populate on the screen. She clicked on the last chapter she had written titled "Recovery". Regardless of how well she knew or remembered it or how long it had been, she felt the need to re-read the last chapter she had written to see if it made sense and fit the plan. And it served as her first human spelling and grammar check.

As she read over it she knew it was good, and maybe the best thing she had done so far. The scene of the party and the toddler's almost demise read like a horror story. Always make your character suffer, she thought, and then the reader will draw closer to her.

She reached the end, hit "save," and opened another file, titling this the temporary "Recovery 2," and read over her notes for the chapter, which said:

> *Parents proud of her recovery but no trust yet. Have some outside babysitter*
> *come over WITH HER THERE for something prescheduled that can't be canceled. At school real pull to hang out with her pot friends. Someone offers and she takes it but*
> *doesn't USE. Social media with ex, friendly, then pleading. Response: No,*
> *we're done!*

Okay, so she's going to have the indignity of not being trusted by her parents (why should she be, right?). Followed by that real pull of her "friends" to hook her again. It would be so easy. Feel so right. She really doesn't have friends right now. She's longing for others. Then taking the joint, putting it in her pocket.

Then the climax is a social media exchange with her ex, and she's just SHATTERED in the end. Good stuff.

She started the chapter *"Jodi, we need to talk to you about something," said Jodi's mother, clearly wearing a worried expression."* and stopped when her phone lit up.

It was EJ, who she had at lunch earlier given her number to. The text read, "Wanna Facetime?"

Not wanting to be ripped from her writer's reverie but also wanting to see what he wanted, Caitlyn typed SURE back to him. Within seconds FACETIME VIDEO EJ appeared. She accepted. He was lying in his bed with a Clash London Calling poster on his wall partly covered up by his head.

"Hey Caitlyn. Wutcha up to?"

"Just doing some writing."

"Writing? What? I thought you finished school for the year?"

"True. Writing a book."

His face appeared confused. "A book . . . like a novel book."

"You are correct. 'Like a NOVEL book'." She laughed.

"Sorry. I know that sounded stupid. It's just . . . that's really cool. Didn't know you wrote."

"Yeah. I started it in Guam and I'm getting close to finishing the first draft. I'll have the whole summer to do it though."

"That's true. Hey, what's it about?"

Caitlyn thought of a quick summary. "A girl who got kicked out of a band and lost her girlfriend because she was getting high all the time. And her trying to get those things back, I guess."

"Sounds great. Gonna let me read it?"

"You want to read my book? Dude, I just met you!" Caitlyn pulled the phone close to one eye, and EJ laughed.

"I like to read, what can I say?" Caitlyn knew that this guy was more carefully than usually vetted by Kristen and wondered if the Clash poster was a continued part of the ruse.

"Well, yeah, when it's done," she said.

"Deal," he said.

"Hey. You gotta Clash poster behind you. What's up with that?"

"You like the Clash?" he responded.

"The only band that really matters, right?"

He laughed. "Yeah, a pretty stupid band slogan, but they are one of my favorites."

"I didn't know you were into music," she said.

"Kristen did mention to me that you were, are, and that you were in a band in Guam."

"True. Now sadly defunct, but true."

"Let me guess. You were the lead singer."

"AND keyboardist," she said.

"Oh AND keyboardist. That's awesome. What type of music?"

The eternal question. "Well, Indie I guess? Pop? Rock N' Roll. Punk?"

"The whole nine yards, eh?"

"Yeah, pretty much. Wildly veering through all of the above I guess you'd say?"

"Yeah, that's cool."

Caitlyn heard a voice echoing through EJ's house and caught the tail of end "me your phone."

"Yeah, okay Mom. Just a minute," he said to his left as he rose from the bed.

"Hey, I don't want your mom pissed at me. Better give up that device, boy."

He laughed. "Okay. Hey, nice talking to you. See you in lunch tomorrow?"

Caitlyn thought of the implications of the call, and the question, and where this might be going. And liked it. "Yeah. Sure. And this time tell your friend Kristen that she doesn't have to leave the table."

"Yeah so about that . . . "

"Don't bother. Saw through that ruse immediately."

"Her idea, not mine," he said, showing her a face-up palm to signal giving up.

"Yeah sure. Okay, Clash boy. See you manana. Bye," Caitlyn said, pressing the end button and smiling. This felt good. This felt overdue. Two years without any attention from a boy. Okay, so there was that one, like for a day or two, but that didn't count. EJ was nice and had cool taste in music and wanted to read her book. Some plus column items.

She looked back to the laptop and fired it up again. She now had renewed energy and couldn't wait to dig into the perils of Jodi and her attempts to get back her life.

Tuesday, May 26

Guess what day it is, diary? Yay, it's therapy day. The day I have to dredge up my shitty life's debris like a giant earthmover uncovering years of topsoil and just dump it bare on the ground for the birds to sift through. So I'll just kind of summarize what the day was and then go into this one thing that we talked about.

*Probably did okay on my language arts and Spanish tests. Language arts is just a joke and I kind of half knew Spanish because one of the guys on my team Mario speaks it so he's taught me some over the years. I can even roll my R's which apparently is a big deal for a non-native speaker. So yeah, I did enough to pass those two.

*Mom started talking about getting a dog again this morning, and I just tried to put her off for now. She tried to tie it into going to graduation, made it seem like if I attended then we could get a dog for sure. I told her that I didn't even know if I wanted one so how could she hold that over me? But I was more aware than usual of dogs in my walk to school, for what THAT'S worth.

*Nothing stupid happened at school today with Kristen or HER. I'm doing my best to ignore them and I guess it's working or Kristen's given up or something. Yeah, probably giving up, because I saw Caitlyn sitting with EJ at lunch and they looked like they were having a grand old time. Kristen talked to me during science. Asked me how I'm doing. She likes to think that she's the Brendan-whisperer at times or something. She asked me about how I felt about the hockey suspension, so I told her. She talked about graduation. I told her again I'M NOT GOING. Etc.

So the thing I want to write more about is the hockey thing, and what I talked about with Dr. Fuller eventually. It started with him asking how I was feeling about the suspension. I will say this for the guy: He pretty much takes whatever I dish out. He doesn't try to control me like Mom does. So I can be honest with him. I told him it sucks, that it's definitely not helping me in any way, and that a lot of the time stupid things adults do like this that are intended as warnings or punishments against future behavior just get under kids' skin. He just kind of nodded and listened. He asked what I was doing to cope. I told him I have friends and through Call of Duty. He asked how video games help. I told him that I can dish out punishment and see things die and not have to actually experience it in real life. He asked if I thought THAT in any way they fueled my anger in real life. I told him that's what parents don't get, that it's the opposite, that any gamer will tell you that. And then he cited some statistics that could have proved otherwise, and you know, today I just wasn't going to sugarcoat things, so I told him where he could stick those. He stopped and smiled at me. The bastard SMILED. Which just made me more upset.

So we sat there and stared at each other for a second. Then he asked what happened in the kitchen that morning. And of course I knew what he was referring to. When I pushed Mom. Obviously she had told him. He patiently waited for an answer. And then I stated it plainly. Why did you do this Brendan? Because I was angry. Is this the first time this has happened? Yes. How did you feel afterward? What do you mean how did I feel? I was pissed off! No, after it happened, after an hour? Really shitty, that's how. He stared. So why did you do it? I told you why. I was pissed off. Why? She made me feel like shit. That's why. And what is a better coping mechanism than pushing your mother? Is he serious? I guess anything but that doc. Such as? Beat the crap out of my pillow. And? Go running. And? Call of Duty, like I said! His smile looked smarmy to me today, like he was sitting in judgement, which like I said he usually doesn't, so I just asked him if we could end things. Before he said yes, he talked about how my mother felt and the need to talk to her about this and apologize (if I thought it warranted an apology? I love this shit. IF?) I agreed so he'd get off my back and he let me leave. I had not come close to the Grandpa George-ism **revere women always,** a further source of shame. Pushing does not equal reverence.

Oh yeah, and as part of my penance for my dastardly on-ice deed I had to call the kid I wracked up—Hill—and formally apologize. Formally, and sincerely. All I thought about while I did it was you shouldn't have hit me first and then you wouldn't have a concussion.

Not sure that counts as repentance though.

-Brendan

Wednesday, **May 27, 2021: Two days before graduation**

One glance at the clock told my fate: One thirty. Which meant I only had fifteen minutes left to finish the test. And--three, four five problems left. No way I'm going to finish. Anabel could feel sweat running down the center of her back and into her underwear. The class was too respectful to Mr. Ridgely to actually talk during the test but the fidgeting and turning and catching glances and hand gestures was in full sway, which proved a further distraction.

She looked at Chris to her right, and he gave her a questioning look that conveyed "Why are you still working? You're the last one?" Maybe even "This is kind of embarrassing to me" to boot? No, I'm just imagining that, as another clock glance showed a minute elapsed. A minute filled with worry, and sweat, and possible recriminations on her part to something that wasn't even said aloud. God! Calm down, Annie! She took two deep breaths and went back to her work. Back to #3, one she had spent over ten minutes on in vain. And it still looked like Swahili to her. Okay, move on. Number eleven. She checked her work, quickly found the error, and somehow just as quickly corrected it and saw that her answer matched "B) 10.3 cm." Yes!

Chris then TOUCHED HER SHOULDER and tried to say something to her, and she mouthed STOP and went back to her work. Sometimes he just doesn't get it. Failing that, he tried to talk to his friend Landon next to him which brought a hard look from Mr. Ridgely, who often ceased actions without a word. Anabel took another breath and looked at 11 again but noticed that her hand was shaking--her pencil hand. She didn't eat breakfast that morning. The scale read 109, that's why. Can't have 109 for Friday. And wait, she didn't eat her lunch either. She went to lunch. Well, not to the lunchroom. To the study room. And then she'd taken it out and put it on the desk. She remembered the hard-boiled egg, celery, and raspberries that had been before her. But then she didn't eat it save for the egg which she threw in her mouth as she got up at the bell. I really bring a lot of this on myself, she thought.

I'm in trouble even with the curve on the test, she knew, and not finishing just expounds the possibility of not making an "A." She had a "B" the third nine weeks and an "A" the fourth, so a "B" here would tip my grade in that direction. Bye bye 4.0. She determined the best strategy at this point was to give her full attention to one more problem and just guess the rest. The squirming and fidgeting had reached a crescendo, and Murray came out with the inevitable "There are students still taking the test. Relax, children!"

Anabel knew she was the last one. Like always. Chris's slow girlfriend. The girl who doesn't belong in all advanced classes. The girl who watched others get plaques for different subjects on awards day and only got the "Principal's Honor Roll" certificate, a flimsy piece of paper she could print out herself. Her head began to throb from the pressure she'd exerted on herself, and with the clock showing 1:38 due to this time she'd wasted in her pity party, her only recourse was to guess. She looked at the four remaining problems and just marked them all "B."

When she got up with her test and started the walk to Mr. Ridgely's desk, the relief from both students and the teacher was palpable. Murmurs now. The silence had lifted. Slow girl finally finished.

When the teacher announced the again inevitable "Does anyone have a test out?" and paused for five seconds and scanned the room, as if he didn't know Anabel was the only one who still did, Anabel cast down her eyes and trudged back to her seat.

School has a way of just beating you down sometimes, she thought.

Right after the Geometry test, when the always popular but still somehow miraculous Wildwood MS policy of giving the students fifteen unscheduled minutes to catch their breath after an exam had just ended, Chris and Anabel walked out of the geometry classroom and toward their lockers. They had spent the last few minutes of the testing time talking about the test, with Chris being far more human and understanding than lately as he tried to pep her up for the results, which usually came the day after when you had that class again.

"Yeah but remember Annie, there's a huge curve on it," he said, hooking a belt loop on her jeans and tugging as they approached the locker.

"I know that," she said, slinging her Vera Bradley pink backpack to the ground and beginning her combination.

"So don't worry about it. You're going to get an "A," he said, touching her face this time.

"Look who's taking an interest in me now," she snapped back at him.

"Yeah. Last night. I was just, really--"

"--being a dick!" she finished.

"Yeah pretty much," he said. "I was trying to figure out this module I've been working on, and . . . "

"No, you weren't. You had just played a game and you were going to start another one. After having seen you play this crap forever it seems I do know the difference."

"Okay, so yeah. I'm sorry," he said, and touched her chin, pulling it forward and kissing her. She closed her eyes and enjoyed the kiss, but almost immediately thought: This is just too easy for him. I make this too easy for him by just lying down. "I'll make it up to you. Let's go to Tasty Swirl after school. Split a sundae with you?" She couldn't crush the hope in his eyes even though she knew she'd take about two small bites of the sundae and let him eat the rest, even though that really wasn't the point of the outing.

"Sure," she said grudgingly, getting a smile from Chris. She remembered that she told Ebony that she would talk to her about what she was wearing to graduation now, and hurriedly got what she needed and closed her locker. "Look, gotta run. See you after school," she said, quickly grabbing and releasing Chris's hand and exited, leaving left him alone at the locker.

Just then around the corner came Sebastian, Enrique, and Billy Brendt. Chris turned back to his locker, but they knew he had spotted them.

"Hey, look who it is, Enrique," said Sebastian, his hand extended open palm toward Chris. Billy's expression was puzzled. Chris turned to see his light green shirt that showed the table of elements.

Chris froze, unsure of how many others were witnessing this and what he should do.

"I see, Sebastian," Enrique said slowly, his hand on his chin in a forced show of contemplation. "It's our old pal Chris. What's up, Chris?"

"Hey guys," Chris said. "How's it going?"

"Sea-bass?" Enrique said.

"Yeah 'Rique."

"Did you just hear that?" Pause. "Did you just hear Christopher Lawson deign to speak with us? Actually LOWER himself to speak with us? Or am I just going crazy?"

"Naw man. I heard it too," Sebastian replied.

"Wonder why that could be?" Enrique returned.

Since nothing like this had happened to him, ever, or ANY interaction with the guys really since Chris ignored helping Enrique when he was being picked on, Chris didn't know how to respond.

"Hey Chris. Wanna talk about the home runs you've hit lately?" said Sebastian.

"Or the beer you drank at some kegger with 'the boys'"? Enrique asked. At this point Billy, not completely understanding what the game was but wanting no part of it, moved down the hall past Chris.

"Or how about how hot your girlfriend is?" spat Sebastian. Chris felt himself in the unusual position of not having the upper hand in an exchange, and though he tried to assuage this with the fact that he could crush them with one punch, it did no good. Chris looked from one boy to the next and awaited their next move. "How about we let him think for a second of why WE stooped to talk to him," Sebastian continued. "Or why we did anything this time other than the usual of putting our heads down and moving as quickly as we can through this part of the hallway where he and his friends hang out so we don't get harassed."

Enrique crossed his arms and cocked his head at Chris.

"Not sure what you guys are talking about," Chris said, closing his locker and picking up his backpack.

"Oh, I think you do, Christopher," Sebastian continued. "I think--Well, let me say I hope--that your mind has been racing, confused, scrambling, off-key as it were. But I doubt it. Since you don't give two shits about anybody other than you."

"Yeah, okay, I've got to get to my next test guys. Nice talking to you." Chris moved to go around Enrique, but Enrique stepped in front of him. As many kids were out in the courtyard, the hallway was clear.

"Christopher," he said, putting his hands in front of his chest to feign stopping Chris. "Come on. We've gotta play this out. This is too much fun to stop."

If there had been any doubt in his mind what this was, Chris knew it now. He was unused to being around people smarter than him and was rusty. But maybe, just maybe, if he took it, there would be a positive outcome. Maybe this is just a penance?

"So, Christopher . . . "Sebastian started.

"You mean Lothar, right? Lothar2236?" Enrique finished.

"Oh, yes. That's right." Sebastian had taken a step toward Chris. "Is it okay if we call you Lothar?"

Despite realizing he was in for a verbal throttling, Chris was still starting to get pissed. "Okay, can we just drop this? It's obvious you aren't going to help me, right?"

The boys looked at each other. "Not a chance in hell, Lothar," Enrique said. "Why would we?"

"Such a clever ploy, Lothar, saying that your mic was broken. And getting help from developers WAY sharper than you. Bravo!" Sebastian said.

Chris then pushed him, and his back collided with the locker.

"Now THAT is what I remember Chris. But then you only watched Enrique hit the locker. And. Did. Nothing. Why don't you go ahead and take a swing at me?" Sebastian said, pointing to the hallway camera, unseen yet undoubtedly recording every minute of every school day.

"Because since you're so pathetic at coding, you might as well be good at something," Enrique said.

"Yeah, really," Sebastian said, taking a step back towards Chris but this time at a further distance from him. "Did you really not think we'd recognize your feeble attempts at creating that module? That crap had NOVICE written all over it."

"Yeah, after ten seconds discovering that it was your bungling, we spent another half an hour laughing our ass off at how bad it was. Why did you even bother to ask us for help with the most difficult thing to do when there were hundreds of other errors you should have fixed yourself."

"Just forget about it," Chris said, and forced his way through the two boys with a stiff arm as he moved down the hall.

"It's forgotten. You jerk. We forgot you a long time, ago!" Sebastian shouted, hoping Chris would react. Rather, Chris turned the corner and moved toward the bathroom, somewhere, anywhere where he could be alone for a second and regain control.

As he sat down on the toilet, he closed the bathroom door, and his thoughts went quickly from his stupidity at asking them for help to wondering why he ever separated from them in the first place. His Dad's words came to him. "If you want to get better at something, play someone better than you." It had worked for him in basketball, chess, and most things.

Had he become so content, so complacent, that he was no longer challenging himself?

Each successive school day was making Caitlyn more relaxed, and, while she wasn't yet a part of everything yet, she was beginning to feel more like she was way quicker than she'd imagined. The old friends. Saying hi to some of the teachers she'd had. Principal Lawson welcoming her for the week. Caitlyn wasn't even a student there and she had gone out of her way to make Caitlyn feel at home. Just walking the school hallways again, although a few of them were strange to her due to the separation of the sixth grade from the two upper grades. And then there was EJ.

She walked into the lunchroom, and despite Kristen telling her that she and Mike would have lunch with her and EJ, Kristen, who got to the lunchroom minutes before Caitlyn, had weaseled on her. Her friend was nowhere in sight. Of course she wasn't. She smiled at him and sat opposite him at the table. She had thought to wear her Sex Pistols shirt, then realized that wasn't going to fly under the dress code so she chose the beige Talking Heads' "More Songs About Buildings and Food" shirt instead. Okay, so maybe, yeah. Maybe for him.

"Talking Heads. Very nice. Don't know that record though."

"Well then that is your homework, sir," she said, sitting down and unzipping her lunchbox. She pulled out her salad and peach and unscrewed the cap of her water bottle.

He read the title. "More Songs About Buildings and Food. I will give you a full report tomorrow," he said dutifully, saluting her.

"Double-spaced, Times New Roman or Arial font please," she returned, echoing her language arts teacher Mr. Rhinesdorf in Guam. They both laughed.

"I was going to ask how your exams were going today, but then I realized that you don't have any," EJ said shrugging.

"So I'll ask you: How are your exams going today?"

"English and Art. No biggy."

For the next fifteen minutes after they were finished eating the pair stayed and discussed everything from America's immigration policy to which hair metal band from the '80's was the funniest (Caitlyn thought Ratt but EJ swore it had to be Twisted Sister). Then there was a pause, and Caitlyn realized he was trying to word something he was going to ask her.

"Okay, so you know, you know how graduation is Friday," he managed.

She knew where this was heading but at the same time tried to shift it slightly. "Yes. I'm going with Kristen. Lawson okayed it. Isn't that cool?"

He opened his mouth, then closed it. "Yes, definitely. Doesn't surprise me because everyone loves her."

"Yeah, so you going? I'll see you there?" Caitlyn offered, but then his mouth opened again, just a bit, and she realized that she wasn't dodging this, at least not entirely.

"So you're going . . . with Kristen?"

"Well, okay, not actually WITH with Kristen. But I'm going to uh, accompany her to graduation."

"So she's going with . . . "

"Oh, Mike. Yeah. She's going with Mike. Of course."

She noticed him relax and start to breathe normally after half a minute of watching his body tense up. "Well, yeah, right. With Mike. Yeah," he said. Come on, just do it. Just ask me, she thought. Not sure what's going to come out of my mouth, but just ask me.

"So, the thing is, um, I don't have a date for graduation, and I was, um, wondering if you wanted to go with me?"

So it was out. Caitlyn now was the one lost for words. Sure she liked him. But that's two days "liked him." Not really enough time to say "yes" to something like that. So how to tell him she liked him but not to that level, yet?

"Well, I've really enjoyed talking to you and getting to know you. But EJ it's kinda too soon for me," she said as kindly as she could.

"I get it. That's okay. I'll still see you there, right?" He had regained him composure quickly.

"Yeah, of course. And we can hang out some. No doubt," she returned.

The final five minutes before the bell was filled with a discussion of what they were planning on doing in the summer, with Caitlyn saying her book and maybe trying to find a band to play with and EJ talking of working with his dad. But those five minutes were kind of guarded, she thought. He's hurt. Some at least. I did what I could. She hoped that he didn't find someone to go with, and that she could spend time with him then.

But if she thought that, why didn't she just say 'yes'?"

That night, with the weight of the geometry exam lifted from her, Anabel had waited until everyone had gone to bed or at least to their bedrooms and she could have the den to herself and pulled out her well-used Blu-ray of CLUELESS.

About five minutes in she realized that she had a visitor, as Nessa must have heard and crept behind Anabel on the couch, looking over her shoulder as she watched.

"Is this CLUELESS?!" she asked.

"Yep," Anabel said.

"I wanna watch it, Annie. Please," she begged.

Anabel tried to mentally scan the film for things that Nessa shouldn't see, and, finding a few like references to losing virginity and a joint, realized that she could explain these to Nessa when they happened. IF her sister stayed awake that long.

"Yeah. Okay runt, c'mere," she said, patting the couch beside her.

Nessa, clad in her Wonder Woman pajamas, plopped down beside her, and Anabel put her arm around her. She willingly accepted it and leaned into Anabel.

"This is like your favorite movie, right Annie?"

"Yes it is," Anabel replied.

"Cool!" she said, and Anabel remembered the thrill of at a young age the feeling that you were doing something that was a little risky.

As the movie was somewhere around halfway, Anabel became aware that her sister hadn't asked a question in a while and was pressing now more firmly into her chest. Asleep. And when Nessa slept she was like a rock. As she pried her from chest and laid her back down on the couch, Nessa's body flopping like a rag doll.

Because she didn't have to consciously construct the story in her mind for Nessa's benefit, Anabel's mind started to wander. To graduation. Then back to the dance. And then she was asleep. And asleep she dreamed a strange dream, as dreams are, of she and Chris in the future. They were sitting on the back patio, she supposed of their house, and their kids were in the yard. Wait, no, those weren't kids, they were cats. And they were chasing each other. And this wasn't her back yard. It was the Wildwood gym. And she and Chris were sitting watching some other kids in sixth grade get crowned, like they had. But the principal wasn't Lawson. It was Cher, Alicia Silverstone from Clueless, doing the announcing. And she looked at Chris and Chris looked at her, and they both were speechless.

When she awoke, the movie was near the end. It was at the wedding, and they were going to throw the bouquet. And Cher was going to catch it. And then a close up of Alicia Silverstone made her pause. She reached for the remote and found both it and the pause button. The bouquet was in the air, and precisely at the moment where Cher caught it she hit "pause."

She looked at Cher's face as she had done dozens of times before. The face that was a poster still in her room, next to her bed. But this time, it was different. This time she saw what had happened. It didn't happen overnight, but more gradually. The hair, the clothes, sometimes the demeanor and personality. It was her. She was Cher, to some degree.

That I should want to emulate the hero of my favorite movie didn't seem like a big deal, right? Then she thought of Chris's comments the times they had watched the movie together. "I wonder what you'd look like blonde." "She looks really good in yellow, doesn't she Annie?" You don't have a yellow dress, do you? I know it's not your favorite color, but damn, look at her." She knew he liked blondes because he always spent just an extra tick checking out an attractive blonde. He commented more about blondes. And then Anabel was blonde. Chris mentioned the dress that Cher had on. And then Anabel had that dress, pretty much that exact dress. And the way Cher was as the title said clueless but always tried to help people out, albeit in her Cher way. Was that his doing too?

Or was ANY of this Chris's doing? He didn't force me to do anything. These were all decisions I made myself. I bought the dress. I dyed my hair. I lost weight. Chris used to comment about my stomach before I did though. What the hell is going on here? How systematic was this, she thought. It wasn't. It was gradual. And if she had been persuaded to make certain decisions, they were still hers to make. Or not make. Probably.

Right?

That night after the obligatory grilling from Kristen on how lunch with EJ had gone, Caitlyn was distractedly watching an episode of Everybody Loves Raymond with her dad when she heard her phone.

"Want me to pause it, Cait?" her dad offered.

"No that's okay. I've seen this one. Thanks anyhow dad. My phone's ringing," she said as she rushed to her room.

She picked up her phone and saw "Facetime Video: Moira." Moira! She pressed accept and the voice of her bandmate (well, ex-bandmate) and her beautiful ebony vision filled the screen.

"CAITLYN!" Moira said, and just screamed for a couple of seconds. Caitlyn laughed and lay down on her bed. "What is up with you contiguous states of the United States of America girl!?"

"Hey Moira," she said, seeing the familiar band posters and artwork Moira had on the walls by her bed. "That was a good one. You thought about that before the call, didn't you?"

"Yeah. Had to look up 'contiguous,' but in the end it was worth it! So . . . again, how you doin' girl?"

"Trying to hang in there. What about you?"

"Girl I miss you already," she said, theatrically putting a hand over her heart.

"Awww. I miss you too. What're you up to now that school's out? Any gigs on the horizon?"

"Yeah, we're opening for The Cure on Saturday night here at old Naval Station Guam." She opened her eyes wide. "WE JUST LOST OUR SINGER. Namely you! We're probably done," Moira said, running her finger over her throat.

"Come on. You'll find someone else. Wait. That something else is you! Why don't you sing?" Caitlyn said.

"I am no Caitlyn Patterson. Besides, concentrating on guitar is enough for me. You want me to be like Joe Strummer too?"

"You have a great voice. You just need practice."

"No, what I need is you to become an island girl again!"

"Not my fault," Caitlyn squeaked.

"Damn. I know it Cait. It just sucks."

"The life of the military brat. We know it well."

"I guess."

"Any news on you getting back to the U.S.? You moved from Houston, right?" Caitlyn asked.

"Hell no. I've been stuck here before you and now after you. Why didn't you just smuggle me outta here witchu?"

"Can't. Illegal. Woulda been arrested. The brig. The clink. Court martialed. Put in the hoose—"

"All right, I get it Miss Writer. Speaking of which, how's that book about me doing?"

Caitlyn laughed. "Just because I told you one of the characters is loosely based on you doesn't mean you're the protagonist!"

"Well she's a lesbian, right" Moira asked.

"Yeah. So?"

"So she's me."

Caitlyn laughed. "Oh that's right, you are every lesbian. How can I forget that?""

"You better damn well not forget me girl, or Imma come cross that ocean and find your skinny Jacksonville, Florida ass." Both girls cracked up. "And Jacksonville's not that far from Houston. I'll just steal me a car and surprise you one night."

God she missed the spontaneity and humor of Moira. She found herself tearing up. "God, I'd love that Moira," she said, this time putting her hand over her heart earnestly.

Seeing this, Moira changed tack. "All right Caitlyn. You need to buck up. Don't go all soft on me. You stay the same so when we see each other again--not Facetime seeing but REAL seeing--I'll still let you be my friend." She thrust her chin in the air.

"You are the best," Caitlyn said. She heard Moira's mother come into her room and announce that she was ready to go, to which Moira responded okay. "Where you going? It's what, like 2:00 there? Shouldn't your mom be at work? Wassup?"

Moira's mom heard Caitlyn's voice and her mom's head suddenly thrust into the top left corner. "Oh, gone only a week and she's pointing fingers already!" her mom said. Caitlyn knew where she got her sense of humor.

"Just kidding Ms. Anthony. Just kidding," Caitlyn replied.

"Caitlyn honey how you doing? How was your flight? You settled in yet?"

"Just fine so far. Flight took a hundred hours. Watched a dozen movies. Slept. You know. But it kind of feels like home again, somewhat."

"Good to hear," she replied. "Listen, we gotta run. Your friend here's got an orthodontist appointment. Talk to you soon."

"Okay, you too. Bye Moira. I think you should choose RED for your rubber bands this time."

"Ooooh, red-sequined to match that shirt I like. You got it. Talk to you soon Cait. Bye."

The screen went blank. Caitlyn had been thinking of investigating whether there was a band who needed a member, and her dad pointed out that now would be a really good time for that, being the start of summer. She was split between wanting to write more of her book and researching, so she decided to do both. Band first.

She Googled "how to find bands that need members" and the first site was bandmix.com. She clicked on it and realized it was just what she was looking for. You could search by genre, age, instrument played and others. A list scrolled before her. Every state in the union was listed, plus many other countries, plus Guam. GUAM was in there. Impossible! She clicked on it and 11 items loaded. Some were bands needing members, others were just musicians, their bio's, and what music they liked to play. This is freakin' awesome! She saw one of a female lead singer who was searching for a band: "Hard rock, punk, new wave, disco" were listed under genre. She was 20. Well, a bit older than her ex-bandmates, but in a band who cared. She'd have to tell Moira about this, about her.

She closed out the girl's bio and clicked on "Florida," then "Jacksonville." 72 results. Aya mia! She chose "filter" and a dizzying variety of possible filters filled her screen. These people take this seriously. Okay, what are the important ones: genre and age. And Jacksonville is a huge place, but I doubt I can search distance. But then she saw it also: distance. She chose "within five miles" then clicked "search" again and it pulled up several individual musicians wanting bands, but only four existing bands needing members.

She opened the first one, which said, "Heavy metal hair band seeking keyboardist chick who can do backing vocals. Our band is 'Hairs to You'". That couldn't be real, thought Caitlyn, then just as quickly realized hair metal was kind of cartoonish itself so it probably was and then closed that window.

The second's opening line was "Barbershop quartet needs tenor" and she stopped reading and moved on. The third band needed a drummer, "preferably one that can slay like John Bonham," and, realizing that much of the musical world, or at least the amateur branch of that world, was stuck in the seventies or eighties, moved on. To the last one.

The opening line was "Teen band in Jacksonville needs singer." No way! Before she opened up the full window she braced herself for "Specializing in good Top 40 like Maroon 5 and Bruno

Mars" and took a deep breath. She closed her eyes for a second, then opened them. "Focusing on indie rock and alt country: Cure, Radiohead, Sufjan Stevens, Jason Isbell, Kate Bush" is what she read. No. Frickin'. way! Too good to be true. Impossible. And because no one was watching she jumped out of her chair and threw her arms about wildly for a second, she sat back down. She read on: "Two middle and one high school student who are trying to write their own music but for now playing the classics. Singer moving away at school's end. Need a new one ASAP! Ready to tryout? Contact Reese." Caitlyn punched the phone number on the screen into her phone and quickly typed in "Saw your ad on Bandmix. I'm a singer/keyboardist who loves the bands that you listed. Going to high school next year. Was in Jax for sixth grade (at Wildwood) but moved to Guam for two years, but back permanently now. Love to audition with you. Just let me know a time and place" and hit send.

She found herself hyperventilating some and took a couple of deep breaths to relax herself. Then she went over the possible scenarios that could play out here and realized that there was only one good outcome and many bad ones. Be realistic, Cait. Be serious, Cait. They don't know you. They may already have someone. You may audition and they won't like you. They might all be heavy users and you won't want anything to do with them. Ahhhh!

She needed something to distract her at this point, so she plugged in her phone and opened her laptop. Writing. Writing and the focus it demanded shuts out everything. Graduation. EJ. Moira. Guam. Jacksonville. Band. Kristen. Begone!

At the start up screen she pressed her novel folder, pulled up the file, and picked up her handwritten notes from her desk. Her notes for this chapter were:

Finds out about ex-band's concert. She'll go. Upset at herself. In room at night, puts
On CD of band's songs. Sings to make her feel better. Cries. It's over. THEY HAVE A

NEW SINGER.

Caitlyn shut her eyes and tried to see the sequence of events she would unfurl. In some ways, Caitlyn thought, this is even more despairing for the fictional Jodi than crashing with drugs and losing the band. That hurt, but her addiction in a way acted like a pain shield. Now that she was sober this absolute reality has hit her and it's got to hurt. So how can she find out about the band's concert? They try to conceal it from her to avoid hurting her. They don't put up flyers all over school like they usually do. They actually tell people to not tell her. They avoid the social media stuff that she'd monitor. But then she finds out at school. She denies it because of the above. Someone tells her the real truth. Crushed. Comes home. Slams door, shutting everyone out. Puts on that first CD that they all love even though it's all covers. She's singing, happy, like SHE is still the singer. Then she cries, realizing that now there's someone else singing those songs. What she considers HER songs. And this person is now dating her girlfriend!

Caitlyn realized the depths she was willing to drag Jodi through to get the sympathy of the reader and wondered what that said about her. Well, they say art is often created through pain and suffering. I don't have that, but can I create that? She'd done her research on addicts. And recovery. So she was speaking semi-authentically at least.

As always, you've gotta get that first sentence, she thought, so this one began: *Jodi knew it would be a bad day when she had an argument with her mom at home, forgot her lunch, then sat down at her desk in homeroom and heard her former friends whispering behind her back.*

And away she went . . .

May 27th

Today was THAT day, the day that thankfully only comes once or twice a year, the day when at times I have to go through pain far beyond a normal day. Where the old times get dredged up and shat all over the place, and no matter how palatable the speaker tries to make them it rarely works and I'm always left with a tremendous feeling of loss and despair.

Of course I'm talking about dinner with Dad.

I knew this was coming, as Dad had called a week before telling me and Mom when he'd be in town, and tonight was the night that worked best for their dinner. For Dad. Not me, in the middle of exams. For Dad. Always, for Dad. Dad was a jet setter, an international hot shot. He was CEO of some kind of tech firm, and he was always traveling. Brendan would occasionally get a postcard (yeah, seriously, a post card) from someplace like Vienna or Dubai or the like with some BS robotic-like writing, something begging to be tossed in the trash at the first opportunity. The last one, from Florence, had read: Having a lovely time. Wish you were here! Like the classic ones from the mid-20th century. I guess he thought that was funny, but it really just showed how out of touch with me he is.

Dad told me that he'd picked my favorite restaurant for the meeting, and of course that was Ruth's Chris Steak House, the one on the water downtown. He always wore a business suit when he had dinner, which was just so . . . him. Sure it was a classy place, but what the hell? He remembered telling Brendan all his life that "clothes make the man," which Brendan had Googled at some point and found it originated not with Mark Twain, as his father had offered, but some dude 400 years earlier.

So yeah, Dad was all pomp and circumstance and little actual flesh and blood, so he had to compensate with gifts, promises, and show. Which did work very well when I was in sixth grade, to a point, but that point is now long gone and I see him for the empty shell of a human being that he is. Someday maybe I'll use therapy, which I imagine I'll be partaking in for quite some time for the future, to sort out who Dad was before he left on that December day of his sixth-grade year. A week before Christmas. The last day of school before Christmas. Coming home not to a house full of family, but to tension and misery at the dinner table. Then the revelation.

Tonight started out innocently enough, with Dad talking about Brendan's hockey team, the fate of the Lightning, his coming summer job as a Y lifeguard (don't think I've mentioned that yet— "Getting out of the house will be good for you"— Mom), and school. The updates on his business, which were always stimulating. Once I started looking around the restaurant as if to escape he stopped the business talk. And I was really good this time, for like an hour. Then I couldn't help myself. Once I had found my voice with him and dared to speak capital-T TRUTH to him a year or so ago I was never going back.

I don't want to paint a picture (so temper the above a bit) that he's a complete asshole, because he's not. But one indiscrete action on his part has made me the person I am today: resentful, angry, distrusting. And for that I can't do anything other than face it head on. I'm not a little kid anymore. When you've got six months minimum to compose something in your head that you want to say you need to get it right. And I think I did. In my head I could hear Grandpa George saying, "**Ask the question**," as in, don't be afraid to ask something if you really want to know it.

"Why would you ever throw away love?"

Dad had just forked a piece of steak in his mouth, which gave him a chance to overcome the piercing abruptness of it all, so he chewed it an extra few times as a delay tactic. I was watching him the whole way. No letting up. I'm through pulling punches with him. And you know the response I got was pretty much the usual BS, probably what I'll always get with slight variations for my age and understanding: "It's not that simple." I willed myself to be calm and watch the theatrics as the worm yet again struggled to squirm off the hook. He adjusted himself in his seat. He stared back. He wasn't used to this—my lack of anger. Because anger is so easy to dismiss, isn't it? Someone loses their cool and yells or hits something and every action since Eve was pulled from Adam's rib is their fault. Not this time.

He hemmed and hawed and stammered and started and stopped and it was pretty damn funny actually. If he had tap dance shoes in his bag he would have put them on and entertained the assembled diners by dancing on the table. But he didn't. So he opened his mouth, took a deep breath, and closed it. I told him: You got nothing, right? He looked down at the table. He folded his hands on its top. He was considering. Which lie to tell? What version of events to spin this time? How to blame Mom for something that she had supposedly done? What? I waited, all the while vowing to stay calm throughout the torrent of shit that was about to come. And what came?

"I screwed up."

My smirk quickly fell and now my mouth opened. What the hell was that? He saw my reaction and repeated his line, this time running his right hand through his hair, then covering his mouth with it and exhaling when done. And then, hold your breath future Brendan/reader: the man then told the damn truth. Praise be! How he had met Rhonda at a convention, in St. Louis, and they had slept together, and then how they'd continue to meet up when they could (she was of course in tech also) and continue their affair. And how great she was. And how she didn't pressure him like Mom did. And she accepted him for who he was. Blah blah blah. And then came the day two months after leaving Mom and moving temporarily into Rhonda's apartment in Atlanta when she just told him it's over. And how crushed he was. Normally I'd be doing cartwheels in my head for any trace of pain I could squeeze from this man, but not today. For today he had told the truth, at least the facts of the truth.

But it still didn't answer my question.

"Sometimes the heart wants what it wants" is what he eventually came up with, ripped straight from a Hallmark movie and vomited all over me. And then he began to cry. I had never seen this before. It seemed he spent his life carefully setting up walls to keep things like this out. Or if not walls then surfaces. Slick. Teflon. Able to deflect the most head-on missives. But maybe not from his son.

So, I wasn't going to hug him or anything, but at least I got some kind of explanation. I mean, what the hell could I have asked him after that? But then, I did.

"But did you ever think what affect it would have on ME, Dad? On me?"

I could give you more of a blow by blow here with further tears and confession and apologies and the like, but I think you/future me get the picture.

FUTURE ME: THIS IS THE FIRST TIME IN YOUR LIFE THAT YOUR FULLY TOLD YOU THE TRUTH. Take note of that.

Not that it does me any good. Now.

--Brendan

(Added later) My night got even better when I watched the recording of the Lightning game. They beat the Canadians and now are tied at 3. With the finale being Friday night. Graduation night. Which is yet ANOTHER reason I ain't goin'!

And another thing. I'm done with this damn diary. It started out as Mom's suggestion, then it became basically mandatory for therapy, but seeing as it hasn't helped me any, I'm done.

So, for one last time

--Brendan

Thursday, May 28, 2021: The day before graduation

The first thing Anabel did every morning was check her phone, like she supposed a lot of people did. What has happened in the world that I just absolutely needed to have at my fingertips to have any way of functioning as a normal human being? Usually her screen was filled with the yellow ghost of Snapchat with an occasional Instagram mixed in, but at the very top, the latest one, was a text, from Chris. A text? That's weird. She clicked on it.

"Hey Annie. Since I'm done with my finals I'm not going to be in school today or tomorrow. I'm not going to have any time to see you between now and graduation. I've got to decorate my crown, plus do the slideshow for Mom. And I'm done with my exams. So, have fun. Love ya. Pick ya up around 6:00 on Friday?"

She definitely wasn't surprised that he left decorating and the slideshow for the last minute. That's his M.O., despite his mother's pleading with him to get started just within Anabel's earshot a half dozen times in the last two weeks. But the "I'm not going to have any time to see you" part is what threw her. Why are those not things we could do together, like most other things? Then the memories of the night before and the Clueless observations ("revelations" seemed too strong a word here) came back to her and these combined with her curse of constantly being on guard/worrying filled her with dread.

She spent some time staring out her window, thinking worst case scenario. Anabel was a worst-case scenario person. Prepare for the worst. It rarely happened. Then what happened was doable. Livable. Survivable.

And then, as always, she talked herself off the ledge. It's not a big deal. It's just a day and a half. It's not like Chris has never done something like this before. And while school was her social hub and sometimes her lifeblood, Chris was fine with missing a day or two a month. So, everything's fine, she thought, mentally preparing for her day with its series of choices and commitments.

Chris opened his eyes to the sun glaring through his window and looked at the clock. 10:17. Good night! In anticipation of not going to school he had stayed up late playing D & D (not in the "Gonna Kick UR Ass" group of course) and hadn't gotten to bed until close to three. He checked his phone for Anabel's response to his surprise declaration of not seeing her, and finding none, clicked on his mother's text instead:

"I have agreed to let you stay home under the stipulation that you will A) Decorate
your crown for graduation and more importantly B) Put together the slide show
that I've been asking you to do for the last three weeks! Do not disappoint me."

He looked over at the crown that he had thrown in the corner, thinking there were few things he'd rather not do before that. Anabel's gonna have a GREAT time with that, he thought, showing all that they'd done or whatever for years. He wasn't interested. But yeah, the slideshow had to get done. It was going to be kind of a centerpiece of the show, going nearly constantly throughout the proceedings. Mom volunteered for it at a PTSA meeting probably knowing it was just going to be all me. Thanks Mom.

Chris mentally ticked off the task: First, the music. Then how many slides there would be. And then how long between each slide. Transitions. Etc. So before he opened up his mom's laptop, he went to his and searched "Graduation songs 8th grade", to which the Internet spat forth:

My wish by Rascal Flatts
Good Riddance (Time of Your Life) by Green Day
The Climb by Miley Cyrus
For Good by Leann Rimes and Delta Goodrem
Graduation (Friends Forever) by Vitamin C
Lean On Me by Bill Withers
100 Years by Five For Fighting
Ocean Avenue by Yellow Card
Don't Stop Believin' by Journey
Seasons of Love by RENT soundtrack
I Hope You Dance by Leann Womack

He then looked up each song individually, and they came to just over 45 minutes. You figure the slides may be up an hour and a half, tops, the songs would only be repeated once. That seems reasonable. He knew most of these songs but didn't know a few. Regardless, he could find torrents of them on the web using his VPN "Nightcrawler," so if some of them sucked he wasn't out any cash for a crappy song.

Getting the songs took about fifteen minutes, and he stored them in a folder titled "Graduation Mix" and walked into the kitchen and disconnected his mom's computer from its charging cable. He laid back down on his bed and put on an NFL highlights video from You Tube on his TV, just to have something going before this boring task.

He booted up the computer and typed in her password, and saw the folder very specifically labeled "2019 Sixth grade dance pictures for 2021 graduation" immediately. I hope it's got enough to stretch out at least ten minutes, he thought. If there are only like 50 though they'd see the same picture maybe ten times. It's not like hearing the same song over and over though. Whatever. He'd make it work.

He clicked on the folder and watched it populate, his face becoming incredulous as the number passed 500, then 1,000, finally stopping at 1,341. What the hell? She expects me to wade through all these pictures, 80% of which were certainly total crap because as Mom explained they'd been taken by all the students? No way!

But as he began looking at the photos, he realized several things at once. Yes he was at least partially accurate that most were crap, but there were a lot of quality ones. Probably taken by the journalism kids. Like that kid they all used to call "picture girl." She was everywhere in sixth grade. Whatever happened to her? Probably switched schools. Anyway, seeing how the kids had changed from sixth to eighth grade was really incredible. Sometimes he couldn't tell who they were in the picture, even IF it wasn't blurry, because some had such a "glow up" as Annabelle liked to say that they dwarfed their former little kid self.

And finally, once he hit the section of the crowns, it was amazing to see how much HE and Annabelle had changed. It was one thing to sometimes see pictures of them that one of their families had taken and think "We were so young," but these were almost always posed and stagnant. THESE pictures, taken together, really told a story. That justified all these pics. A good many were candid, dynamic. He hadn't thought about the dance much since then, really only when Anabel wanted to relive it, but that frequency fortunately had decreased over time. Now though he was reconstructing that night in his mind. Their expressions. What he was wearing. Ugh.

Oh, God. Annie so young . . . and so heavy. He at this point looked to the picture of her in a bikini at Daytona that he'd taken this past spring break on his wall and to his screen and the dance photo of her expectantly about to receive the crown as she was perched on that platform with him on the other side that night two years ago. They were the same person. Wow. What she'd become! What she'd become, with his help. Sure, she loves looking the way she does, but did she appreciate his invisible conductor's baton that had played a symphony over her rough parts? Or, conversely, did she care? They both got what they wanted. I just . . . helped her.

He had spent an hour just looking at pictures without any kind of sorting system, so he decided to restart more with the task at hand in mind then a starry-eyed onlooker. He scrolled to the top and began. The TV distracted him at times, this time for one of those incredible Gayle Sayers runs when it looked like the defenders were in slow motion, but after just under an hour he'd pared about 90% of the photos down to "trash" and "keep."

He was getting hungry, and the clock showed 12:49. He realized at school he'd almost be starting lunch now. In the kitchen he took the easy way out, popping a tray of green chili verde burritos into the microwave and grabbing a can of Coke from the fridge. After three minutes they were done, and after slathering some sour cream and hot sauce on them took his meal back to his room. He set the plate down on the bed in front of the laptop and watched some other highlights while he ate.

Finishing, he set down the plate on the floor and picked up the laptop again and laid down onto the two propped-up pillows. He checked the "keep" photos and found just over 300. 300! He decided that to do this right he'd need a second set of songs and calculated the time that would take. Hearing the songs a second time would be weird really.

He vowed to go through the next section even quicker than before, and maybe shoot some hoops, take a shower, then begin the real work of paring down what he'd chosen, arranging, setting the music, etc. There were just over a hundred pictures left. This might take five quick minutes. He opened the folder and the scan once again began. Blurry picture of the floor. Toss. Smiling picture of Principal Lawson. Framed really well. Good lighting. Keep. A close up of someone's mouth. Um, heave. Two shots of the food stands—there are better ones. Out you go.

Some blurry picture of the back of the auditorium and a table. As his mouse grabbed the picture and was preparing to move it to the trash, something caught his eye. While the surroundings were somehow blurry, the center of the picture wasn't. Chris's eyes lit up, and he enlarged the shot to full size on the laptop's screen which served to pixilate it further. He couldn't be seeing this. This didn't happen. He made it smaller again, and the reduction confirmed the action. He found himself breathing heavily, aghast, confused, stunned. He pulled the photo onto the desktop and in a state of near shock attended to the remaining photos, now not really caring which went where. Then he clicked on the picture again. Then reached out to touch it, as if he could change what it showed.

There is no doubt in his mind that the hunter had become the hunted.

He closed the laptop and paced around his house for a while, trying to come up with a plan. He went through shock, to sadness, to anger, to focus.

Arriving back at his room, he first transferred the downloaded songs onto a flash drive, then to his mom's computer. After this he rammed the charging cable he had retrieved from the kitchen into his wall socket, sat down, and knew what he had to do. This discovery had given today's task new purpose, he thought. He opened up Power Point and proceeded his attempt to try to affect what changes he could.

As the morning show and announcements ended, Brendan waited for Mr. Loxler to begin their last American History class before the test later that extended period. The teacher soon finished typing on his keyboard and looked out at the class.

"All right. You guys ready?" he said, his voice as always bouncing and echoing off the walls of the room, walls that were filled with events from America's fight for independence from Britain to Reconstruction after the Civil War. He really loved his subject.

To the teacher's query the students were mainly silent, but turning Brendan could see a few thumbs up, one kid giving the "so-so" hand flutter and Morgan Riley, never without something to say, responding, "Let's go Mr. L!"

Every other teacher so far had just given the students this extended time to study, either by themselves or with a partner or group, unsupervised, but this wasn't Loxler's way.

"So, here's the plan folks," he said, palms open to the class in a grand gesture. "Let's play a game." The class murmured, some interested and some bummed from the loss of individual time. "We're going to choose teams, and then you'll compete with a slideshow of questions and answers that I've made." With this he unfroze the screen, which now showed: The Roots of Independence to Reconstruction.

Some kids whooped and started making eye contact with their friends, but Brendan inwardly groaned. Not that he didn't know the material. Not that he wouldn't be an important member of a group. But just that he might get a jerk in his group. Marco Sutherland. Jeremy Brisco. That loudmouth Morgan.

Brendan looked back toward the teacher, who had hushed the chatter while carefully arraying the familiar manila folder cut squares on his desk that contained each kid's name in the class on them.

"And we're going to do a modified schoolyard pick," he chirped, which was met by looks of silence. "You know. Schoolyard pick, like when you choose teams at PE?"

Jeremy raised his hand and spoke simultaneously and with a smirk. "That don't let us do that anymore, Mr. Loxler."

The teacher was happily surprised. "Really?"

"Yeah. No one wanted to be the last pick," Jeremy said, causing some muffled chuckles from his friends.

"Yes! That's exactly it. So rather than me picking the teams, which although may be more fair it gives you less choice, I'm going to draw captains, then they'll pick. But these captains can't say who was picked in what order. Capeche?" The class understood. "If I pick your name and you DON'T want to be captain, then just tell me. Okay?"

"Got it Mr. L," Morgan said. The teacher then quickly called out the names, making sure he had gotten everyone. This year's COVID nonsense necessitated a lot of period switching, and the teachers weren't doing a good job of keeping track who was in what period.

When he got to the end, he said, "Anyone I miss." Kristen's hand shot up from the back. Oh no, Brendan thought. She's going to say Caitlyn. Why? She wasn't even enrolled here . . .

"You forgot Caitlyn, Mr. Loxler," she offered.

"Oh, that I did. Caitlyn, did you take American History in your old school, to Reconstruction? Feel that you could help a team out?"

Caitlyn thought a moment. "We went through Reconstruction, but we started out at the colonies. Isn't that what you guys did?"

"Precisely," the teacher returned, reaching into his desk and pulling out his ever-ready supply of blank manila-folder squares on where he wrote each student's name to draw randomly at times. "Okay, then you're in, okay?" Caitlyn nodded. Kristen looked at her and smiled.

Great, Brendan thought again. Now she could get into a group with me. That happens? I go use the bathroom. I'll find a way to take a colossal dump. Or die trying.

The teacher visibly counted students in the room. "Somebody double-check me. I got 19." A few students did the same.

"Yep. 19 is what I got," Amy Cowson said.

"Okay, so the easiest way to split 19 is four 4's and a 3. I'm going to draw for captains. Then when I get done, the captains will come up to my desk. Everyone's name is here," he said, pointing to the squares now in the bowl. "Don't SAY the person's name aloud, but rather point to their square and I'll move it to your team. Make sense?" The class got it. "Remember, you can say no if you don't want to be a captain." The teacher then drew the first three names, all of whom said "Yes" to being captain.

Brendan didn't know if he wanted to be a captain or not. If he were he might keep an idiot off his team. If he weren't he just took what he got. The teacher read the fourth name. "Brendan Ellison." Brendan froze a second and could feel the weight of eyes who wanted him to say no so they would have a chance at captainship.

What came out was "Sure." Loxler chose the final captain and a few of those not chosen moaned and looked to newly captained friends, beckoning to be chosen.

"Okay, so captains, come on up," the teacher said.

Brendan walked to the desk and looked at the displayed names, each written in a more- precise blue ballpoint pen except for one, Caitlyn's, which was hurriedly scrawled in pencil. As Mr. Loxler went over the instructions again to the captains, this time quieter, the image of Caitlyn's name held his eyes.

"Okay, so we'll just go in order of selection here." He looked to each for misunderstanding.

Katie Mickler, picking last, saw the inherent unfairness of this and said, "Can't we do a snake draft? Like they do in fantasy football?"

"I'm not sure what that is, but let's just do it this way," Loxler said. Here he addressed the whole class again. He reached into a drawer in his desk and pulled out a small basket of candy. Not just Airheads or Jolly Ranchers, Brendan noticed, but whole movie theater packs of candy, arranged neatly so the tops of the boxes and wrappers were sticking out so you could easily pick out the name. The students' eyes became large at the possibility. "One to each member of the winning team," he said. "Nothing to anyone else. You gotta win!" The class, seeing more than bragging rights were in store here, perked up. "And since the numbers are odd, the last captain, that's you Katie, will only have three on your team." Katie pouted at the now double handicap but nodded at the teacher

"Okay, Taylor. You're first."

Taylor moved the name square of his best friend Terry underneath his name, and the draft was on. Brendan was picking fourth, then he'd pick ninth, so he'd get a few smart kids. On his turns he chose Molly Martin and Randy Wilson, and he knew that he'd have a decent shot at winning.

But as the picks came "off the board" so to speak, Brendan's eyes once again fell on the one written in pencil. No one had picked her yet. Kristen wasn't a captain, so he wasn't sure anyone would. He wondered how much these kids remembered her. Next he picked Ryan Rossler at 14. Her name was still there. There were only five picks left. If no one selected Caitlyn she would automatically be put with him at pick 19. Brendan looked out at the students and saw that she was turned to Kristen saying something. The picks continued: Aiden Smith at 15. Leslie Grommler at 16. Emmanuel Montez at 17. Brendan looked at the two remaining names: Adam Leibowitz and Caitlyn Patterson. Adam was just a goofball, but people liked him. And then there was Caitlyn. It was Ross Dunworthy's pick, and Brendan saw the boy weighing the two options in his mind. Five seconds passed.

"So Ross," the teacher whispered, "Who's it gonna be?"

"I'll take . . . "Brendan tried to see on his lips the open-mouthed "C" to Caitlyn's name on Ross's lips, to no avail.

"I'll take Adam I guess," he said, and the teacher moved him under Ross's name, then Caitlyn's name under Brendan's. Good God. What are the odds, he thought? Brendan now felt that he couldn't look at her, but his mind scrambled for how to get out of this.

"Okay, class. Here are the teams," Loxler said. It was tough to catch 8th graders not trying to be cool, but there were some tense moments during the year when you could. Like seeing who they'd be paired up or grouped with. The teacher then read each captain's name and carefully scrambled the order that the students had been chosen in so it wasn't apparent to the class. After this, he pointed to regions of the room where each captain and his/her team should gather.

Brendan's team was in the back corner, near where Caitlyn and Kristen had been sitting, so Caitlyn just stayed in her seat when the teacher pointed to that spot. Brendan started to feel flush as he walked the leftmost aisle to join her. The other kids had already beaten him there because he had taken a few extra seconds to prepare for this.

"Hey, I remember you," Molly said. "We had science together."

"Mr. Shipman, who we called SHEEPman, right?" Caitlyn said, bringing a laugh from Molly.

"Yeah. What a creepy dude," Molly returned.

"Dude looked like a sheep. That's why he got his name," Randy chimed in, and the three of them continued to laugh.

Brendan sat down in the seat behind the trio.

"That guy still here?" Caitlyn asked.

"Naw," said Molly. "He left after sixth grade. I think he retired."

"Or died!" Randy said, bringing a quizzical frown from the two girls.

Molly turned to look at the just-arriving Brendan. "Aye aye Cap'n. Why don't you join us up here?"

Brendan's attempt to remain sequestered ruined, he nodded as they moved their desks apart and created a hole for him. A hole for him . . . right next to Caitlyn.

"Hi Brendan," Caitlyn said, smiling at him.

"Hi Caitlyn," he replied. "Long time no see."

"Been living the life in Guam!" she said.

"Guam? I have no idea where that is. Is that like a U.S. territory or something?" Molly asked.

"Yeah it is. It's part of Micronesia, in the south Pacific. Most of the countries though are independent now. Samoa. Marshall Islands. Palau."

"Samoa. Okay. I've always wondered where that was too," Randy added.

"It's about 2500 miles from Los Angeles. Western Pacific Ocean," Caitlyn supplied.

"2,500? That's like pretty much from here to LA," Molly said. "It's THAT far away?"

"Think DESERT ISLAND and you've got Guam. I mean, there are 100,000 people on the whole island I think, but if isolated is your thing, Guam's your place."

The teacher was plugging in the widget to control the slideshow, and right before he read off the first question, Brendan was reminded by this exchange how easily charming Caitlyn was.

"Okay. Only captains answer. On your white board. Any other random outbursts and the team doesn't get the point. And these questions are all over the place from what we studied. Don't want you to get too comfortable. And ALL of you, whether you care about winning the game or not need to pay attention, because you'll be seeing some of these in that county test in about 45 minutes I'm sure." He clicked the first question: "What is a carpetbagger?"

As they turned to one another, each knowing the answer, Caitlyn spoke first.

"It's what the Southerners called the people that came down from the North post-Civil War who they felt tried to get rich off Reconstruction," she blurted.

"Um, yeah. That," Molly said, taken aback by the precision of the answer. Randy smiled.

"Okay, boss. There's your answer," Randy said to Brendan, who wrote his best-remembered version of what Caitlyn had said. When he looked up, she was smiling at him. He returned the smile.

Nearing the end of the game, Brendan's team was in the lead by a point over the team led by Taylor. Caitlyn had proved to be instrumental, and Brendan was now glad he chose her, but then remembered he didn't have the guts to choose her.

"Okay, this is the last question. And it's the hardest one. Brendan's team up by one. Only Taylor's team has a shot. The other three teams. You gone!" The teacher's attempt at humor was booed by someone in the crowd. Loxler held up the remote like Moses about to cast down his staff to become a serpent and pressed the button.

"What general famously burned through Atlanta in the Civil War?"

Taylor said, "What?" drawing a glance from the teacher. "We didn't study that!"

"I told you it was hard. It was in the video you watched the day I was gone."

An indistinguishable voice from the front said, "You gone!" to the teacher, and the class broke up.

Brendan couldn't help but smile at that, remembering that no one in class had watched that video. He hadn't given them work to do so everyone was just on his/her phone. Seriously, what do he expect? No one in his group knew it, but since they were in the lead and it was obvious Taylor's group was blank on this one too, it didn't matter.

"Just write something funny," Caitlyn said.

Brendan smiled at her, and wrote "Wutchu talkin' 'bout Willis?" Molly said, "Classic!" Brendan looked at Taylor's group, who appeared now at least a bit more confident.

"All right, let's see boards in three, two, one." Brendan and Taylor raised their boards. Loxler saw Brendan's first. "No, that's not the answer, Brendan. But pretty funny." Some of the class laughed at the answer. "So that leaves Taylor and his group's answer of 'Ulysses S. Grant'. And while, class, of course Mr. Grant---"

"Later PRESIDENT Grant," Morgan of course had to interrupt/append.

"You are right, Miss Riley. Later PRESIDENT Grant was of course in charge of the entire Northern army, but it was in fact General William Tecumseh Sherman that nearly destroyed the great southern town of Atlanta in the Civil War. Point, set, match to Brendan, Molly, Randy, and Caitlyn. Come up and grab your booty," Loxler added with a flourish, pointing to the basket of candy on his desk.

Caitlyn reached out and grabbed Brendan's hand and pumped it quickly as a victory display. And Brendan let her. Then the kids all fist-bumped each other and claimed their prize off the teacher's desk.

Mr. Loxler looked at the clock. "Okay, so ten more minutes until the test. Do what you wish. Back in your seats in ten."

Molly and Ryan left the group and found their friends and sat down. Caitlyn, happy that she and Brendan were at least talking amicably, tried to continue that trend.

"So how have you been, Brendan?

"Well, not great. You know," he responded. He now looked down as he realized that she wanted to talk personally.

"Kristen told me about your hockey suspension. Sorry about that."

"Yeah. That's hockey I guess," is all he could manage. He decided to deflect the spotlight from himself. "So what're you doing back in Jacksonville?" he asked.

"Dad. Transferred."

He again looked at her. He'd forgotten how lovely she was. "That must be really weird—moving all the time."

"You get used to it. Not that it's ever fun, but you know it's coming usually, so . . . "

"How long did you know about this one?" Brendan asked, and as he did he could see Kristen saying goodbye to a group and coming their way.

"This one wasn't typical. Two weeks."

"Two weeks?! That's crazy," he said.

"You're right about that."

"So, congrats guys," Kristen said, touching each of them on the shoulder. "Kicked some ass there, didn't you?"

Both Brendan and Caitlyn started to say "It was . . ." and then the other's name, but Kristen, never missing a chance to carrying on both ends of a conversation, answered her own question.

"Yep. A real team effort." Her efforts at matchmaking were always so thinly veiled but her manner was so disarming that you just couldn't hold it against her. Caitlyn noticed that Brendan had also pointed at her as the impetus for the win and smiled. "All right, so yeah. Cool," she continued, clearly having a hard time with the idea that this was happening--the two of them were talking.

Brendan didn't know what to say next, so he started to make an excuse about spending a few minutes going over his notes before the test, but before he could, Caitlyn seriously put him on the spot.

"So Bren. Kristen tells me you're not going to graduation tomorrow night. That true?"

Brendan stared blankly and her and opened his mouth slightly.

"Something about the Lightning playing, right? Come on Bren! You can record that game. You can't miss graduation. You gotta come. Plus I bet your mom would KILL you if you didn't. And best of all, I'LL be there!" Kristen said, spreading her arms open as if to hug him.

Kristen was that person who always said what you were thinking but what you'd never say. Occasionally it would get her in trouble, but pretty much everyone liked her and she was honest, so that made up for a lot. So Brendan was waiting for the inevitable, "And come on, you guys can get to know each other again. Won't that be fun?" Or the like.

But somehow, for once, it didn't come.

What came into Brendan's head was Grandpa George's **keep hope alive**.

At lunch that day Caitlyn went to her usual table, but rather than finding the expected and anticipated EJ found Kristen and Mike. She and Kristen talked about it, with Kristen saying that he just probably wasn't in school that day, that some kids have talked about staying home or coming late because they either just had one test to take or were done. Still, she wondered of the effect of her refusal of his graduation request on his absence. But that really made no sense. She'd only known him a couple days. Why would he THAT be the reason he's not here?

Anabel's only exam that day was "office assistant," some joke of a multiple-choice thing that was about careers you could have, one of those tests that were so demoralizingly easy that you felt compelled to choose the stupid answers just to be antagonistic. After having to semi-focus during that morning test, her mind raced with what she was going to do to finalize her crown, her dress, how happy she was that she'd hit her goal weight of 102 (she'd taken the blocky numbers and writing on the glass surface and imagined it as a smile, which was rare), and graduation in general.

One of the strictest rules in testing was that you could not under any circumstances have your phone out while anyone had their test out, but when after sitting for over an hour staring into space Anabel's phone buzzed once, she knew she had to break it. Despite the heat today she had worn jeans, so her phone was in her back pocket, making her task easier. Trying to be as casual as possible, she reached her left hand slowly around her body until she felt the tip of it just sticking out from her back pocket. The teacher was shuffling some papers around on her desk and the others around her were either doodling on the ubiquitous piece of scratch paper students were always given for tests or had their head down. She slowly worked it out of her pocket and when it was free quickly jerked it to the seat between her legs.

She pressed the start button and since it was too dark for Face ID to recognize her she punched in her code. The latest message was from Ally. It read: Hey squirt wanna do something tonight— you me and Nessa? Your exams are over today, right? Mine too.

Anabel's first thought was no. She had to finish her crown for tomorrow's soiree. But then almost as quickly came the fun she'd have with her sisters. Ally's high school life was so full that she rarely got to see her much in the evening. It WOULD be fun. And the few times she'd gone out with her since she got her license felt so liberating without the watchful eyes of Mom and Dad 24-7. She didn't have much left with her crown; it could easily be finished in a short time. She'd do it.

After closing her legs to hide the phone from the now-circulating teacher, she uncovered it again once she'd resumed her seated position at her desk. She responded: I'm in. What do u wanna do?" After ten seconds came the response: Don't know. We can talk. Later."

Anabel checked the time, then turned her phone completely off and slipped it back into her pocket. She had ten minutes left in the ridiculously-long TWO HOURS the county allotted for these tests, and then it was lunch. Just then the idea of signing out early hit her, and she wondered if her mom was available to pick her up. Worth a shot, she thought, quickly texting: Pick me up? All tests done. Love you!" and awaited a response. A minute later her mother wrote back: Sure. I'm running errands for graduation right by the school. Be there in ten. Love ya back!

At the last minute before the bell a student assistant came into the testing room and handed Anabel's sign-out slip to the teacher. She collected it and tried to quickly reach the entrance before the explosion of humanity that happened each time the end-of-class bell rang which only doubled or maybe tripled with the end-of-exam bell. She waved the pink slip at the front-door monitor and just as she pressed the bar to open the door the bell sounded. Score!

As she moved from the walkway that bisected the manicured grass lawn of Wildwood Middle and onto the sidewalk she knew something had changed. Although she'd of course come back tonight for graduation, for maybe the last time, finishing that last test signaled to her the end of 8th grade and of middle school. The freedom of the summer and high school was on her mind as she opened the door to Mom's dark-blue BMW.

"Hi Honey. How'd you do on your test? Office assistant, right?"

"The lamest test ever. Took me twenty minutes and then I stared at the walls and doodled for the next 100."

"Sorry to hear that," Mom returned, accelerating as she pulled into traffic on Eisenhower Boulevard. "So what's your plan for the rest of the day."

"Gotta finish the crown for tomorrow. Try the dress on again. And go to the gym before all that. Can you drop me off now please?"

"Sure," her mother started, then pursed her lips. "Do you really think that dress needs to be tried on for the fifteenth time, Annie? I saw you do it last night. How much could change since then?"

Anabel thought: A lot. I've gained three pounds in a day before. While eating very little. Scale weight makes NO SENSE. "Plenty Mom. And why should you care?"

Her mother looked at her, then back to the road, and sighed. "Because I keep wondering when you're going to break this obsession you have with your weight. Look at your waist. It's practically non-existent."

Anabel then looked at her own waist and then her mother's. "Mom. Look at your waist. It's the same as mine. And you're like . . . 50 or something!"

"Okay, that was a low blow. You very well know I'm 44," her mother said mock-indignantly.

"You're missing the point. You know that you obsess over your weight as much as I do. You always have. That's probably where I got it from!"

Her mother's mouth opened and she violently whirled her head to Anabel. "That is SO not fair, Annie." She tightened her grip on the steering wheel. "I'm not saying you're wrong, about me, but I have never done anything to bring that about in you. Why would you say that? Tell me one time when I did!"

Anabel realized her claim was a reach, so she back-pedaled. "Okay, so maybe you haven't, but don't you think that that's rubbed off on me or I've inherited it or something?"

"Inherited? Child what are you TALKING about?" her mother returned. The car was now stopped at the light on Eisenhower and Main, and Anabel sulked while looking at hers and Chris's hangout, Panera. "You've gotta be joking, right?" Anabel crossed her arms, then looked at her mother. "When have I not complimented your looks, praised your work ethic, built you up in every way I could?" Silence. "I need an answer here, Annie."

She didn't want to say it now, but Anabel thought her mother had done all that and more. She wanted to think more about this, so she offered a quick "I guess you're right" to hopefully end this thread.

Ms. Donan studied her face for sarcasm and finding none looked toward the traffic light in anticipation of movement. The phone rang and her mother pressed the "Accept" button on her car's touchscreen and began talking with her friend Fiona. Although it was about some detail for the coming graduation, which usually garnered all of Anabel's attention, she took the opportunity to pop in her earbuds and start a music mix. She almost instantly realized that her mother most certainly didn't have anything to do with her weight obsession. Anabel had read books with anorexic or bulimic characters, gotten information at school, and been well-educated on eating right. The only excuse she had for it was her. Sixth grade. That's the time this started. The pressure of middle school. Fitting in. The struggle all that year. Then getting together with Chris. And things changed.

Changed? "Changed" seemed a light word for the task here. Progressed? Mutated? Taken over her whole being? That was less poetic but more like it. Starting that sixth-grade summer she had dieted drastically, exercised more, thrown up intentionally some, fought in her brain to think of something, ANYTHING, other than food. Even though she was with Chris at the time she thought it probably the worst period of her life. Then one day she woke up sixth months later with the scale's number five pounds less and her body four inches taller. And she had given all the credit to herself for that. But now she wondered what glory or blame Chris deserved in the matter.

"Anabel, can you hear me," Mom practically shouted, and Anabel pulled out her earbuds.

"YES I CAN!" she responded.

"I can never tell if people with those things are listening or not," she fumed. "So you see where we are. I'm going to get the dry cleaning and my dress for tonight, go to Fiona's, then pick up your brother. I'll see you back at home around 4."

"Sounds good, Mom. Ally and Nessa and me are going to do something just after dinner, okay?

Her Mom looked at her, thinking. "Well, I guess that's okay since you're both finished with exams, but I don't want Nessa out too late, all right? She's really excited for her end-of-the-year party tomorrow."

"Okay," Anabel said.

"What's the plan? Where're you going?"

"Not sure yet. Me and Ally will talk at home I guess."

"Okay, Annie. Let me know when you know."

"Okay, Mom," she said, grabbing her backpack and closing the car's door. She watched her mother pull away and turned to the double doors of the gym. I bet the gym is pretty deserted there now, she thought. When she pulled on the door it held fast. The hours posted on the glass said "Monday-Friday, 4:00-10:00." Damn. Try totally deserted. I wouldn't know that because I'm always in school. But wouldn't Mom? The sign below it said, "Summer hours Monday-Friday 8 AM-10 PM. Begins week of June 2." Of course, she thought, pulling absently on the handle again and getting the same result.

I'll just call Mom. She couldn't have gotten far. She pulled out her phone and went to call her mother, but then realized that this would be a good opportunity to start thinking in earnest about tonight. Her house was only a mile away. It WAS hot as hell. But I'M SUPPOSED TO BE IN SCHOOL. Anything at this point was just gravy. So she began the trek back to her house, slinging the backpack to one shoulder rather than covering her back entirely to try and stave off some heat. And, trying to find shade when she could, started walking.

Later that night at the skating rink, the three sisters were sitting down to eat pizza after nearly an hour of time on the floor. Annie saw her little sister's eyes widen as from behind Anabel Ally was coming with the pizza.

"Here we go," she said with a flourish, setting down the 20" pie in the center of the table. Ally sat down and the girls all took two slices each and set the half-full box behind them on a small table so they'd have room to eat.

Nessa was about to shove as much of her pepperoni slice into her mouth as physically possible when Ally said, "Hey Ness. Slow down. See how hot that is?" Nessa reluctantly nodded. "Gotta let that cool a minute."

"Okay," Nessa said, and took a drink of her Sprite.

"Hey thanks for taking us out, Ally. This was a great idea, Anabel said.

"Glad you guys are having a good time. I figured it had been a while and now we're free. Whoo hoo!"

"I know. Awesome," Anabel returned.

Nessa was looking expectantly at Ally for the green light to eat, and Ally nodded and said, "Blow on it first." Her sister complied and took a tiny bite off the tip to check its warmth.

"You sound like Mom," Anabel said with a laugh.

"Mom? Thanks," Ally said with a smile.

"You know what I mean . . . In a good way."

"Well thank you for acknowledging my maternal instincts."

"Absolutely," Anabel said.

Although Nessa was somewhat following the conversation with her sisters, she was too focused on picking the pepperoni slices off her pizza and nibbling around the perimeter of each and watching the size diminish. But she did say, "This is REALLY good pizza," and both sisters smiled.

"You know, we COULD do this more often," Ally said, raising her eyebrows.

"Well, sure," Anabel returned. "Wait, what is that supposed to mean?"

"Annie. How often are you available to do anything?"

"I don't know. More than you. During swim you're gone like five nights a week or something."

"Swim was done two months ago," Ally said. "Seriously? Like you don't know?"

Of course she knew. She'd known for two years. Most of her non-committed time revolved around she and Chris. When they had first gotten together it had weighed on her even more, but over time she had become resigned to the fact that she put him over everything else. Outings with her sisters. Time with Mom and Dad. Watching TV or playing games at home with the whole family. Yeah, everything.

"Of course I realize that I spend a lot of time with Chris. But hey, you spend a lot of time with your boyfriends too, right?"

"You're really going to compare those two things?" Ally's mouth was agape.

"Well . . . yeah," Anabel managed.

"Annie. Come on. Not even close. Even when you're with us it doesn't ever feel like you're really with us."

Nessa, who had been watching the skaters fly by them just a foot or two sometimes from their table, turned and nodded at Anabel. Ally noticed this and held up her palm towards Nessa. This had a greater impact on Anabel than any other thing her older sister could have said, and Anabel slowly looked back and forth between them. Anabel started to protest but couldn't deny the accusation. How many times was she just not present with them? Thinking of something to do with Chris, FOR Chris during family TV time. On her phone during vacations, texting back and forth with him, eager to share her experience with him rather than sharing it with her PRESENT family. Planning how she'd lose that pound she'd gained the day before during meals in a restaurant when phones were forbidden. Guilty as charged. Both sisters looked expectantly at her. What could she say to make this better?

"You're right."

Although they still had fun the rest of the night finishing their pizza, continuing to skate, and wasting money at the games for tickets to get five-cent prizes, the revelation weighed heavily on Anabel. She knew that something had to change.

That night, close to bedtime, as Anabel was putting the finishing touches on her crown, that antiquated symbol of some fifties-era sense of privilege that was forced on the girls and boys of Wildwood Middle but still she had taken as her own and cherished, she started crying as she thought of the night she got it. Remembering her nervousness beforehand. Thinking the worst but praying for the best. Their names getting announced by Principal Lawson that night. The surprise on Chris's face. Getting the crown put on her head. That awkward "first dance" that was again part of the ceremony. And then just them together. The bad times and mostly good over two years. The life they shared. And still share. It was all she ever wanted. And tonight, tonight was just another chance to show what each meant to the other. Writ large again though this time, in front of everyone, not just in the private moments. They've survived, folks. Beaten the odds to be together two years. Two years! In dog years that's like 15, she thought.

And just as before, Anabel wouldn't fail to take advantage of her opportunity.

She had just set the needing-to-dry-crown down on the very top of her bookcase where it couldn't possibly get damaged when her mother popped into the doorway. "Time for bed, honey. Big day tomorrow." Noticing the crown on its perch, she said, "Oooh, it looks great. Can I see it?" and stepped into the room. Anabel moved to block her way.

"Uh uh uh," she said, wagging her finger back and forth in her mother's face. "Not until tomorrow. Just like everybody else."

Her mother looked puzzled. "Annie, you know this decorating the crown business is nothing really formal, right? That it's just between you two to share? The whole school's not gonna see it."

"Yes mother. You've briefed me already."

"Then what's the harm in—" Ms. Donan took another step toward the crown, with the still-blocking Anabel backpedaling but now putting up both hands to fend her off.

"Mom. Please!" she said, getting a face drop of resignation and the crossing of arms from her mom.

"All right All right. I think that's kinda WEIRD, but sure, I'll wait." She said, "Love you," and kissed Anabel on her forehead.

"Love you too Momma." Anabel started to the bathroom to get ready for bed.

"But you know . . . I could just sneak in here at night and see. Maybe take pictures and post them . . . on Facebook . . . "

This froze Anabel, who spun and said, "You better not!" Her mother shrugged her shoulders. "I'll lock my door!" she countered.

"Now YOU better not!" her mom said as she smiled and closed the door.

When she was finished in the bathroom she texted Chris: "Hey. Hope you're doing well today. See you tomorrow. Nite Nite". She turned off her light, turned her phone completely off, and lay down for sleep.

That night at dinner (Caitlyn's favorite—Mom's Chicken Marsala) the topic of the graduation came up near the end.

"So how you feeling about tomorrow, girl?" Julianne Patterson asked her daughter. "Any better?"

"Yeah Mom. Some people this week have gone out of their way to make me feel welcome, kind of at home again. I'll be with Kristen. There's a boy I wouldn't mind seeing there."

`Her dad was trying to get the last three peas from his plate to his fork but stopped this to look at her.

"Now that's a passive sentence if I've ever heard one. A boy? Already?" This brought a "Why?" look from Ms. Patterson.

"Why is that so strange, dad? You do realize I'm not 10 anymore, right?"

"I noticed that about the time you started wearing shirts that exposed your stomach. Not something I ever really WANTED to see."

Her mom laughed. "Do you have any idea how hard it is to even BUY appropriate things for her to wear at school, honey?" she replied to her husband. He rolled his eyes. "Yeah, I thought so. They're either t-shirts that go well beyond her waist or cute shirts that expose her stomach. Not much in between."

Caitlyn held up her palm and her mother high-fived it.

"What's wrong with long t-shirts, and why do I feel like this is a conspiracy?" Warren Patterson said.

"Dad if this is a conspiracy then the entire United States of America is in on it," Caitlyn returned.

"Besides Warren, if you want to see exposed midriffs I can show you some on teenagers WAY more out there than the stuff Caitlyn wears."

"That's okay. I'll take your word for it," he said, rising to take his plate to the kitchen, where he spooned another chicken breast and plenty of sauce on it and returned. Caitlyn loved her dad despite his being stuck in 1962 at times. "So who is this 'boy' that you're going to see," he said.

"His name's EJ."

"Okay. Tell us about him," her mother stated.

"Okay, so I've known him like three days guys. It's not like I know what brand of toothpaste he uses or what position he sleeps in yet," Caitlyn said, suppressing a smile.

"Come on Cait, give us something," her mother cajoled.

"I don't know. He's a regular kid. Kinda cute. Brown hair. Is into a lot of the music that I'm into. I don't know," she said, throwing up her hands.

At that point her brother Luis came in the front door.

"Excuse me," Julianne said to her son, her demeanor doing a 180. "What time do we eat dinner in this house?"

"Mom. I tolja I was going to be at Alex's house and that we---"

"I'm waiting," she said, cutting him off.

Luis looked from his mom to his dad, and quietly said, "6:30."

Caitlyn's mother looked at the Jaguars clock on the wall above the kitchen. "And it's now what time?"

"6:52."

"And 6:52 is not . . ."

She and Luis had gone through this same interrogation several times, so each knew the rehearsed and correct response, which was the only way to end it.

"6:30," he glumly repeated.

"Yes. 6:30," she said. Luis knew at this point his sentence had been commuted, and he moved to the bathroom to wash his hands and face for dinner. "Not sure there's any Marsala left for you, straggler!" Julianne said, bringing a cry from the bathroom.

Caitlyn smiled at her mother. "Hey Mom. Can you help me try on my dress later tonight? See if it needs anything?"

"Sure honey," she said. "But it fits though, right? You've had it on already."

"I did in the thrift shop, yeah, but that was pretty quick."

"Okay," her mother said. Let me get dinner cleaned up and I've got a couple phone calls to make, then I'll do it. Around 8:00?"

"Yeah, that's fine," Caitlyn said, and then cleaned up her dishes.

When she had just turned off the water and dried her hands, her mother came into the kitchen with a brown tube.

"Hey Cait. Forgot to tell you. This came for you today."

"For me? What is it?"

"I don't know honey. It's from Amazon. Open it and let's see."

With scissors Caitlyn cut through the tape at one end and wedged out the white stopper on one side of the tube. She carefully stuck a finger in and pulled out the rolled-up poster.

"You ordered a poster?" her mom asked.

"Uh, no. I didn't."

"Then who sent it?"

Caitlyn unrolled the poster and saw the familiar image of Clash bassist Paul Simonon ready to smash his bass onstage and the words THE CLASH and LONDON CALLING.

"It must have been EJ, the kid I was telling you about earlier," Caitlyn replied.

"He bought you a poster? For what occasion?"

"I don't know, Mom. He knows I like the band."

"Is this one of your friends from sixth grade?"

"No, I just met him on Tuesday. I told you that."

"You . . . just met him, and he's already buying you a poster?" Her mom lifted her eyebrows.

"What?" Caitlyn asked. "What's wrong with that?"

"Nothing. I guess. It's just that it's a little—"

"Soon?" Caitlyn said. "Yeah. That's kind of my first thought, too."

"This boy doesn't EXPECT anything from you, does he?"

"What is that supposed to mean?"

"Well. I don't know Cait."

"Mom, it's okay. He's harmless."

"Whatever you say, dear. I believe you." Her mother put her palms up and walked out of the kitchen with a smirk.

Caitlyn took the poster back to her room and scouted out a place on her wall for it.

After she had successfully tried on the dress with her mother later that night and between the time she had planned to work (and maybe finish!) her book, her phone lit up with "Facetime Video: EJ". Caitlyn pressed the button and his face filled the screen.

"Whoah there. Kinda close pal," she said, which brought a repositioning on his end. She now could see a different a window in a different wall in his room in the background and an acoustic guitar on a stand in the corner.

"Hiya Caitlyn. How ya doin'?"

"Hey. Good. What about you?" she said, then added "Where were you today?" as he started to answer.

"I've finished all my exams so I didn't need to go in. I told you yesterday, right?"

Caitlyn wracked her brain for this knowledge but came up empty. "I guess you could have. Yeah. I forgot." She felt a vague sense of . . . relief?

"Nice to know that you're looking for me though," he said smiling. "Sit with Kristen?"

"Oh yeah. And she was going on about something that happened before school. She was a one-girl animated insane monologue. I tried to get in a question and she'd hold up her hand to stop me and just keep going. I swear I don't know how she does it."

EJ said, "Best friends. What are you gonna do?" Caitlyn laughed.

"So, wutcha doing?" he asked.

"Getting ready to write," she replied.

"Ah yes William Shakespeare at work. Or should I say Virginia Woolf? Toni Morrison?"

"Oooh, look at you. Naming some favorites. I'll go with Woolf today because I am in a room of my own."

"Clever clever," EJ said, nodding at the connection. "How close are you to finishing?"

"So close I can taste it!" she said. "Sometimes I think that I just need to produce when I'm into it. Just keep writing—"

"Until the muse leaves you, right?"

"Okay that's just weird. I was seriously going to say that," Caitlyn replied.

He laughed. "Like the Beatles, eh? Just spit out Hard Day's Night/Help/Rubber Soul/Revolver in like two years."

"Sure EJ. That's me. You haven't read my writing yet, so PLEASE do not compare me to anyone with actual talent."

"If you write the way you talk I bet it's great," he said.

"Okay, you just keep thinking that and we'll just be swell." Caitlyn made an "OK" with her thumb and forefinger, bringing a laugh from her friend.

"By the way," Caitlin continued. "That link you sent me to that Jam video didn't work. I was looking forward to hearing that song."

"Oh, really. Sorry. I'll try to resend it later tonight."

"Okay, thanks," Caitlyn said.

"So, switching gears. Given any more thought to going with me to graduation tomorrow?"

She paused and looked away from the screen. Deflect it. She moved the phone closer to her face. "You see we were having a perfectly wonderful conversation and you have to spoil it by asking THAT?" EJ didn't know how to take this, so he opened his mouth, probably to apologize she thought, before she preceded that with "I'm just kidding," which caused him to sigh with relief and nod his head.

"That was mean," he said, smiling.

"I don't know about MEAN. I think of it more as FUN."

"Fun for YOU. Not so much from the person that's only known you for a few days staring at a likeness of you on a five-inch phone and just STRAINING to see if you're joking."

Caitlyn laughed. "Point taken."

"So. Gonna answer the question?" He WAS persistent, Caitlyn mused.

"Yes, but the same way I answered before. I'll see you there and we'll hang out."

Silence. "See, and I was going to buy you a corsage and everything. A pink lily. Stargazer," he replied.

"And if you had done THAT I'd never speak to you again."

"Okay," EJ said. "I get it. I won't be in school tomorrow either but I'll see you at the shindig tomorrow night."

"All right. Sounds good," Cait said.

"Um, okay, but . . . before you hang up, I have something to confess."

"To . . . confess?" she asked.

"Yep."

"Well okay then. Shoot."

"I really do know that you write the way that you talk."

"Huh? Okay. I guess. What are you talking about?"

"Because I've read your novel."

"You've read my novel."

"Well, yes. Parts of it anyway."

"Okay, I get it. So you're a mind reader, right?"

"Well, not exactly. You see, I—"

"So what's my protagonist's name, wise guy?"

Silence.

"Caitlyn. I know her name."

"So . . . guess."

"It's Jodi."

Caitlyn froze.

"I didn't tell you that."

"Right. Like I said. I know it because I've read it."

Caitlyn tried to wrap her head around this possibility and had nothing.

Seeing her puzzled look, he said, "I hacked into your computer."

"You what?" she screamed. "You invaded my privacy. How?"

"Well, actually, I sent a worm through the link that I sent you that allows me to see what's on your hard drive. Just to read some of your book. That's it. Nothing malicious."

"What the hell is wrong with you? You don't call THAT malicious? Stealing my thoughts. Who are you?"

"Okay, so I just wanted to see how you wrote. So we could talk about it. And . . . you wouldn't let me. So I just read a little."

"Wow." Caitlyn began to breathe heavily. "You. You're a maniac."

"Caitlyn. Listen. I'm sorry. I didn't think it would affect you like this or I never would have done it."

Caitlyn composed herself enough to say, "You creep. Don't you EVER talk to me again. You hear me. Never. And—" Her mind grasped for a threat. "Good luck after I tell my dad what you've done, you jerk."

She ended the call and slammed her phone down on the bed. She worked to control her breathing but could feel her face flushed. Closing her eyes and letting her face go blank usually helped, so she tried that. Nearly immediately she knew what she had to do first. She Facetimed Kristen. When her friend picked up.

When Kristen saw Caitlyn's face she said, "Cait. What's up honey?"

"You'll never believe what I'm about to tell you," she said.

"Cait. WHAT?" Kristen's eyes were wide and her mouth open.

"That kid. EJ. He hacked into my computer. HACKED INTO MY COMPUTER."

"What?" Why? Did he steal something from you? Money?"

"He stole my privacy. He read my book!"

"Wait. He broke into your computer to . . . read your book?"

Caitlyn nodded.

"Are you sure that's all?" Kristen asked.

"Well, no. That's just what he said he did. There might be more."

"Oh my God Cait that's insane! I mean, I knew the guy was good with computers but I had no idea he was a—"

"Fiend?" Caitlyn offered.

"Well yeah. At least. Damn."

"What should I do, Kris?"

"Unplug, disconnect from the internet for a start."

"Tell my dad?"

"Yeah. For sure."

"My dad's gonna kill him.

"Yeah, probably," Kristen replied. "Not your problem though, right?"

"But do that now, Cait. Right now. Disconnect. Sign out."

"Okay I will."

"I'm SO sorry girl. My God."

"Yeah. I know, right? He seemed normal and well, even like a nice guy."

"Well yeah. I never would have set you two up if I knew ANY of this."

"Not your fault, Kris. So sorry. Okay, so you all right for now?"

"I'm good. Thanks Kris."

"Okay, so I'll have my mom pull his place card at our table, like now."

"You had him sitting at OUR table? Oh Kris."

"Yeah. I'm the idiot here, but I'll take care of it."

"Ok. I'm going to download my book, disconnect, then write."

"Good for you. Resiliency."

"Writing always makes me feel better."

"Okay, see you tomorrow girl."

"Love you," Caitlyn said.

"After this? You da bes'."

"Always." Caitlyn smooched at her friends and ended the call.

She plugged in her phone and sat heavily at her desk. She downloaded her story quickly and then signed out of every program she could think of, even Windows. She then turned off the computer and pulled the power cord from its socket. She had no idea what further damage he could possibly do at this point but at least she could make it harder for him. She started a file with the final chapter of the book, "Redemption," and stared into the bright whiteness of the Word document. At first she couldn't shake the thoughts of EJ's violation and just how and when to tell Dad but decided that could wait until after graduation tomorrow night. After a few minutes she'd decided that he probably really wasn't trying to steal money or passwords or whatever from her and really DID just want to read her writing. He was way more into her after three days than she was into him. Whatever, no excuse. What he did was just creepy.

After processing these thoughts for close to five minutes she put in her earbuds and put on something classical to blot out any ancillary house sounds. Use this, she thought. Use this anger to fuel your writing.

Her notes read: *Jodi, on restriction, sneaks out and goes to the concert. Before she gets there, texts from parents. Busted! Arrives at club. Local record producer is there. Band sounds great. She doesn't get near the stage because she doesn't want to be seen. Overhears producer saying that he loves the band but hates the singer. After the first set, the lead guitarist Jack asks the producer what he thinks. He tells him (the above). Jack spots Jodi. Jack says to producer "Well, she's not our REAL lead singer." Explains in a simplistic and mostly masked way what's happened to Jodi. Introduces her to him. Jodi nervous before performing the second set, sitting behind the stage with the band, going through the songs, asking her if she's ready for this. She says yes. Jack tells her this is it though, no more chances. He leaves. Ex-girlfriend acknowledges her with Jack gone—at least she's not hostile! Performs second set. Producer impressed. She's back!*

And this is how she finished:

Jodi stood alone on the stage and surveyed the now-emptied club save for a couple of bartenders restocking for tomorrow. This is her place, and these are her people. She wouldn't do anything again to sabotage the electric feeling she gets every time she's up here performing. The net effect of the drugs and alcohol was to blur her dream. She wouldn't take this for granted again. She was home. To stay.

Caitlyn hit SAVE, then stared blankly into the computer screen. That's the best creative burst I've ever had. Although it was only three hours ago, the EJ incident felt like a month ago, and while she wasn't exactly over it she now felt positive enough about tomorrow night. It was doable.

Friday, May 29, 2021, morning and afternoon: Graduation

Anabel woke up, and the first thing she did was check to see if her teacher had posted the geometry exam grades yet. She saw a notification and held her breath. She opened up her class and scrolled to the end where the test would show. She deflated when she saw the "B." That means she got a "B" for the semester. That's a "B" with the curve, meaning she maybe had gotten a "C" or "D" as a straight percentage. She pulled the covers over her head and went back to sleep. She awoke from a good dream two hours later, and, despite the memory of the grade hitting her flush in the face once again, thought about graduation: I got this. One more piece of business. She texted Chris and asked him what songs he had chosen for the slideshow. He explained to her that because there were so many slides and given the time he'd have to cover he had made two playlists and sent them to her. She thanked him and realized how perfect Miley Cyrus's "I'll Always Remember You" at second to last and Death Rattle's "Forever" being the last song were for the evening. The Cyrus song had always been one of her favorites, it being a sentimental look back on good times. The Death Rattle song was of course the song that had been playing when they had their first dance when they got their crowns in sixth grade.

Caitlyn woke up, spent four hours finishing her unpacking, listened to a couple of records, went for a run, and lay down to take a nap before graduation. She woke up to a visit from Kristen intended to console her about the EJ fiasco and assuage any fears she might have about the graduation that night. As usual, it worked.

Brendan woke up, went for a long bike ride, watched some TV, played some NHL 2K, thought about how stupid it was that he would miss game 7 (at least live) of the Stanley Cup finals with the Lightning playing to go to freakin' graduation, and somehow made an uneasy peace with the fact that yes indeed he WAS going to graduation (lest his mom cancel hockey "for the foreseeable future") and realized that there were worse things in life (probably) then events with 200 people attending and little control and possibilities of things going crazily wrong (he referenced the sixth grade dance here). The only possible Grandpa George saying that fit this was **suck it up.**

Chris awoke and showed his mother how awesome the slide show he'd made for graduation was. She'd told him to show her the night before but he was still finishing, and he had pleaded that she could count on him. She was pleased. Chris was pleased. It was different than game design, and I may have struck out there for now I did not strike out but rather hit a grand slam. They'd all love it tonight. And some would be really surprised. After his mom literally patted him on the back he resigned himself to no frustration on design and to play some hours of Neverwinter, which he lustily did and was highly successful at it, going up two levels in one day. And then he finally got around to decorating his crown and admired the results. Tonight was not only doable, he thought, it was necessary. The king is back ya'll.

Friday, May 29th, 2021, evening: Graduation

The gymnasium at Wildwood Middle School was set up similarly to the way it was set up for all three end-of-the-year celebrations, those being the sixth grade dance, the seventh grade party, and the eighth grade graduation, but each event had its own particulars which had to be catered to in keeping with the traditions at the school. The "founding fathers" back in 1944 used their military-borne foundation of discipline and tradition to establish rules, guidelines, and standards that had remained consistent with little variation through the years. Since a fair number of the kids were military kids whose mother or father worked at the Naval Air Station, there always seemed to be plenty of support for keeping the "old ways." When a brash PTSA parent reared her head and suggested a revamping she was usually quieted by the old guard. 67 years later the decorations were glitzier, the hair longer, and the wealth more apparent, but the ceremonies themselves remained preserved as if in a time capsule that was unearthed yearly for those nights and then securely stored again lest they be sullied.

The 8th grade decorations were less frilly and colorful but more pompous, with the colors black and gold setting the tone for all else that followed. The stage which to the sixth grade Fire and Ice Dance was red and blue and for the seventh-grade party was multi-colored was now in the more somber and regal black and gold. Now from the raised baskets hung not tendrils of ice and flames of fire but simple black and gold streamers. The dais steps were gold and the dais was black. The arch over each was a combination of the two.

Gone were the garish food stands of hot and cold of sixth grade, replaced by the formal dinner serving trays served by seventh grade honor students and their parents clad in dresses, suits and even an occasional tuxedo, and white gloves. The regular lunch tables that were wheeled into the gym for sixth grade gave way to rented tables and padded chairs. One of the few nods to modernity was that the "tablecloths" were taped together white poster paper that teachers used for their bulletin boards. Sometime in the '90's this became a thing after a PTSA member was so taken by them while eating at Macaroni Grill that she forced a vote after a short battle at one PTSA meeting and it passed by one vote.

Another tradition held that the parents and students be separated, or at least seated separately in different parts of the gym. This made it more fun for the kids, who didn't have to worry about their parents breathing down their necks for these last moments of middle school. The parents didn't mind either because they sat with their friends and chatted. The only snafu with this was the need for the principal to turn continually to address each group separately. Parents have joked that she needed some kind of Lazy Susan rotating disc to spin her around slowly, which made Principal Grayson remember the Fun House's trio of whirly discs on the top floor in Cleveland at the Greater Ohio Fairs of her youth.

The main difference in graduation however was easy to see upon entering: the video screens. At the back wall of the gym above the now-pulled-to-the-wall bleachers was an enormous screen measuring 80 x 20 feet and controlled by a ceiling-mounted projector. The size made it such a commanding sight that almost demanded it to be watched.

At the sides of the gym were smaller screens for those who couldn't see the big one. Projectors on the dais cast the images for these screens. Here would be projected the kids as they were in sixth grade, which always proved to be fun for all involved. One always shone on the entrance and exit doors, something Lawson had reluctantly agreed to despite it temporarily blinding those who entered because it was another source of humor for the kids and it reminded her of some of the shenanigans her grandmother had told her about from her days as a girl at Coney Island.

Principal Grayson strode around the gym with more than a cursory eye on everything that had been decorated, designed, or placed. She knew she probably didn't need to worry this year, as Chris Lawson's mother Marion was in charge of Blue Key and hence essentially the night's activities from dinner to awards to the slideshow and everything in between but worry she did. The worst disaster they'd ever had in 67 years of these events was a call from the commanding officer of the Naval Air Station concerning the need to conserve power for military use in May of 1945 near the end of WWII, thereby ending the sixth-grade dance prematurely. By an hour. And back then, she thought, people would have lived in the dark for a year to support their country. Hardly a calamity. Still, she didn't want anything on her watch to supersede that. Her last two years were going to go smoothly and then she and her husband Bill would retire together and their traveling would begin.

Her final check before taking half an hour for dinner (she sometimes didn't have time to eat with everyone else for various reasons) on her longest working day of the year were the three projectors set up for the slideshow. She turned on the projectors and booted up the computer and inserted the flash drive given to her earlier by Marion Lawson and saved the slideshow to the hard drive. She took out the portable drive and put it in her pocket and clicked on the slideshow itself and then "Slideshow" to get it out of production and into presentation mode. Marion had told her it would run automatically and have music throughout which would basically serve as the DJ too, so she relished that $500 saved for a live DJ. The first slide was for some reason of her on the dais. She didn't really want pictures of herself at the celebration but knew she couldn't do anything about it because it would throw off the timing of the whole presentation. After previewing about a dozen slides she was satisfied. She powered off all the equipment and started to her office and her Jimmy Johns turkey sandwich awaiting her.

Anabel was the first non- "working" student to arrive at graduation. She was always the first one to arrive. At any school function. Including each day at school. When your mother is the school secretary you are going to spend way more time at school than you wanted. She had gotten used to this over the course of the last three years at Wildwood, and whenever she could she resisted the urge to be on her phone and therefore had gotten to know other adults at the school that she might never would have otherwise. She remembered the conversation with Mom at the beginning of sixth grade about who the other people were at the school other than teachers. At the time she was overwhelmed with titles like social worker, psychologist, ESOL aide, speech pathologist and the like, and she was still pretty iffy on most of these people because they weren't at school, at least not at her school, every day. But people like the custodians, office staff, and administration were all well-known to her.

One of her favorite people at the school was the head custodian Mr. Banks. "Tyrone Banks: Head Custodian" is what it said on his office door, which was her first stop in the school at least a couple days a week. Getting there an hour and a half before the other kids gave you PLENTY of time, she thought, and she gravitated toward this probably at least 70-year-old black grandfather of eight because of his friendliness and supply of fruit in his dorm-size office fridge that he freely offered to her each morning. When Anabel had first told her mother of the fruit her mother had said, "Don't take fruit from him, Annie. Do you have any idea how little that man makes as a custodian?" Anabel had protested that he was such a nice guy and that she loved to visit him in the morning and her mother slowly relented and said that his generosity should be accepted. And in her mother's mind to compensate for this Ms. Donan made sure he was the first one offered any extra duty or overtime chances that arose. It was a win-win.

Before she had come to the gym, she and her mother entered through the main school hallway because Ms. Donan needed to get some keys from her office and a few supplies. Anabel carried her newly revised crown in a specially made black bag that was cushioned in a way to keep both the original crown and the re-decorated band at its top from getting damaged. Tyrone Banks was mopping an intersecting hallway and spotted them right away.

"Anabel Donan. As I live and breathe!" he said, putting down the mop and walking over to the pair. "Hi Mrs. Donan," he said to her mother.

"Hello Tyrone. Happy that the kids have gone—for the year—and you can get some work done—in peace?"

"Absolutely. Absolutely. But you know," he said taking Anabel by both shoulders. "I am so gonna miss this beautiful young lady." While Anabel blushed the custodian drew her in for a huge bear hug, and Anabel held her crown in its case away as much as possible. Her mother smiled and put both hands to her face.

"That's right," Ms. Donan said. "This is her last day. God with everything else happening . . . But still, how did I forget that?"

"Well I guess I been saying my goodbyes all day, but I missed you because you didn't come visit me," he said to Anabel.

"I wasn't in school today Mr. Banks. My exams were done," Anabel said.

"Oh okay. So you were planning on saying goodbye to me tonight, right?" he asked.

"You know it," Anabel said, and this time she initiated the hug. The two held it longer than before, which caused Valerie Donan's eyes to tear up.

"Girl, I remember when you were yay high to a grasshopper, about this tall." Here he put his hand below his shoulder level. "Now look at you. So much taller and more beautiful. And smart. Dang this girl's smart," he said to Valerie.

"That she is," Ms. Donan replied. "She's . . . a handful she is."

"Now wait a second," Mr. Banks said. "Who am I gonna give my fruit to if not you?"

"Good question Mr. Banks. You know there's no one as special as me," Anabel said.

"I know that's right," he replied. "Maybe it'll just be more fruit for me. But truth be told I am REALLY going to miss our chats in the morning, girl."

"I'll always come back and visit. Mom's not going anywhere. You're coming back next year, right?"

"They're gonna have to drag me outta here kicking and screaming, Anabel. Kicking and screaming. Sure, I'll be here. Don't get too high and mighty as a high schooler that you'll forgot your old friends you leavin' behind."

"I could never forget you Mr. Banks. You'd be the LAST person other than Mom at this school I'd forget."

"You comin' over to the graduation, Tyrone?" her mother asked.

"Naw. Not 'less they need me. I'm going to start onna coupla rooms cleaning now. Graduation's for the kids. They don't want some old janitor toddling around in there."

"Before you go," her mother said. "Where's my hug?" She stepped forward and hugged him. "I come back in early July, so I'll see you then Tyrone. You take care."

"Goodbye Mr. Banks," Anabel said.

"Goodbye Annie. Don't forget to write," he said and chuckled as he moved back down the hall to his bucket and mop.

Minutes after that Anabel had entered the gym and she appointed her first task as seeing how it was decorated and its layout. The layout was less important to her than the sixth-grade dance mainly because then she was so full of anxiety and doubt and now she felt more a sense of relief—and its coming release. Things were coming to an end. A new chapter in her life would begin soon. And she was ready for it.

The only bit of uncertainty of the night for her was the crown reveal ceremony, but her mother explained what that would look like to others and where she and Chris would be standing when they revealed their crowns. Unlike the private and flamboyant and totally over-the-top crowning ceremony in sixth grade, her mother said this one is much more private, despite the spotlight. This was to be a reminiscence of the last two years to be shared between the Ice Queen and Fire King. They would be announced, a song would play, the spotlight would come, and they'd privately to each other share the photos and talk about how they decorated them. And that was it. Anabel was still unsure how private this actually would be but her mother assured her that eighth graders really didn't care anything about it, and that this tradition of the school's was one that had narrowly survived PTSA votes to get rid of it. Ms. Donan had said that usually the other kids either danced or talked but certainly ignore what happened in that spotlight. Yeah, eighth graders are different beasts than sixth graders, she thought, and was content that her personal choices and pictures she'd chosen would be shared with just her boyfriend.

Task #2 was to find where the placard that determined who she sat with was placed, and she found it at a table near the dance floor and the spot of the crown revealing. She immediately saw Chris's next to her. No surprise there. Checking the other cards she saw the familiar names of her friends and their dates: Courtney and Peter; Alan and Aria; Lydia and John. Although she never had a problem talking with unfamiliar people it was still reassuring to have the kids that deferred to her on this night, this night to end all nights, or at least all middle school nights, seated with her.

The next task for now was to put her crown up on the dais for the later reveal. As she approached the steps the nervousness and glory of her first walk up them during the crowning ceremony flooded back to her. Upon reaching the top, she realized she had not taken the steps she'd used but rather Chris's steps. She looked out to see what would have been his view on that night. Not so different than hers. But he'd been more surprised. You bet he was.

She found a place out of the walkway area and set her the black crown case down and returned to the main floor. The final task she had was to see how she looked at this point and so exited the gym proper and went to its attached girls' bathroom. It had only one mirror, with she and her friends sometimes jostling to see how they looked in it after PE and before returning to class. She centered herself in the mirror and first stood with her hands at her sides. Face/makeup? Check. Conservative but more than usual. Hair? Not doing exactly what I wanted, but fine. Check. Chest? Double check. Stomach? The eternal question. The bane of her existence. Even a hint of stomach depressed her, and here she didn't see one. My stomach? Not check. Choosing a dress that hides said stomach? Check. Overall she'd take a B or B-minus and be happy.

Then she thought: today doesn't really matter much, does it? Merely a rite of passage. After today, she'd begin anew. A new summer with all its possibilities. A new school year soon, a HIGH school year, with many of these people gone either to military-forced locations across the USA or world, or private or IB schools. And she herself leaving Wildwood, which at this juncture was the craziest of the thoughts. And leaving her mother, her friend and school companion for three years. Mom was right there when she broke up with her first boyfriend, or was out of tampons, or the time she slammed into the fence in PE and was knocked out briefly.

Changes don't scare me now.

At home getting ready Chris knew that he would not be getting surprised at the graduation tonight like he was for the last gym ceremony in sixth grade. One surprise like that was enough for one lifetime. No, tonight . . .he was in control. He had chosen the music and pictures for the slideshow, so he was essentially its DJ and photographer to some extent that would control over half the ceremony. And he was satisfied with the job he did on his crown that morning. He was just getting ready to put on his white with thin blue striped long-sleeve shirt when his mom yelled for him.

"What?" he yelled back.

"Do you need help with your tie?"

"Of course I do. I wear a tie like three times a year."

"You know you need to learn this sometime Christopher. I won't always be here to do it for you," his mom said.

"Got it. But today is not that day, Mom. Just give me a second and you can come in and tie it."

"All right," she said.

Just as Chris was buttoning the top button on the shirt and flaring up the collar, his mom appeared.

"Well, aren't you looking sharp tonight?" she asked. "Where's my phone?"

"Yep. Doing the dress up thing. Sometimes you just gotta," he returned.

"You know I have to do this from behind you, right?" she said, taking the offered tie and looping it around his neck as she moved.

"Yes'm."

She looked beyond her son and at the mirror in the bathroom as she began the process of measuring the distance, starting to loop around twice, and shoving the tie between the created space. She stepped around and pulled it through and took up the slack.

"Not bad, Marilyn. Not bad," Chris said.

"Why thank you my dear. Thank you," she returned, bowing. Chris straightened it and stepped to the bathroom to brush his hair. "I need about ten minutes to finish my makeup and I think we're ready to roll."

Shortly after dropping his brother Liam off at his friend Kieran's house for the night, his father pulled the BMW into one of the few spaces left in the Wildwood parking lot and killed the engine.

"Man, look at this," his father said. "Packed!"

"Well, that and we are ten minutes late," his mother said.

"Notmyfault," his father replied via a cough, which brought a stern look from his wife. Chris got out first and retrieved his crown in its case from the trunk.

"You ready, son? One last time at old Wildwood Middle?" his dad asked.

"Yeah, completely ready for high school dad," Chris returned.

"Sooooo much more freedom. That's for sure," his mother said.

"Yeah, but leaving a school is hard. Remember how tough it was for you leaving Pinewood Elementary after six years. You were bawlin'," said his father.

"Sure sure," Chris said, and the trio entered the black wrought iron gates festooned with black and gold balloons at the side of the school and soon into the gym itself.

Chris saw Anabel right away and after his parents said hello and his dad gushed about how beautiful she looked (and he was right Chris thought) they moved to the side of the gym reserved for parents and found their seat, which suited Chris just fine.

"Hey, howya doin' Annie?" he asked, setting down his crown case on the table and kissing her cheek.

"It's about time you got here," she said half-playfully.

"You know my mom. C'mon . . . "he said.

"Sure, right. Your mom. I bet you were decorating your crown until the last second."

"Guilty . . . as charged," he lied.

"Hey, get that thing offa the table. It's the size of a Tesla," Anabel said. She pointed to the dais and the spot off the walkway where she had stashed hers. "See over there, up by that rail. That's where mine is." He strained to see but couldn't.

"Where?"

"Here, grab it and come on. I'll show you," she said.

They got up and Anabel noticed that he was swinging the case at his side as he walked.

"Chris. What are you doing? The crown is fragile. Frah-jeel-eh," she said, using the dad from *A Christmas Story*'s pronunciation.

"This?" he replied. "It's got like six layers of protection. I think I could throw it up there and it wouldn't get damaged.

"Okay so let's not do that," she said.

He looked at her quizzically. "You okay tonight?" he asked.

"Sure. I'm fine."

"Not pissed because I haven't seen you in two days?"

"No."

"That's longer than we've gone since sixth grade, right?" he asked.

"Not true. The week you spent at camp summer of seventh grade."

"Oh right. Well you survived then. I'm sure you've survived now," Chris said, drawing a furrowed brow and narrowed eyes from his girlfriend. "What?" he again asked, and she pushed him in the back as he hit the final step. She pointed where her crown lay. He went to descend the steps but she stopped him.

"Do you remember? What it was like?" she asked.

"What WHAT was like?"

"Don't play, Chris. The crowning. Sixth grade. Standing up here?"

"You mean when I was scared shitless? Don't think I'll soon forget that," Chris said.

She looked at him. "You scared shitless now?"

"Now? Why would I be scared now?"

"I don't know," she started, then trailed off.

"I'd call it more like 'content' now," he said.

"'Content' huh?" Anabel said. "I guess that's . . . something."

When they reached the bottom of the stairs, he asked her the same question.

"I guess 'relieved' is how I feel right now. Relieved at things ending. That I've survived getting through them," she said. "I'm surprised I'm not feeling more nostalgic now though."

"I guess I've got that sense too. Middle school over. Seems weird. I remember walking in that black gate we just came through nearly three years ago. I must have been a foot shorter."

"And I was 50 pounds fatter," she said, causing him to laugh. She punched him on the shoulder. "And no way you would have had anything to do with me."

"I didn't have anything to do with any girl at the start of sixth grade. I looked like a Munchkin with my Pinewood Elementary shirt on."

"Hmmpph," she voiced.

"You're too funny with that stuff. Look back at yourself then. You were never fat. During the dance you weren't fat either. That stuff's just in your head. It controls you."

They had arrived back at their table. "Yeah, try being female some time," she said.

"No thank you!" Alan said, bringing a smack from his date Aria.

"Thanks for the support, ALAN," Anabel said.

"At your service ma'am," he returned.

The talk then turned to what each of them was doing for the summer and confirmations of which high school they'd be attending. Of the four boys and four girls at the table only two others, Chris included, would be going to Lakewood High, Wildwood Middle's feeder school. Anabel reassured herself once again that at least some of these relationships that she'd created or had been created for her were temporary, which made their separation easier.

Still and always following Grandpa George's advice, Brendan was one of the first students to arrive that evening. He took notice of how the gym was decorated and found the hugeness of the screen set up on the far wall fascinating. Very quickly he was ushered to his seat by a tuxedoed waiter (What was up with that?) and as he sat down noticed the placard "Brendan Ellison" perched atop his dinner plate. Around him were some kids he barely knew, so he walked around to the other side of the table to see who else was there. He saw the names "Mike Blanchard" and "Kristen Rothstein" and was happy to be seated with his friend.

And then the ephemeral happiness dissipated when he knew the name that would be next to Kristen's. Sure enough: "Caitlyn Patterson." And next to her there was a plate with no placard. Of COURSE she was going with Kristen. Kristen told me she would be. Sitting back down Brendan looked out at the other 20 or more tables and realized that this was no coincidence. Kristen, through her mother, arranged this. Brendan stared at the table and realized he wasn't too far from where he was in sixth grade. When IT happened. And now again he was at a table with her. He tried with difficulty to block out those associated emotions but his brain made him revisit that night's ending and its ensuing destruction of life as he knew it for months and months. The struggle continued from the other side as he remembered yesterday's win in the American History game and getting to be around Caitlyn again. Before the battle inside his brain was done, Kristen and her boyfriend Mike walked in through the doors.

"Bren-dan!" she said and ran to him. He tried to rise to greet her but she wouldn't let him, pouncing on him with a hug. The surprised Brendan looked at her as she found her seat and sat next to Mike.

"Hey dude," Mike said. "How ya doin'?" Mike stood and leaned over the table for a fist bump. Mike played on a different team than Brendan but they'd faced each other several times over the years. He was a good guy. Mike was wearing a light-yellow shirt and yellow tie with a blue jacket, and Brendan paled in self-comparison with his white short-sleeve shirt and bow tie. His mom had struggled to even get him to dress up that much as he fought her every offered suggestion for half an hour in the store.

"Hey man. Pretty good," he replied.

"Sucks that we're missing Game 7 though, right?" Kristen glared at him and he shrugged.

"Okay, so don't tell me ANYTHING about the game?" Brendan replied.

"Brendan, seriously? I know you're recording just like I am. Why would I do that?"

"Okay. I was hoping you'd say that. Just remember to shut notifications off on your phone."

"Hey. You two," Kristen said. "No more hockey talk tonight!"

"Yes ma'am," Mike said. Kristen turned to Brendan.

"Brendan! You came! You said you wouldn't but I knew you would. Yay!" Kristen's smiled encompassed her entire face. Although it didn't really matter what Kristen wore because she lit up most rooms she entered with just being Kristen, her pink floral print dress and string of pearls looked both classy and attractive.

"Well, as I told you. Mom was gonna take hockey away for the 'foreseeable future. Couldn't have that."

"A fate worse than death," Mike chimed in.

"You two are too much," Kristen said, and began looking around for people she knew.

"Hey, I wanted to ask you. How is Steve Hill doing?" Brendan asked.

Mike paused for a second, then shook his head. "From what I hear not as good as was expected. A slow recovery."

Brendan had begun to think more and more about what he had done to the kid, the ferocity of that hit that caused his head to slam into the boards and pretty much mandated Brendan's suspension. It was probably the hardest hit I've ever dished out in hockey. And it was unnecessary. Out of control.

"What do you mean?" Brendan asked.

At this point Kristen rose and said "Hey Joanna. Where you sittin'?" This made her leaving imminent. She patted Mike on the head and he waited until she had left before answering.

"Well, yesterday, that would be what, five days after the game? Yesterday Miller told me that he hadn't been back to school yet. That he's been in his 'darkened' room for a while. He's now able to watch TV, but still gets bad headaches. That he's going to be doing his exams in the summer. Kinda sucks," Mike related.

Brendan felt horrible. He tried in his mind to justify the hit because hey, it was hockey, and hey, he had given me a cheap shot first, but it wasn't happening.

"Damn . . .Yeah," Brendan said fumbling. "I never meant THAT."

"It's hockey, Brendan. You know what you've signed up for. At least by our age, right? We've been playing awhile. Who hasn't taken dozens of shots that rattled you, right?" Mike said, clearly attempting to assuage Brendan's immense guilt.

Having already determined before this that granted there may be some truth to that but that THIS hit was a vicious outlier, he didn't at all feel there was any truth in his response. "Yeah. I guess you're right." Brendan wondered how Mike would have spun this while talking to anyone but him.

"But they are talking about year-long suspensions in the future for something like that," Mike said, shrugging. "Most guys think that's BS and would totally change the game but I wanted to let you know. Devon said pretty soon hockey will be like that stupid quarterback rule in the NFL where a defender can barely touch them now."

"Yeah, that's just not hockey," Brendan said, now wishing the subject to change.

"I mean. Waddaya gonna do? Not let us hit anyone? Like ever? That's just completely unrealistic and just not what the sport is."

Brendan realized Mike could keep discussing this for a while, and normally he might have, but the inherent tension of the occasion was for him starting to creep in along with his egregious other just-spelled-out transgression. He tried to think of another topic to engage Mike in, to get HIM talking while Brendan could nod and smile and "Really?" or the like but failed.

He got rescued a few seconds later however when Kristen bounded back with a friend in tow. Not just A friend, but THE friend. Her.

Caitlyn smiled at Brendan, saying, "Hey Bren. How ya doin'?"

Brendan froze at the suddenness of being confronted with his former girlfriend slash tormentor, but he recovered and answered with more than usual confidence, "Hey Caitlyn. Pretty good." Caitlyn and Mike exchanged a quick hug, and before she sat noticed that she had straightened her hair and gotten a haircut. The only way he could tell was that it was straight across in the back, something he'd always found attractive. Clean looking. Her dress was light blue with sparkly elements in it, which made him think of the Elsa dress she had worn to that fateful sixth-grade dance.

Kristen said, "Look at you. Her hair looks amazing. Got it cut today, right? In that style that we saw online together?"

Caitlyn turned her head so Kristen could see the back also. "You right, girl. Glad you like it! I thought it turned out well."

"It looks great," Mike said.

"And that works really well with your dress. Can't believe that was $20 at Thrift City. How is that possible? It looks like a classy throwback from the early sixties," Kristen said.

"Like something from that movie *Hairspray*," right?" Mike asked.

Both girls looked dumbfounded at him. "How would you know that Michael?" Kristen said. "Hairspray?"

"Ahhh I watched it with my sister last year I think. Better than I thought it would be."

"Score a point for my boyfriend," Kristen said, then leaned over and kissed him. At this both Caitlyn and Brendan turned from them and just so happened to glance at the other. Caitlyn shrugged, which produced a smile from Brendan. Mike separated from Kristen and seemed to sit a little straighter in his seat.

"Hey, let's go mingle Cait," Kristen offered.

"Sure thing," she said.

"That okay with you guys?" Kristen asked, bringing a nod from Mike and a hands-up sure gesture from Brendan.

After they left Mike started talking hockey again, but this time Lightning hockey, so Brendan leapt into and was fully engaged in discussing the season and strategy in tonight's Stanley Cup Final game in particular. But this was good, easy conversation for Brendan about what he was most passionate about, so it filled the time until dinner. And it almost drowned out the thoughts of the two girls that had just left their table—especially the blonde. Almost.

"All right students and parents and faculty," started the familiar voice of Principal Grayson. She waited five seconds, counting it down in her head. "All right 2021 8th grade Graduation attendees." Another five. The crowd by that time had gotten the message.

Caitlyn and Kristen arrived back at the table, and Mike had to shush his almost-always- too-loud girlfriend as she was telling Caitlyn about something someone had whispered to her.

"And might I add 67th ANNUAL Wildwood Middle School Graduation attendees," she said, beaming. "So first I think we owe a round of applause to all the teachers and staff who made this all possible." The applause ensued and as quickly died. "The next commendation is due to Mrs. Marion Ellison, the leader of our very own Blue Key Society, of course patterned after that superior college to our southwest, the University of Florida." Some vociferous applause and a smattering of booing FSU fans were heard. "Now I assure you Marion and Blue Key those catcalls were not for your effort but more for my Gators shout out. Right everyone?" Here the applause tripled in intensity.

"All right everyone. As you know, Wildwood Middle is a school steeped in tradition, and tonight marks the 67th graduation ceremony we've undertaken. I've only been here ten years but I and most everyone who walks through that door feels connected to something larger and grander, and I assure you we work hard every day to uphold the values of our forefathers. And foremothers." She paused a few seconds and took a deep breath as she was smiling. "Tonight is about the celebration of all the wonderful memories and accomplishments over your three years here. You're the first class to lose a seventh-grade ceremony, but we persevered through that virus and still had our 66th class graduate last year, albeit virtually. This is due to what you parents and you students do every day to make this school what it is. I think you owe YOURSELVES a big round of applause!"

Knowing of her tendency to be long-winded, most of the crowd decided not to feed too much into this lest it lengthen, so the ensuing applause had been diminishing. Sensing this the principal cut to the chase.

"So I know you're all hungry, and these Blue Keyers are ready to serve you dinner, but first let me go over the night's events. The plan is first dinner, 45 minutes, then the journalism teacher Miss Thorssen will announce the superlatives for eighth grade that were voted on by the students and tallied by her. That's always fun and only takes about 15-20 minutes. Then we get a bit more serious with the awards. Students will receive awards from teachers in the form of plaques that each of them will present to their winners. But I want to warn you that we cap the number of plaques at two per teacher per subject, so your child will most likely NOT be receiving one of those tonight. Sorry I have to put it so bluntly but every year we get parent complaints. These are hard decisions for the teachers I assure you. There are however plenty of certificates that will be handed out. Awards take about an hour. Then there's dancing or just chatting for another 45 minutes. We hope to be done before 10:00."

Someone blurted out "Lightning game" which brought a great collective rustle from half of the men in the crowd and some women.

"Yes, we are aware that there is an important hockey game for some going on tonight, so that's why we're getting out by 10:00. Hopefully you are recording it?" Lawson said, chuckling. "Okay, without further ado I will let the students and their mentors do us the honor of serving dinner. There is a lot of food to be distributed, so even though they have plenty of help tonight . . ." she said, waving her hand in their direction, "we must be patient. Bon Appetit!"

Chris at this point was standing on the floor by his mom's laptop and trying to gauge when to start so the slideshow would finish close to the end of dinner. As Principal Grayson finished her speech and descended the steps to get to her table, Chris moved to intercept her.

"Excuse me. Principal Grayson?"

"Yes Chris. Ready to start the slideshow?"

"Definitely. But I just wanted to check that now would be okay. Is it looking like 45 minutes is realistic for dinner?"

"Yes I think so," the principal returned, surveying the scene of the heated food trays now pulled back for serving and the number of seventh grade students and adults serving. "I think we're right on schedule."

"Sounds good Mrs. G. Starting in a second," Chris returned, and moved back to the laptop, quickly pressing "Start Slideshow" and watching the first slide of the principal on the dais and hearing the piano introduction to Rascal Flatts' "My Wish" start simultaneously.

As Chris was creating it, he thought that this was good practice for game design. Not in any way the same thing but having to blend different creative elements together was similar to figuring out problems in gaming. He may be stuck on his game for now but he had mastered THIS. And this for now was more important.

Back at his table the servers had already served dinner rolls and drinks, and Chris noticed that Annie had ordered him iced tea. As he sat down four uniformed servers brought their meals, which consisted of a chicken breast with some kind of white sauce, green beans, and mashed potatoes.

"This looks really good," Anabel said, determined for once to eat all her meal and maybe even seconds and not beat herself up for it.

Lydia responded, "Well, if you're not vegan I guess it does." Chris noticed Lydia's low-cut dress and how she had pinned up her bright red hair on her head and wished that she hadn't. Bisected on her plate were some kind of garden salad with the other side of possibly quinoa and cottage cheese or yogurt.

"John, how do you stand for that, man?" Chris said to his friend, who laughed. "Do you guys like have to go to different restaurants, like pick up food for you before you end up in Callie's Flowers."

"That's gotta be the weirdest name for a restaurant that specializes in CAULIFLOWER," Alan said. "Get it? Callie-Flower! And it sounds like a florist shop!" This brought a raucous laugh more because of Lydia's vegan choices than the restaurant name from the boys at the table.

"You guys are so mean," Anabel said in defense of her friend.

"Okay, so you want me to start on one of my lectures on the benefits of a vegan lifestyle and the detriments of eating meat?" Lydia responded.

Chris and Alan in unison said, "Please No!"

"Then be nice," Anabel said, nudging Chris, who held up his hands to indicate okay.

Chris had just tasted the first bite of the chicken when Principal Grayson came up to him.

"Hello everyone. How's it going tonight?" she asked the table. A few nodded but no one responded, so she asked, "How's the food?"

Anabel had just swallowed her first chicken bite so she felt truthful in saying, "Really good Mrs. Grayson." A few others at the table then murmured their approval.

"Good to hear. At $14 a plate it better be!" the principal said, not bringing about the intended laughter. She then leaned down to Chris. "Chris, I've had a chance to preview the slideshow some and I wanted to tell you what a masterful job you did with it."

"Thank you Mrs. Grayson. It was all those great pictures that did most of the work."

"Nonsense," she replied. "I've put together a few of these myself and I know how much work it takes for the effects and music and choosing pictures and timing."

"It was a labor of love," Chris said, playing to the audience.

"That is true. And of course there are so many of you and Annie in there because of the crowns . . ." Chris nodded and she felt this was a good time to exit. "Okay, so you all enjoy the night, and let me know if you need anything. This night is for you."

"We will Mrs. Grayson. Thank you," Anabel said. Then to the table she said, "I'm gonna miss her."

"You are going to miss . . . Grayson?" Aria questioned. "Why? Other than these events she's just on our butts all the time. I swear I've still got MP3's playing in my head of her screaming at us in sixth grade."

Chris responded, "Guys. She's just doing her job. She's not that bad."

"Yeah, and I know her differently than you do because of my mom. She's always treated me different," said Anabel.

"Yeah, that's true. Nothing you can do about that," Alan said.

"But anyway, what she was saying about the slideshow is true," said Courtney. "These pictures are amazing. I've already seen two that I took back then."

"Yeah . . . you the man . . . Christopher," said Courtney's date Peter between chews and laughs.

"You know," Courtney said, staring at Peter. "I'm hoping that some of you BOYS grow up some over the summer so you won't embarrass yourselves OR US in high school."

"Grow up what?" said Alan. "It's just us here. We all know how to act around adults."

"Sure sure," she said, forking a bite of mashed potatoes in her mouth.

At that point Anabel swallowed and whispered to Chris, "They're right, though. This slideshow is really amazing. Great work."

He was going to respond but just then on the giant screen came a picture of the two of them at the dais, the coming crowns held hovering above their heads for a moment. Chris pointed to the screen and Anabel saw it. "Wow," she replied, and when Chris looked at her she was in rapt attention. "LOOK at us." Chris looked at the screen and the picture and went over the feelings associated with it after he had chosen it as he lay in his bed Thursday night. Well, technically this morning. It's funny how in such a short span of time how feelings can change, he thought.

After this and until the beginning of the superlatives portion of the program the conversation groups were myriad and diverse, with topics ranging from the Lightning game to what people were wearing in summer to high school. Early on, seeing that the topics were mainly split along gender lines, the boys moved together, as did the girls, so Chris didn't talk to Anabel again for a while.

"Yo best fren," Kristen said, hugging her. "Who now is with you agin." Having never gotten a hug from Kristen that didn't feel like a boa constrictor, she didn't disappoint here, and the spontaneity of it made her return hug stronger than usual.

She picked up on whatever dialect Kristen had affected and said, "You da bes'!" back.

To Kristen Mike said, "This is so weird, you know, seeing you with such a good friend and how close you guys are after not seeing each other for so long . . . "

"Girls never forget things, Michael, and definitely we don't forget people or BEST FRIENDS!" Caitlyn said. "Like remember that time in fourth grade when you wet your pants in class?"

Mike's mouth opened in an "O" and he stammered, "Bu-, but . . . I had just had surgery. I couldn't help it. My mom made me go to class two days later, which was insane."

"Aww, I still love ya Mikey," Kristen said, kissing him. "Some can't hold your liquor. You can't hold your pee."

Mike glared at Kristen. "So unfair!" he protested, and she kissed him again.

Brendan had done his best both carrying on his part of the Hedman conversation and listening to Caitlyn and was partly successful. Seeing her with another guy was strange to him. Well, not WITH with another guy, but even talking familiarly with another guy. He had felt just the tiniest pang of jealously which he instantly held in check. She was not his anymore.

Caitlyn turned from the snogging and back to her dinner and noticed that Brendan was looking at her expectantly and realized now that his sixth-grade cuteness had not entirely left him but was now pushed back some in favor of a stronger chin with a cleft, facial hair, and some acne. But he still had those piercing brown eyes.

"Hey, I really like your dress," he said, causing her to look down and straighten it. "It's the same color as the Elsa dress in sixth grade."

Caitlyn froze but hurriedly thought of something to say in response. "Well you know you were SUPPOSED to wear blue if you were a girl that night and that's all I had."

Brendan had hoped she would pick up on his lead and that the conversation would go somewhere, but her summary dismissal of it took him aback.

"Sure, yeah," he said. "Still I like your dress."

"Thank you," she said automatically. "You look nice too."

She then again stared at her plate and pretended she was having trouble cutting the rest of her chicken. When she looked up Brendan was looking at the slideshow.

Motioning to the screen, Brendan said, "Hey Cait. These are pretty cool right? I wonder if there any of us in there?"

"Of us? Why would there be?"

Brendan paused. "Well we were there together all night, and there are just so many random pictures here of everybody. Whoever made this did a good job of choosing the pictures. Not just of the king and queen you know?"

"Yeah, I guess so," she said, again looking down to her meal.

"Cait, I'm sorry if I said something to offend you. I didn't mean to."

"No, you didn't. It's just that . . . I've tried to spend two years forgetting that night. And I thought we were getting along well . . . I really liked being in your group for that game in history . . . "

"Yeah, that was fun," Brendan smiled briefly. "But I get it. That night wasn't exactly my favorite either."

She studied his face for sincerity, but then realized that he had always been sincere with her. He smiled empathetically back at her.

"Okay, so let's just not talk about that night again, okay," Caitlyn said.

"No problem. Done. But . . . can we still have a dance together?"

What flew through Caitlyn's head was: Is that a reference to what happened to us again or maybe to that dance those popular kids had and is he serious and could I possibly do that and would that just be inviting pain and but he's a nice kid and it's just a dance and he couldn't possibly have any INTENTIONS here beyond a dance could he and but we haven't seen each other in two years and that was one of the hardest things in my life to overcome and yeah but you know each other SOME and it's just a dance and what could it hurt and I'm sure Kristen would LOVE that.

What came out of Caitlyn's mouth after the above five-second pause that felt like a hundred to Brendan: "Sure."

"Great. Maybe they'll play a song you like."

Caitlyn had regained most of her senses now. "I doubt that will happen. This music is pretty predictable, and I'm pretty sure it's a timed slideshow, to the music. Not like there's a DJ here."

"Yeah you're right. Doesn't matter to me. I just thought that would be cool for you."

Trying to get over the creepy EJ deal, one of the selling points of her going to graduation tonight had become meeting up with the two 8th grade Wildwood band kids that she was going to audition for tomorrow, which due to getting used to Brendan again Caitlyn had forgotten about, until two kids walked from behind her and stood to Mike's right at the table.

"Caitlyn?" the girl asked. Caitlyn saw she was Hispanic, tall and thin, with a pierced nose and beautiful hair.

"Yes?" Caitlyn asked, then realized who she and boy standing next to her were. "Reese?"

"Guilty as charged" she said as she put her palm up.

"Heyyyy. How ya doin'?" Caitlyn said.

"Really good. Fun party tonight. Hey, this is Clive, our drummer," Reese said, hugging her bandmate. Clive was a few inches shorter than Reese and Caitlyn thought he didn't look anything like a typical drummer. Or maybe he did. She imagined the picture of REM drummer Bill Berry onstage in the eighties with a heavy unibrow and linked the unbroken brow of Clive in front of her to Berry's. If he's Bill Berry then he's good she thought.

"Hey Caitlin. Reese tells me you have good taste in music. That's awesome," Clive said, and she noticed he had drumsticks sticking out of his front pocket, thinking that those guys just have beats in their heads that they've gotta instantly be able to pound out. AND that this was a serious musician.

"Hi Clive. Good to meet you. Were you not at Wildwood in sixth grade? I was here then," Caitlyn replied.

"I moved here middle of seventh grade. From Texas. Navy," he said.

"Me too. Well, not Texas. I just got back from Guam a week ago," Caitlyn said.

"Aww man. Guam. Naval Base Guam. I had a friend go there once. That is SO far away, isn't it?"

"Yeah, just thousands of miles in the middle of nowhere," she said.

"My condolences!" said Clive.

"Clive! Be nice to our new maybe band member," Reese said, grabbing a stick from his pocket, hitting him on the shoulder, and then replacing it. That was good, Caitlyn thought, almost like it was rehearsed. Or maybe just "rehearsed" was on her mind now. "Hey, listen. We've got an extra seat at our table. Can we steal you for a few minutes to talk?"

Caitlyn looked at Kristen who was nodding Kristen-style almost like a bobblehead.

"Sure," Caitlyn replied, and rose to go with the pair.

After five minutes Caitlyn returned and noticed that everyone else was finished with their dinner so she set about doing the same.

"So?" Kristen asked. "Spill!"

Caitlyn took a drink of her water. "Went well. They're really cool. Gonna try out tomorrow at noon. I was so surprised when I answered that ad on Bandmix and then found out it was Reese."

Kristen slung an arm around her friend. "See? I told you it would be easy to get back into things. Look at all these people you know. Brendan. Mike. Reese and Clive."

Chris's table had been finished eating for some time, and most people in the gym at this point were either waiting for their dishes to be cleared or for awards to start, so much attention was being paid to the slideshow, with each successive slide met with either a groan or laugh or mock cheer or "Yessss!" by some boy wanting attention. Chris of course also watched his handiwork but watched more for reactions and how his program looked on the big screen than anticipated each slide as the others were doing. He had been cognizant of the timing for sure at the end of the first segment as people were through eating and awaiting awards and the beginning of the second segment post awards and his and Anabel's crown reveal. Judging from memory the images shown led him to think that this had to be close to the end of this segment. The principal was also watching the show with an eye on the laptop and the time, so she looked up just as the final slide, the funniest one in Chris's opinion that showed that dork Adam's attempt at breakdancing, spent the last of its 20 seconds on the screen. The audience roared for most of that time, and Chris knew that was a good choice.

The principal motioned to a PTSA mother who had been monitoring the show to turn off the laptop and projectors, and this happened in concert with the spotlight appearing and awaiting the principal on the dais and the sound of a few crashing plates that was caused by the sudden darkness.

"So again, thanks to Blue Key and Marilyn Lawson for the fabulous dinner and to Marilyn herself for the slideshow," the principal began using that principal voice that the kids knew all too well, and the spotlight swung abruptly from her to Marilyn, who though being instantly blinded by this unexpected tribute still managed to squint her eyes and wave. The light swung back and quickly found the principal, caught with a "What the—" expression on her face caused by the too-active spotlight person.

"And so . . . on to the awards," she said. "First we have some superlative awards to give out. The students like these because they have actually VOTED for these, unlike the teachers who choose theirs. In some schools these make the yearbook, but traditionally we've given them out at graduation, which is yet another reason it's so special. Our yearbook sponsor Theresa Thorssen conducts the poll with her journalism class but only she knows the winners and she keeps these under lock and key until tonight. So here she is."

Miss Thorssen was still unmarried at 55 and looked every part of the classic schoolmarm teacher from days of yore. She started climbing the stairs from her waiting position at the bottom. Despite sporting a throwback look of a hundred or more years, students really liked her because of her good-natured charm, this proven here by most 8th graders applauding. She thanked the principal and took the mic.

She started with her own brand of folksiness that was in sharp contrast to the rigidity of Principal Lawson.

"Hello students. Good to see you all again, and you looking so fine in your fancy clothes." Here she put a hand on her hip. "Now why couldn't you dress like this every day?" she said, smiling. Getting little reaction, she continued. "So, you all know that you voted in homeroom, first to nominate and then to choose winners, for twenty categories. I know you're itchin' to know the winners, so here we go. Winners, come up these steps," she said with a gesture, "take your certificate from Principal Grayson," then pointed to the steps that she had just ascended, "And go down those." She pointed to the opposite steps.

       Back at Caitlyn's table, she was thinking that other than being with Kristen and a few other close friends seeing her former yearbook teacher again was the highlight of returning to Wildwood. Upon entering her class with Kristen on Monday the teacher spotted her and just lost it, running up to her and hugging her. Miss Thorssen had then re-introduced her to the class and Caitlyn had felt at home. She just has a way of doing that, Caitlyn thought.

       Mike and Kristen were whispering to one another, and Brendan noticed Caitlyn deep in thought. He had been stealing looks at her, and this done quite successfully for the better part of the last half-hour, picking and choosing his spots and not holding the gaze for long, but this time she started out of her reverie and saw him. She looked back at Brendan and he smiled, which brought a return smile from her. Since the principal was still speaking she just mouthed "What?" at him, but he just kept smiling and then shrugged.

       "So our first winner, for "Best Smile' is . . . drum roll please," Miss Thorssen said, which brought a half-frown from the principal and dozens of table-drummers and one that sounded real. Caitlyn thought maybe THAT was why Clive had brought the drumsticks, then dismissed it. I'm sure he carries them everywhere, like I do a book.

       Miss Thorssen nodded approvingly to the drummers and then said, "Brendan Ellison." Some people applauded, probably mostly parents, and some kids laughed. Caitlyn looked to Brendan and then saw him shrink two sizes. He stared hard at the table and blinked a few times, not making eye contact with her. This was clearly a joke, she thought, a bad one, and probably really destructive for him. They were punishing him for not being friendly without any clue who he is or what has made him that way.

"Brendan? Where are you?" Miss Thorssen asked. Shame and embarrassment shot through Brendan's mind, but he realized he could probably walk the distance to the dais and up the steps and back without killing anyone, so he willed himself to get up. At this point Caitlyn started clapping loudly to encourage him. He turned and looked at her before he left and she saw his blank expression. Well, it could be worse, she thought.

After Brendan left, Kristen was incensed. "That's a really shitty thing to do," she said. "And they know what effect it'll have on him. Jerks." Caitlyn rarely saw her friend get angry, although for this it was justified. And then Kristen, being Kristen, stood up and took turns staring at each table, her face a mask of pissed-off. This stopped the chatter that was taking place after the initial reactions, and then Miss Thorssen noticed her yearbook editor standing at her table. Thinking she was going to say something related to the superlative awards, she waited her out.

Caitlyn placed a hand on her friend's back. "Kids are such jerks," she said. "C'mon Kris. Sit."

Kristen felt her hand and heard her words but was intent on staring the other tables down and forcing them to feel the blood that was on their hands. After Brendan received his award and was exiting the steps the silence stretched out for 15 seconds.

"Our next award is for--. Kristen, is everything all right?" Heads that were not already turned to her now did. A few seconds passed. "Kristen, are you okay?" Caitlyn knew that Kristen and Miss Thorssen were like white on rice. Kristen was THE yearbook editor, her right-hand man. The teacher noticed Caitlyn next to her. "Caitlyn honey. Is everything all right?"

Caitlyn started to respond, but Kristen, still sporting that stern look, swung her head to the teacher and said, "No, things really aren't all right, Miss Thorseen. That was a low blow guys." Miss Thorssen didn't understand what was happening, so she paused and hoped that her star student would finish soon and sit. Principal

Grayson was weighing whether or not she should intervene. Outbursts such as this could spoil the whole festivities, she thought. Do sit down, girl! Kristen sat down.

Principal Grayson looked to the still-shaken teacher who was holding the mic down at her side and realized that she needed to do something. Taking the mic temporarily from her, she said, "Okay, that's our first award. What's next Theresa?" and held out the mic for her to take. This had the effect of forcing composure on Miss Thorssen and she took the mic and continued with the second superlative.

The effect of the Brendan superlative award brought different reactions at Chris's table, still seated by gender and now separated by reaction. The girls had murmured "That's terrible" and "That's mean" and "Who would do that?", while the boys had stifled laughs into their hands and one had even said "Got heem!"

Anabel noticed this. "You guys are such jerks, you know?" more to Chris but to them all.

Chris recovered to say, "Annie. It was just a joke. Seriously."

"Joke or no joke you KNEW the effect it would have on him. On the kid who RARELY smiles." The three other guys looked properly chastised, but Chris didn't.

"Like you've never played a joke on anyone, right?" Chris said.

Anabel glared at him. "Not a vicious one like that. No," she returned. Chris shrugged. "Did you not think that this would happen? Did you see Brendan walking up to get the award? He looked devastated."

"EVERYONE looks devastated doing that, getting in that spotlight. WE were devastated back in sixth grade, remember?"

"That was different," she said. "That wasn't a joke, Chris."

"Wasn't it?" he said. The others at the table, theirs faces in fearful anticipation, were now wishing they were anywhere except in the middle of this lover's spat.

"What does THAT mean?" Anabel shot back.

"Well, I mean. Why did we win, Annie? Ever think of that? Us winning I mean? I mean wow. THAT was an upset, right? THAT was a vote, just like this one. Maybe THAT was a joke on us, right? Do you know for sure that it wasn't?"

"You are such an asshole," she said, and threw down her napkin and left the table.

"Dude," said Alan. "Go get her."

Chris waved at him dismissively. "She'll be fine. Been through this dozens of times. She storms off. Cools off. Comes back. And usually even apologizes."

"I don't think you're going to get that here, Chris," Peter said, which brought a nod from his date Courtney.

"Yeah man. What we did wasn't cool. Brendan's a good guy," John said.

"How would you know, John?" Chris said back. "Ever talk to the guy?" John shook his head. "Yeah, that's what I thought. Anyone here ever had a conversation with the guy?" The table was silent.

"Yeah that's what I thought," Chris said, believing his point made.

Lydia, the smallest and one of the most sheepish girls in eighth grade, got up the courage to say, "But that doesn't mean he deserves that." Chris looked at her in surprise that she had spoken. "People go through all kinds of things that you never know. My sister has a friend whose mother had cancer and was dying, and---"

"Yeah yeah yeah," Chris said, turning from her, hearing someone mutter something about him being a dick as he did. Chris tried to blot out his table by acting like he was paying attention to the awards.

His thoughts in an attempt to blot all this out wandered to his game and what he could do to fix it when he was snapped out of it by Miss Thorssen saying, "The next award is for 'Best Glow Up'" At the time he had voted he knew that his girlfriend was a shoo-in for this one but now he didn't give a rat's ass. "And our winner is . . . Anabel Donan."

Anabel had been standing against the gym's wall during this interval and was likewise jolted out of her thoughts by this announcement. She straightened her dress before slowly making her way toward the dais. She accepted the award from the teacher amidst much applause and a catcall or two but thoughts of Chris being such a jerk wouldn't leave her head. Despite this, she thought it made sense to return to her table.

She sat down, and Chris put his hand on her thigh and said, "You okay now?"

She glared at him, then brushed his hand away. "Sure Chris. I'm 'okay'." He withdrew his hand. Anabel sat and stewed.

Chris whispered "Get ready" to her, and she mouthed "For what" back and then realized what was probably to follow. As the superlatives continued, no one could have been surprised at the final one. "For 'Best Couple' the winners are . . . Chris Lawson and Anabel Donan."

Chris rose and grabbed her hand, and despite her near repulsion for him right now she plastered a smile on her face and allowed herself to be led to the stage. They each took their certificates and Chris brought the ire of the principal when he lifted his up over his head in celebration. Anabel looked at him dumbfounded but then realized what they must be seeing on her face and changed it to a thin smile. Chris made a motion to her hand that was holding the award to grab it and hoist it up likewise and she parried it with her free hand. She then started down the steps in hopes of beating him back to the table and ignoring him there for as long as possible.

Principal Grayson was handed the mic by Miss Thorssen. "All right, students. Congratulations to those of you who got superlative awards. After just a five-minute break we'll begin the academic awards. This is a good time to use the facilities!" Many in the crowd stood up, if not to take her advice at least to take a stretch break.

When Brendan had sat down with his award Caitlyn could see suffering writ large over his entire body. She had to try to talk him off the ledge, so she started by saying what jerks those kids are, and that he was friendly if you bothered to get to know him, and that he should just throw that award away, and somehow—it worked. Kristen chimed in too, and Brendan told her how much he appreciated what she did. Then, right at the end of her pep talk was the early stages of the promised five minutes of break time from the principal, so Brendan grabbed his award and started walking with it by his side purposefully. Kristen, Mike, and Caitlyn all watched as he shielded the crowd with a back turn from a trashcan on the wall and threw the award in. They all applauded when he arrived back at the table, including Mike, who said, "That shit is gone!" and gave Brendan a fist bump, which made him smile.

Caitlyn then thought of another way to cheer him up. She was sitting directly across from him, so she took a tube of lipstick out of her purse and wrote on the tablecloth, white poster paper stitched together, "I'm so sorry that happened Bren," then held up the end of the paper on her end so he could more easily see it.

Kristen noticed that and said, "Hey. That's a great idea" and reached for hers. Seeing her intention and relishing the chance to participate, Brendan pointed to Kristen's lipstick and then to himself and put on a sad clown face and clasped his hands in prayer. "Oh. All right," she said, realizing this would facilitate the game for them. She tossed it to Brendan.

The rest of his and Caitlyn's conversation was in Red Dahlia and Electric Orchid, with the two taking turns writing something and then raising that portion of the paper so it could be more easily read by the other.

Thanks. Yeah, that was pretty stupid

Why would they do that to you, Bren?

Cause people suck

That's not fair. Kristen doesn't suck. I don't suck. Right?

There are exceptions to everything. But . . . few

People are not that bad, if you give them a chance

People like that? Seriously Cait?

They're just immature. Boys are late to that you know!

Not ALL boys

See, you're making my point

Arrgh. Score one for you

You forgot how smart I am, didn't you?

Most definitely! Hey, I have an idea

Mike, lost in his own oral conversation with Kristen, noticed what was happening. He nudged Kristen, who smiled.

"Hey, what're you two doin' over there?" he said.

"Look at you two, gettin' all chummy again. Lovin' it!" Kristen said, her forefinger raised in triumph.

"Have you guys ever noticed how my girlfriend likes to take all the credit for things?"

Caitlyn broke her silence. "Credit? Kristen? Never!"

Kristen hugged her. "Love ya sis."

Brendan then broke his silence with "Hey. Would it be possible for me to switch seats with you guys? I'm out of writing space."

Kristen quickly replied, "Sure, sure. Anything for you Brendan. But not for you Cait." She stuck her tongue out at her friend. Kristen was worth more than all the tea in China, as Caitlyn's grandmother said.

So the pair switched seats. Caitlyn at first thought that this proximity was intimidating but then remembered she was seated right next to him in class and did fine. Brendan thought that this was really feeling right, that anyone who could that easily snap me out of a funk that deep was special. Then he thought: Of course she's special, and of course she's done that before, recalling a few times she had pierced his veil of anger previously. They chatted all during the academic awards segment, as neither was receiving any, and although Kristen and Mike each received a couple of awards that distracted them from their "getting reacquainted" conversation, Caitlyn a few times saw Kristen stop their talk and look hers and Brendan's way. And just smile that Cheshire Cat smile.

As the awards commenced and student after student went parading down the stairs clutching their shiny plaque or embossed certificate Caitlyn and Brendan took little notice. During this time Kristen returned with her journalism plaque which was laser-etched with the front cover of the three books Kristen had worked on and Miss Thorssen's signature and tried to show it to Caitlyn, but her friend was too preoccupied to see it.

Since Chris's table was filled with some of the brightest kids in the school and the most athletic, their table was well-endowed with hardware and certificates, and as it went on each pushed theirs to the center of the table to allow themselves more room, creating a nucleus of wood, metal, and paper in the center.

Anabel had received certificates for art and Principal's Honor Roll for three nine weeks, but this was sullied by her knowledge that she wouldn't have received it for the fourth because of that Geometry "B." Chris as usual got more awards than her: PE, Principal's Honor Roll, DIT, and a plaque for "Best Scholar Athlete." Anabel knew they were almost done because her mother had told her that the final awards were for individual subject, and Ms. Saunders was just giving her for the first academic subject— language arts. Her mother had also said that a student couldn't win more than one "plaque" award because Mrs. Grayson was against the idea of one student winning several. She vaguely wondered which award Chris would receive. Probably history. Mrs. Heller LOVED him.

After another ten minutes their Geometry teacher Mr. Ridgely stepped onto the dais and started talking about the student that was getting his award, but without mentioning his/her name. This was a common strategy among teachers, this drawing it out, but torturous for those who thought it really might be them. "This award goes to a student that had the top average of all my students. Who in class helped others when I asked this person to . . ." At this point Anabel knew who it was. The one person whose win would disturb her most. Because it was the class she just never really got. The class she struggled in all year. The class that this person found effortless. And the person that sometimes refused to help HER when asked to. "So the award for top Geometry student this year goes to . . . Chris Lawson."

Applause at their table was overly loud and instant, startling Anabel, who did her best not to look at Chris as he arose and strode to the dais. When he was at the top with the teacher Mr. Ridgely pumped his hand repeatedly and then HUGGED him. This just added to her misery, and she did her best to smile at him as he returned. Knowing that she had to break out of her funk before the crown reveal, she closed her eyes and took five deep breaths. She could do this. Chris got up and walked to the laptop once again, receiving congratulations from a few students on the way.

Principal Grayson said, "And those are our academic awards for the year. We are so proud of the accomplishments of our students. They all deserve a round of applause." The crowd obliged her again. "So now we begin the dance and chat portion of our show. I'm also told there is dessert to be had in the form of brownies and apple pie, soft drinks and coffee, at the tables to my right. Enjoy everyone!"

Chris had prepared to start the final slideshow segment with its second set of chosen songs, and with the principal's announcement now did so with Blackpink's "Ice Cream," a popular song Chris was sure the kids would love. He thought of the later crown reveal that he and Annie would do at the slideshow's conclusion which would serve as a fitting end to their middle school lives together.

When Chris returned to his table only Anabel was there.

"Ha! I knew they'd love 'Ice Cream'. A good first choice," Chris said.

"Oh yeah. Kids love this song," she said, finding the rhythm and starting to move to it from her seat as she watched others on the dance floor.

"I don't know why."

She stopped moving and looked at him. "Then why did you choose it?"

"It's not for me. It's everyone. I figured they'd want to listen to crap music so I'd give it to them."

"Are you just trying to piss me off tonight, Chris. Just because you don't like it doesn't mean its crap. What's your deal?"

"What 'deal'? Just telling the truth.

"Just because these kids don't know every Led Zeppelin song like you do you think they listen to crap?

"No. Not for that reason, although that IS a good reason. But they still listen to a lotta crap," he said.

She turned away from him and again looked toward the floor. The song had ended, and the other kids at the table returned.

"Great choice, Chris," Courtney said, adjusting her dress.

"See?" Chris said to Anabel.

"Sure!" she replied. The others realized that this ongoing battle between the two had not abated.

"You two need to make up and play nice," Aria offered.

Chris said, "You're right," and leaned in and kissed Anabel on the cheek, causing her to move away from him. He shrugged. "But it was still a good suggestion Aria," Chris said, shrugging.

"Hey, listen man. I'll take her off your hands for a dance," John said.

At the prospect of escape Anabel quickly rose and said, "Let's go!" John came around and the two of them moved onto the floor and started dancing to the next song.

Chris thought he'd reciprocate. "Lydia, may I have the pleasure?" he asked, holding up his upturned palm.

"Anything for you, Chris," she replied.

As the pair danced Chris was able to admire Lydia and her red hair more closely and briefly thought that maybe he could get Annie to dye her hair red and imagined what that would look like. She would do it for him. Just like she'd become blonde.

At the end of the dance the four of them returned to their table.

"Have fun?" Chris asked Anabel.

"Absolutely. You?" Clearly she had seen him with Lydia.

"Definitely."

Anabel attempted to turn to talk to Courtney, who was seated next to her, but Chris leaned in and whispered to her "Hey." She turned to him. "What would you think if I asked you to dye your hair red?"

"What is wrong with you?" she whispered back.

"No. I'm just asking."

"You're 'just asking' because you just danced with Lydia and became so entranced by her hair that you just couldn't help yourself."

"That's not true. It's something I've thought about before."

"When you were fawning over Emma Stone you mean?"

"C'mon Annie . . . "

"Okay so I'll just end this by saying NO. Done."

"You didn't have this reaction when I asked you to go blonde."

"That was . . . a long time ago," Anabel said, turning from him fully now.

Chris laughed. "Yeah. In a galaxy far, far away, right?"

While talking to her friends Anabel was keeping an eye on the time, and as it was getting closer to the crown reveal the songs were getting slower and less danceable and she was getting more anxious. She asked Chris what the song before the crown reveal was, and he said it was Miley Cyrus's "I'll Always Remember You." Perfect. She asked him to dance that dance with her, and to give her a few minutes warning before it came on and he agreed. Chris walked over to the laptop and checked the time. Seeing that the song was just minutes away, he walked back to the table. He tapped her on the shoulder and she turned around. "It's almost time already."

"Okay, sounds good," Annie returned. "Hey ya'll. This next song is the next-to-last song. Anyone else wanna go out with Chris and me?"

Alan and Aria looked at one another. "Yeah, let's do it," he said.

To Anabel Chris said, "You do realize that's not a fast song. It's more like a power ballad."

"Yeah. I know that song. That's fine," she said. She smiled at him and took his hand and kissed it which REALLY confused him. Not the gesture, which she did sometimes, but . . . Annie usually holds a grudge for a long time, he thought. Too long. Maybe she's just done with arguing? Chris stood up.

"Okay, you ready?" Anabel said to Alan and Aria.

"Yep," said Alan.

The four dancers made their way onto the floor. Chris noticed Principal Grayson standing looking at the laptop and she nodded at him. She looked happy that he and Anabel were in position to be ready for the crowns right after that. He returned an "OK" symbol to her.

Back at Caitlyn's table, Brendan looked at Caitlyn and squeezed her hands. "Okay, this may be crazy, but I'm still going to ask." He took a deep breath. "Do you wanna dance with me?"

"Dance . . . with . . . you?" Shock registered on her face. Brendan looked at Kristen and her mouth was agape and she had grabbed Mike with her right hand.

"Yeah. That's what I figured. Bad idea. I'd embarrass you and—"

"Of COURSE I want to dance with you. Sure you're okay with that? Wait? Did Kristen put you up to this. Cause we really don't have to do that, Bren. I'm fine with just sitting here and talking you know."

"No, she didn't. Well, yes she mentioned it to me but I actually LIED to her because I had thought of it first. It's just . . . something I'd like to share with you." She smiled at him. "The problem is I have no idea how to dance, so here's my strategy. I'd like to watch a couple of dances to see how kids are doing it before we get out there. Okay?"

"Brendan! That's really not necessary. No one's going to be watching us. They're just doing their own thing."

"Cait, I just agreed to DANCE with you. Just humor me, okay?"

"Um, okay. We watch a couple then we hit the floor. Got it."

Caitlyn was seated in front of him, so Brendan had to lean in closer to her to see more of the action on the floor. When he did this he smelled her hair, which served to instantly take his focus off the dance floor. Then of course this led to looking at her hair, wavy and blonde and just past her shoulders. She turned around and said, "See. Really not that hard," and he nodded. When she turned back around he got another whiff, thought about touching it but decided against it, and decided to lay his chin gently on top of her shoulder. At first it startled her, but she turned slightly and said "Hey" and completely allowed it. They stayed that way for a few songs and then Caitlyn said, "You ready?"

"As I'll ever be," he said, and the pair walked out onto the floor.

As the Hannah Montana song started, Chris and Anabel leaned into one another and moved rhythmically. After the brief guitar introduction Anabel started quietly singing and it was clear to Chris early that she knew every word.

"Man, you got this song down," Chris said, pulling away enough from her to be seen.

"I've always loved this song," Anabel returned. They went back to Anabel putting her head on his chest turned away from him. She sang the second verse even louder, and Chris realized by listening to her sing that this was probably the perfect song for their graduation. It mentioned laughter and tears, which there were plenty of this week around the school, and then how hard it is to say goodbye, which was perfect. He didn't get the "so much pain" lyric, which unless he was mistaken Anabel sang louder than the rest.

As the song continued Chris continued to listen to her singing but tried to focus to see if she actually was highlighting certain words, phrases, or lines. When the song was just about over, Chris again separated from her. "Great singing Annie."

"Did you just compliment me, Christopher? Does that mean you're stopping being a—"

"Yes, I'm done."

"Well that's a relief," Anabel said, wiping her brow of imaginary sweat.

"I'm curious though why you emphasized certain lines in it. Like your voice got louder and higher on some."

"Oh, I don't know. I didn't realize it. Isn't that what everyone does to favorite lines or parts of songs when they sing?"

"They just seemed to mean something. Like the line about keeping the times she's had like a photograph," Chris said.

"Well yeah okay that's just about perfect for what's going to happen next, right. Totally makes sense. What else you got?"

'   "Something like 'every day we had I'll keep 'em here inside'?"

"Well that fits us and this situation, right? We have had a LOT of days together," Anabel said. "What else?" He looked at her, and it looked like she was having . . . fun?

"Something about crying today."

"That totally fits this too, doesn't it? We may never see some of these people again. It's a time of separation. Peoples' lives will be different after today . . . "

"Okay," Chris said. "Makes sense I guess. But then the bit about 'crying'."

"Oh, I'm sure there will be tears tonight, and beyond."

"I feel like there's something I'm missing here," he said, studying her face. She leaned in and kissed him full on the lips and held it for a couple of seconds. As she pulled away his face was still puzzled.

"Hey, you're the one who picked the songs. Don't blame me."

"I just used a playlist," Chris returned.

"Sure," she said, and the song ended, sending the pair up the stairs to get their crown bags for the big reveal.

Caitlyn and Brendan had let the song that was on end before starting to dance. When the Hannah Montana song came on Caitlyn started moving her shoulders and hips to the beat. Brendan was looking at her for a cue as to what he should do. She gestured at her moving body, and Brendan started a pale imitation of her. But at least he's doing SOMETHING, Caitlyn thought. She let him try to find some groove for 20 seconds and then intervened.

"Your shoulders are too stiff and you're not moving your waist much. Loosen those!"

Brendan took a stab once again at mimicking her and exerted more energy into his movements back and forth.

"You're getting it. Good. Now watch my feet," Caitlyn instructed. She moved her feet back and forth in rhythm, picking one at a time up off the ground. "See that?" She pointed down. "When you move your feet your body has to go with it. It's forced to."

He again tried to copy her movements and found this made everything easier.

"Yeah, so most guys just stay rooted to the ground and it looks funny," Caitlyn said. Brendan half-frowned. "But not you Bren. Just lookit those feet move." This of course made him more self-conscious, so he stared at his feet a few seconds to make sure he was doing it right.

Once finished tutoring, Caitlyn started to sing the song, eventually belting out the chorus loudly. Brendan looked around. "This doesn't sound like your kind of music, from what I've heard."

"It's not," she said. "I used to watch Hannah Montana all the time as a kid. This was an important song in that show."

"Okay," he returned.

The song ended, and Caitlyn started walking toward their seats.

"One more?" Brendan asked. She turned around to see him looking very cute in his same spot, beckoning her with his body, his outstretched hand, and his eyes.

"Brendan Ellison. I think this DANCING thing suits you well!" Caitlyn said, eagerly joining him for round two.

"Well, I'm enjoying dancing with you," he replied.

"Likewise, sir," she said, bowing to him.

"Isn't that supposed to be a curtsy?"

"I am continually surprised by the breadth of your knowledge," Caitlyn said, and did her attempt at a curtsy."

"That's better," he said, bowed to her and then took her hand in his and pulled her closer.

Caitlyn noticed Chris and Anabel walking up to the stage. They retrieved cases and walked down the stairs.

"Oh, is this like that dance thing in sixth grade. These same two are gonna dance again I guess. But what are they holding?" Caitlyn asked.

Brendan explained to her the crown decorating tradition.

"And you know this . . . how?" Caitlyn asked.

"Morning show," Brendan replied.

"Oh, okay," she said. "Does that mean we can't dance anymore? Because this is probably the last dance . . ."

"Dunno," Brendan said.

The spotlight then was trained on a center spot on the floor near where they were.

"Bren, come on. Let's move over here," she said. They moved closer to the entrance doors but just out of range of one of the projectors whose images had been changing for most of the ceremony but was now paused. The kids moved into the spotlight and looked toward the dais. After they got situated, the light moved back to the principal.

"All right everyone," Principal Grayson said. "Tonight has been wonderful, hasn't it?" Applause. "And to anyone and everyone who had a hand in its success, I thank you." She slightly bowed her head and touched her heart. "So Wildwood Middle School Eighth graders, about to scatter to the wind for the summer and high school, with some of you going to our feeder school Lakewood High and others elsewhere. This is the final piece of tradition we have for graduation. This will be the 63rd crown reveal, and I still think it's a fine idea."

Chris and Anabel had begun unzipping the covers and pulling out their crowns. Anabel didn't know what to do with hers, so Chris took it and his and disappeared for quite a while. When he returned, Anabel whispered to him, "What took you so long?"

"I had to remind AP Blaisdell to start the slideshow when Grayson finishes."

"This is crazy. I can hardly see my crown."

"That's the idea," said Chris, which drew a questioning look from Anabel. "Hey," he added. Let me go first with the crown, okay?" to which she nodded.

Grayson continued. "Usually our Fire King and Ice Queen from sixth grade are still here as graduating eighth graders, so their job is to show how they've changed in those two years, and to share this with their opposite. What makes this year so special is that our couple has stayed TOGETHER for two years. Usually I have no idea who is dating whom in our school." A few snickers.

The principal continued. "Well, who could blame me. I'm NOT a student and some of these things last a day and then they're gone. But everyone at the school for two years has known about Chris and Anabel. So yes this is a special one." She paused a second. "Now, this is their time together, but since this IS the last song, please everyone dance one last time if you want to." She looked toward the laptop. "I see my trusty right-hand man Mr. Blaisdell is ready. So, once again, thank you for coming. Thank you for raising such wonderful young people parents. I truly wish each of you the best in high school and in your life."

Brendan and Caitlyn had been standing inches from one another, she still trying to comprehend his newfound confidence on the dance floor. Brendan noticed her puzzled look. "It's you," he said.

"What's me?" she returned.

"That's why I'm smiling. It's just you," he said, and pulled her in for a hug.

"Aw, Bren. You too." She pulled back some. "Isn't this crazy how we have just clicked again after so long?"

"Well, like Kristen said, you're not just some OTHER girl." Caitlyn again was puzzled. Brendan backpedaled. "Oh yeah. I mean you're not just like other people. Sorry, that was out of context." Caitlyn smiled at him.

The guitar and drums then kicked into the Death Rattle song "Forever" and it only took Brendan a second to place the song and the accompanying feelings came quickly. He swallowed and took a step back from her. At the same time Caitlyn's eyes widened and she put her hands up in front of her in a "wait" gesture. Unsure of what to do, Brendan froze. Caitlyn put a hand to her forehead. She began shaking her head slowly from side to side and breathing heavily.

"No, no, no. This can't be happening. Can't be happening," she managed.

"Caitlyn, it's different now." He moved to her. "That's a long time ago."

Staring at the floor, she took a deep breath to still her hyperventilation and willed the shock to leave her. Brendan touched her and she took a step back. "Okay, okay," he said, retreating. "Just tell me what you want to do here." Caitlyn was still trying to compose herself, so he suggested, "Let's just go back to our seats, okay?"

Caitlyn looked from the floor to him and took a few more breaths. "No. I'm okay. I can do this. Let's just keep going."

"You sure, Cait. Really? I mean, I don't want this to spoil the night," Brendan replied.

"It won't. I can manage. You're right. Long time ago. Water under the bridge. Okay, let's go," she said, starting slowly but eventually finding a faster back and forth movement that she knew he must try to emulate.

Chris realized that to time out what he wanted to happen that the slideshow needed to be paused a couple of minutes. That's why he had thrown a glitch in the system that would lock up the slideshow for a few minutes if someone else decided to try to solve the gremlin he'd inserted but one that Chris could easily undo in a few seconds. Both Anabel and Chris held their crowns behind their backs. Just as he was going to begin, Anabel looked up at the screen behind Chris and saw the frozen shot of them when they had just begun to dance.

"Wow. Look Chris. Look how little we were then."

"Yep."

"Why isn't it starting? The song?" she said.

"Dunno," he lied.

Then a second slide projected, and this was the surprise on Chris's face when he was announced the Fire King winner.

"You were so surprised then," Anabel said.

He smirked. "I wonder why that was?"

"What does that mean?"

"I mean," Chris said, "I wonder why I wore a deer-in-the-headlights look there." He smirked at her.

"I'm not following," she said.

"You're right. You didn't follow. You led."

"Can you just get on with showing me your crown, Chris?" Her face showed exasperation.

"Sure thing Annie."

The crazy thing about this song, Caitlyn thought, is that it was one of my favorites---WAS being the operative word. Then the necklace thing happened. Then I've avoided it like the plague.

"Hey, you all right," Brendan said after another minute had passed. He had found her rhythm and had matched or exceeded her movements.

"Sure. And I can see you are." She smiled. "I think dancing is your thing, Bren." She moved more exaggeratedly to mimic him. He laughed.

"No. You know what I mean. Are you okay with this . . . this song?"

"Apparently so. Just look at me go."

"Oh, I'm noticing you go, believe me."

Chris carefully pulled out his crown from the black carrying case and Anabel could see at first glance that he had done a passable job of not destroying the delicate inlay the school had made that fit inside the crown proper. And that he had attached all 7 pictures as prescribed by the great-great grandparents of yesteryear at Wildwood.

"I'm impressed that you followed directions and kept it so nice," she said.

"I follow directions when I need to," he returned. He held the crown in front of him. "Okay, so we've been briefed on this, right? First we state the theme of what we did and next why you chose each picture'.

"Um okay but Chris this is just us. You really want to do that? Not just exchange and see for ourselves."

"We must adhere to tradition, because tradition has put us here, and tradition we will follow until we're out of here," Chris said, the smirk returning.

"Sure. Whatever. Just go," Anabel said.

"My theme is the path from right before I met you until now."

"That's not really a theme, Chris." Still the smirk.

"You know what? I'm going to do this the way I want to do this. You can stay or leave, Annie."

"Wow. Just that quickly you snap back to whatever you've been intent on being tonight. I'll just stop trying to name it."

"Yes. You just stop and sit back. I'm the architect tonight." She rolled her eyes. "And architecture, at least metaphorically, is something you're pretty good at too."

"Just get on with it. This is bullshit."

"Okay, here goes."

Anabel had since set her crown behind her, so here she crossed her arms on her chest and waited. His first picture was of his shock at being chosen Fire King from sixth grade. Chosen for obvious reasons. The second was a still little Chris connecting perfectly with a pitch at the plate. To show how he'd gotten better at baseball. The third was winning the speech contest in 7th grade. Because he used to be scared to speak in front of crowds.

Chris saw the alarmed look on the principal's face and said to Anabel, "Hey, the song's still not started, and the slideshow is stuck. I'm gonna have to start it" and moved toward the laptop. When he was gone the three pictures collectively just hit her. There were none of her. Chris then reappeared and picked up the crown. The song "Forever" had just started.

Anabel gestured to his crown. "Chris, do you have any of me on there? Of us on there?"

"All good things come to those who wait, Anabel."

"Sure. Can you end this soon please? This game you're playing is like an 'in-joke" I'm watching but not getting."

Chris explained that his fourth picture was a picture of him atop the geometry board in Ms. Ridgely's class, showing him with the highest average: 99.5%. Again he had said for obvious reasons. The fifth was a screenshot of his Neverwinter module, in progress. Chosen because he was proud of what he had done, even if it wasn't finished.

"Of course the damn game picture gets in there instead of me."

Ignoring this, he continued. The sixth picture was of he and his male friends posing like bodybuilders at the beach. He said these were friends he'd had since elementary school and they were still together, like brothers. The seventh picture was a split screen shot of his yearbook pictures in sixth grade and then eighth grade.

Anabel shook her head slowly back and forth.

Just as Caitlyn and Brendan had found a workable flow for dancing together and Caitlyn had calmed herself, the last picture that she had seen on Rachel's phone back in sixth grade came on once again. The picture that had literally haunted some dreams. That made her feel like a guy could never want her. Brendan saw her eyes widen, then looked up to see the photo that had ruined his life.

Caitlyn backed away from him. "No no no," she said wildly. "I just can't. I just can't. I can't do this again. This was a mistake." Brendan again felt helpless, this time from his own shock as well as hers. "I'm sorry, Brendan. I just can't."

She slowly backed away from him and toward the gym doors.

"So you had NO pictures of me? No pictures of us? What the hell, Chris?"

"This is true," Chris said, pulling in his lips and then letting them out with a slight smack.

"Is this some kind of message that you're sending me, Chris? Is that what your behavior was about tonight too? Are you just out to get me?"

"The message will be clear when the night is done," Chris said smugly, nodding.

"Okay, so let's just end this now. Here's my crown. Just take it and look at it." She thrust the crown in his direction. At this Chris set his back down but didn't take the offered one. "Why won't you take it?!"

"We have traditions to uphold here, Annie. You have to tell me your theme, show me your choices. Just like I did."

"Why are you so hung up on TRADITION, Chris? You can't stand ceremonies."

"Well, it was tradition that led us to this moment, right? So let's play this thing out for all its worth."

"Okay, whatever, I'll do mine, FAST, but then I think we need to talk."

"Fast would be good. And indeed we do—need to talk that is," Chris said.

Anabel screamed with her mouth closed and started to explain her first picture.

Chris interrupted her. "Um, breach of protocol. Must do the theme first."

"The theme. What? Sure, okay? My theme is becoming my own person. Good enough." He nodded. She continued. The first picture of she and Chris at the beach she chose because it showed them as a couple. The next was of their families at the restaurant because their families were close. The third was she and Nessa in a heap after a game of Twister. Because I love my sisters. The next was cooking a Thanksgiving meal, the first she had ever cooked in sixth grade with her mom chosen because her mom was the best. The fifth was of her doing an ocean clean-up day at Jacksonville Beach because over the last two years she'd volunteered more. The sixth was of her studying Geometry. Chris chuckled.

"You are an ass," she said. He shrugged.

She had chosen that one because even though she'd gotten a "B" this last semester she was proud of herself because she used to be an average math student. The last was of her in sixth grade, the brown-haired version of her, and a starting position before she did a tumbling routine at the gym. I'm proud of myself because I worked hard and became better.

"Done," she said.

"That you are. Noticed only one picture of us there. That's surprising. When you did that scrapbook that one time your mom had to beg you to put some family pictures in it. They were all of us. Or of you."

"Yeah, well times change, don't they Christopher?"

Before Caitlyn hit the door she turned around and looked pleadingly toward Brendan. Did she want him to stop her? She was standing in front of the projection of the Rachel picture now, and Brendan saw that the necklace's gold heart charm was superimposed on her chest via projection, where it should have been that night instead of on Rachel. Much larger than it should have been, but the blue tinge it took on from the opposite neon blended in perfectly with Caitlyn's blue dress. The rest was of Rachel's chest, neck, and half her smile, with the neon "Fiery Foods!" cut off behind her. Caitlyn was mostly blinded by the projector's beam but continued to stare in Brendan's direction. Brendan pointed to the necklace in its rightful place on her chest. He saw her face but words wouldn't come.

Chris then answered the question that Anabel had asked. "Yes, Anabel, times do change. And people change. And truths are uncovered. And life goes on."

"Okay, so what's your grand finale here, Chris? What great TRUTH do you want me to see today? The truth of you being a jerk? Learned that already."

"You are so beautiful," he said, stepping back to take her in from head to toe, then leaning forward to kiss her.

She put up a hand to block him and then sighed. "Thank you . . . I guess? Is that supposed to make up for tonight?"

"Not in the least," he said, now backed off from her.

"Okay, so I think we need to take a break, Chris. You and me." She looked to see his reaction. Blank. She continued. "Going through the pictures has shown me that. And the ending of eighth grade has shown me that. And just thinking what I've turned into has made me think of that. I just to find ME again."

"I agree," he said, crossing his arms on his chest.

"You . . . agree? I've been thinking for most of this week how I was going to tell you, how crushed you'd be, how it was just going to be temporary . . . "

"Not temporary. Permanent," he said, uncrossing his arms and stepping towards her. "Permanent. Complete agreement." Anabel's face was aghast. "My crown was more about what I've become WITHOUT you. I needed to search deep to see who I was, by myself. Because of what I discovered."

Anabel felt her face becoming flushed. "So we were on parallel paths, huh. They say couples know when to call it quits. I guess this is it." She shook her head while looking down. "But what's the game you've been playing? What do you DISCOVER? Couldn't you have just played it straight and broken up with me like, you know, a normal person?"

"Because there is nothing straight about us being together, Annie. It's crooked as a dog's hind leg, as my great-grandmother Eliza used to say." She started to speak and he put a finger to his lips to quiet her. "Just wait a second." He pointed at the projection screen behind her, and she turned around.

"What?"

"Just . . . wait. And if you get bored for a second, sing the song."

"I don't know this song. This is the song that was chosen for us, Chris. It was never OUR song."

"Well, it is now. You'll always remember this." He started to sing the last lines of the song, which were simply "Now I think of forever" repeated. When he sang this she looked at him, and he nodded. "I used to think we might be forever. But now I just can't be with you. Here's why."

"Is this supposed to mean something to me, this picture of some guy grabbing a necklace from a girl?" Chris didn't answer. Hey isn't that Rachel? Serves her right."

"Just wait," Chris said.

Caitlyn was now crying. She turned to leave, and then as she did the slide changed. The next slide showed what transpired after the first. Brendan, standing there by Rachel, his face blazing, reaching out to snatch the necklace from around her neck. Rachel's angry/surprised look at his action. Two other girls jumping back quickly to avoid the rushing boy. And the photographer, thrown off, must have jerked the camera to blur the picture some. All this spoke of suddenness, and of violence. But most all of surprise, of the lack of premeditation, all of which proved Brendan innocent. Brendan found his voice.

"CAITLYN!"

Kids all around stared at him, searching for a reason that the angry guy was going off again. Her hand on the gym door, Caitlyn turned around. He pointed at the screen behind him, the one she could see now. He felt adrenaline rush through his body and his legs become unstable.

Caitlyn moved forward out of the projector's beam and saw the slide. "Oh my God!" she said and put a hand over her mouth. She stared at his face, her face, all their faces, saw the intent there, the violation committed there. And in two seconds she got it. He had been telling the truth. Rachel must have somehow taken the necklace from the case at the table when he was gone to the restroom, tried it on, and someone took a picture of it. It was all right there. And I'm a bloody fool, she thought.

She stepped to him and he ran to her.

As the song ended what came on the screen was something Anabel could never have imagined. She had checked out the gym's layout. Knew when her mother would have to go let the custodian in. Carefully searched to make sure no one was watching her. Who would have watched the fat, nothing me then anyway? I just blended into the background.

Chris then spoke. "I came across this from over a thousand pictures I looked at last night. At first I just thought it was a blur. Look at it. It's pretty blurry, right?" Chris scanned the faces that were looking at the picture. "Look at them," he said. "No one can even see it. See it for what it is." Anabel looked and saw that he was right. "Now, maybe if they stare at it long enough they might. And someone might ask me. And, well, I guess I could tell them."

Anabel's face was white and her voice was flat as she turned to him. "You wouldn't. You wouldn't. Would you?"

He waited for a few seconds, making her suffer. "Naw Annie. I couldn't do that to you. Too many good times together." He paused. "But you know, how REAL were those times? I mean, what's that legal idea. Something like a poisoned tree can't bear good fruit. Was that us? Were we poisoned?"

Anabel stared at the picture that showed her taking her pre-marked ballots, 40 of them, in shades of red ink, blue ink, black ink, pencil, even a couple in marker, and stuffing them in the ballot box. How she'd agonized over the that number before she'd arrived at 40. This was the number that she determined would give she and Chris the crowns but would not arouse suspicion. Ballots that over and over repeated the names Chris Lawson and Anabel Donan.

"How did you know that was me? You didn't suspect anything that night. I've never told anyone."

"Well, because I know you Annie. I used to steal glances at you, just so happy I had a girlfriend that beautiful. I could draw your profile, like a silhouette. I could do it from different ways you do your hair, too. I've got so many on my walls." He paused. "And that same profile, you can see, coming in from the left on that picture. I guess that's your hand reaching out, to stuff the ballot box, right? Don't know about the details, but I know that's you. And I know what you did. And that's what matters. No way you . . . or me was gonna win those stupid crowns. You poisoned our tree, Anabel. And nothing worth a damn's gonna come from that".

She started to cry. "So nothing, nothing we did, nothing we were to each other, matters anymore?" Chris sighed. "All the times with our families. All the things we did together. All the intimate moments we shared. Just . . .nothing?"

"I wouldn't say nothing. It's not like I didn't enjoy having the hottest girl in school as my girlfriend. And I did love you. I really did. That wasn't fake."

Trying to recover, she wiped her nose with her hand. "Not fake like what you made me, right? 'Lose some weight, Annie.' 'Buy this yellow dress like Cher from Clueless, Annie.' 'Dye your hair blonde, Annie.'"

"You loved doing those things. That's who you are. Who you MADE yourself. Your identity. The image YOU so carefully maintain. I never forced you to do them!" Chris was getting red now.

"Sure, okay, right," she said. "I'll take the blame for them. Your constant nagging about them was something I could have just ignored, right. Like you would have just taken my NO and moved on."

"Good question. Not sure. But your changes have made you ANABEL DONAN, the pride of Wildwood Middle, the envy of both girls and boys. And that's what you wanted, right? Or else for what other reason would you have done . . . that." He pointed to the screen, and Anabel realized the image was still there.

"Can you take it off already?" she said. She just wanted to cower under a rock somewhere. Chris walked over and hit the X and canceled the presentation. Blue screens came up around the gym. He walked back to her.

"One more thing. I lied about the theme of my crown. The theme is how proud I have become in myself . . . without you."

"Thanks Chris. Is this like in Shakespeare? You first stick a knife in me and then you off yourself? I'm sure Principal Grayson would love that."

"No. That's all I got."

"Okay, so I have one more thing," Anabel said to him.

"What's that?"

"Since everyone is probably now staring at us, can you—"

Chris looked around. "Actually fewer than you think. They are people, and they have lives too."

"As I was saying, since I've been crying here, can you give me a big hug to show them that everything's okay with us."

Chris slowly shook his head. "Jesus. Sure. Why not?" he replied. "One last time."

As they had done so many times, the couple embraced, and, knowing this was it, held it for an extraordinarily long time.

Brendan was able to narrow the space between them quickly. Caitlyn took his hands and through tears said, "Brendan. I'm so sorry. So so sorry. I was a fool. Just stupid." She then thrust her head into his chest and hugged him.

"Shhh, shhh, shhh," he repeated, trying to calm her. "It's okay. It's okay." When her tears turned to sobs he pulled back from her and held her head in his hands. "We're together now, right? That's all that matters. We're good." She nodded. "We're fine." Kids with parents who were wanting to beat the rush from the parking lot were now coming towards them to the exit, and some were just staring at what was happening, so Brendan maneuvered her around the outside of the tables and back to theirs, easing her into her seat and then taking his.

"You guys. Oh my God. You guys," Kristen said, ready to pounce on them. Mike touched her shoulder to keep her seated. She looked at him and kissed him. "Mike. Look."

"I see Kris. Pretty great," Mike said. "Stay here," he then whispered to her.

"But I'm a part of—" she began.

He looked at her. "Stay. Here." He waited until she nodded before removing his hand from her shoulder.

Although Brendan had heard Kristen and Mike, Caitlyn apparently had not. He waited for her to turn towards them, but she was just looking at him. With gratitude. And kindness. And wonder. There were a lot of things I could say right now, he thought, but then thought against it.

He leaned forward and kissed her gently on the lips and loved the surprise he saw there.

"Mike," Kristen said. "Their first kiss!" She was like a stick of dynamite ready to explode. He nodded to her and watched to make sure there was no outburst.

When Brendan had kissed Caitlyn she had just gone limp, and when he pulled her into him and wrapped his arms around her she closed her eyes and just let herself feel.

They held that embrace for a few minutes, and then Brendan heard Principal Grayson get on the mic and tell them that the event was ended. He looked toward her at the dais. She gestured to them. Maybe for the inappropriateness of the embrace. Maybe just to leave. He held up his hand in acknowledgement.

Sure. They'd leave. At some point. But, Brendan thought, I haven't had many moments in my life like this. I'm going to ride this one out. Although many thoughts filled his mind he tried to enjoy the smell of her hair. The feeling of her body. And the peace that filled his mind.

As he closed his eyes he knew the perfect Grandpa George-ism to capture the moment. The one that he said was his guiding light all his life and that made all his major life decisions simpler. Brendan pulled away from Caitlyn slightly and she opened her eyes. He smiled at her and she smiled back, and then he shared with her those three words.

She's worth it.

Made in United States
Orlando, FL
10 July 2022

19608859R00157